M000190112

f/32

A RICHARD KASAK BOOK

f/32

eurydice

With an Introduction by Patricia Coleman

f/32
Copyright © 1990 Eurydice
Introduction © 1995 Patricia Coleman

All Rights Reserved

No part of this book may be reproduced, stored in a retrieval
system, or transmitted in any form, by any means, including
mechanical, electronic, photocopying, recording or otherwise,
without prior written permission of the publishers.

First Richard Kasak Book Edition 1995

First Printing September 1995

ISBN 1-56333-350-3

Cover Art © Tara Striano
Cover Design by Dayna Navaro

Manufactured in the United States of America
Published by Masquerade Books, Inc.
801 Second Avenue
New York, N.Y. 10017

To Dad who created the mirror.
To Bob Steiner who showed me the periphery.
Thanks to those whose words I have stolen.

CONTENTS

Introduction

From the start, Eurydice's novel, *f/32*, insists that the reader believe in Ela's cunt. The fragmented information of the body builds it/her up in our minds—insists on the point, through ellipsis that Ela's cunt does exist, whether embodied in part of Ela's body, attached to Ela's body, or, finally, separated from Ela's body. In habituating the reader to a new form of imagining, Eurydice also habituates us to a new form of reading: the very work, "Cunt," passes from the vocabulary of shock (and all that that shock embodies—the disowning of the self and violence against the self or against an other, or, as Ela later terms it: "decuntation")— into the perfect expression of that disembodiment of the essence from the self.

Is "essence" encased within and protected by the body or does it exist in some space which eludes the body? In Denis Diderot's "Libertine" novel, *Les Bijoux Indiscret* (1747), a bored sultan, Mangogul, has his Sorcerer, Cucufa, invent for him a ring which will force women's vaginas to speak of adventures, of intrigue, and of duplicities. All of this occurs outside of women's wills and, at first, only to fill Mangogul's empty days. The essence Mangogul seeks, he seeks within—or rather—*from* the vagina. The stories, which are normally hidden from men (lovers and husbands and sultans) and wherein lie the identities of the women, cannot help but be admitted by vaginas once Mangogul turns his ring towards his chosen genitalia. For the sultan, it becomes apparent that it is the vagina which embodies the woman (and her virtues or false-nesses) and only by conversing with it (or listening to it) will he be satisfied that he has plumbed the female depths.

And here, as in *f/32*, the cunt takes on the characteristics habit-ually attributed to women in literature. In the cunt, hides the mystery. Where the mystery is often expressed and sought in psychological or social doubles, it is here found in the anatomy. In *Les Bijoux Indiscret*, the source of the elusiveness which so tortures men in literature is discovered as the absolute measure of a woman's virtue or wickedness. The dependability of Mangogul's ring puts an end to that famous elusiveness. By forc-ing his weapon upon vaginas, the sultan forces the mystery into the light and, so, thinks he comes to know women.

What happens when a woman appropriates her own parts and fragmentation? More than two centuries later, in *f/32*, the vagina not only divulges stories which are otherwise hidden by its propri-etor, but now experiences a life entirely separate from her. Ela and her cunt co-exist: Its insatiability is not Ela's, but its separate-ness speaks for Ela's fragmentation.

However, fragmentation is not the antithesis of essence in *f/32*. The metaphors for the split self exist in a camera, in mirrors, in reproduced images of Ela's cunt. It must not be forgotten that in all of Eurydice's metaphors there is also the parody of the notion of essence: not only from literature, but also from mass media, and from religious and romantic iconography. From this perspective, *f/32* may also be regarded as a mock-*Bildungsroman*, the classic novel of education in which the heroine discovers and develops her essence. Ela is introduced to the reader as happily fragmented in her co-existence with her cunt. However, Ela's privacy (she is barely tolerant of the men and women swarming around her and her only cohort is the mirror) is in certain conflict with the sociability of her cunt. This discrepancy calls for her re-education.

The violent rape of Ela, which occurs mid-novel, is not inevitable, yet it is also not unexpected. It is an act which furthers Ela's fragmentation. Although the separation of Ela's cunt from Ela, "is not a metaphor," it is this act which makes her aware of how much she needs her cunt.

The hindrances to a straight line of Ela's self-discovery and education are innumerable. Further fragmentation occurs: shortly after the rape, Ela's cunt is stolen by a nameless first-person narrator who splits from the initial narrator. While this narrator prepares Ela's cunt for penetration, the cunt escapes. In its subsequent adventures (to the zoo, to prisons, to television, to prostitute's crotches), Ela's cunt eludes the novel's characters: former lovers, Johnny Carson, David Letterman, Ela, and the nameless narrator who later joins Ela's search for her cunt.

When the mass media get hold of Ela's escaped cunt, they grab onto it and mass-produce its image for the general public. Wearing it as a badge and aping its attitudes, the public thinks they have captured the essence of sexuality and freedom and, in so doing, have become sexual and free.

In true *Bildungsroman* fashion, Ela's experience of herself develops in the novel from one of unconscious fragmentation to completeness in fragmentation.

The literary parodies of the *Bildungsroman*(as well as many others which I leave to the reader to discover) and of notions of essence and absence are necessary components for the focus of this novel. For the re-affiliation of the self with the self (as in Virginia Woolf's *Orlando*), it is necessary to go over and through history and, in this process, to appropriate the self through history's remarks in literature.

—Patricia Coleman
New York City, May 1995

We should have been excused from lugging a body: the burden of the self was enough.

—E. M. Cioran

CHILDREN'S MATINEE:

Beauty met the Beast on a crystal path strewn with hollow silver hearts, one day when stiff gusts of wind stirred the hearts into a storm, whirling them like clouds of dust.

Beauty, who had just emerged fully grown from the egg of her mother, felt a heady perfume from her frail pudendum trickle down like a fertilizer on to the roused ground.

At first Beauty thought the Beast was her twin who mirrored her physical abandon, her swaying hips, her swollen lips, and her delicate bodily scent of children's bedrooms.

That night Beauty listened to the difficult dance of the Beast in the adjoining bed, then watched it erupt and pour glowing cum on their pink sheets next to the royal monogram.

Afterward, the Beast purred: "I am the mirror that doesn't reflect you back; every night I take a fresh maiden as my slave and a virgin boy as my wife, but now I give up my kingdom to be in you; so let us descend together the countless steps to my wet shrine, and remember not to speak, for I am blind and only silence guides my footsteps, and do not light our path with your beauty, for darkness is my ally."

So Beauty faced the Beast in mortal battle for years, and on her face were seen erotic escapes, open umbrellas, monsters swimming around gilt hooks, smoking chandeliers, gleaming amoebas, but no images could cover and protect her naked little body from desire.

In the end, after the blood dried and the ashes settled, it was impossible to know who had won; the survivor of that epic carnage of love was a new, unrecognizable creature.

"What a splashing intimate balcony," men prate pouring in, "its sweet shade spouts from your swelling cactus which adds a sober touch, like sliding into an empty spiral warehouse," they wink, and promptly break into moist four ounce chunks under the roving oily leaves of my tongue. "What a dainty tornado you are," they splutter, staggering, yet struggling to be decisive and undrilled characters, as I grind my greedy teeth on their slick cores and suck their sore limbs dry and clean until they snap, as their startled penises squirm blindly toward my shimmering curtain, and I act as hostess to their spry explosions and smooth submersions into the vast obscurity of my carnal past.

My swinging villa, suspended over a dark roaring gorge, is built from the white secretions of my body; my wise ancestral insatiability is indestructible, and every turn of the screw leads me to the stark spoilage of any ephemeral dam erected against my torrent.

Stagnated in my victories, I dream about a staid horned stud feasting on me. Stalking among scattered carcasses of ravished rotting insects, lying above leftovers from my sloppy splurges, surrounded by sodden victims spiked on their own stakes or choked by their own sprinklers, I imagine that a dark winged rider will come, coil around me sweeping me off my comfortable habit of lusty murder, and here, on the precarious luminous edge of my web, eat me, while I spill profusely from my mouth.

Why She Lost It

Ela* has the tightest cunt in the world. Every blessing is a curse, Ela reminds herself.

Ela's cunt creates a corrosion around her like a protective moat.

Ela considers her cunt to be implausible, like a caricature, a lush and obvious imbalance of nature.

Ela's cunt is her stigma, her credential, her legacy, her shield, and her shadow.

Her cunt gives Ela a transparency she likes. She lives in its illusory infinity. Its grip on her at times becomes unbearable.

Ela supposes that, like a mirror image, her cunt is a trick, like throwing ashes into people's eyes: mere diversionary tactics.

Ela cuts a heroic figure living with that manic cunt of hers, the restless flickering light that flashes from her thighs guiding wolves and sheep, dupes and deceivers to its haven, saving lost souls, welcoming all comers: like a legendary pharaoh, and like a lodestar in the firmament.

Ela wants to have a good look at her cunt one day, and laugh.

Before Ela has sex, a strange fight takes place. Outraged by her cunt's demands, Ela asks: "Will this ever stop? I can't keep up." Her cunt: "…!(hi-hi?)" Ela: "Spare me. Try to resist! Just this once." Her cunt: "…! (poww?)" Ela: "Please. I need rest, babe, it will be for your good, too." Her cunt: "…! (tsk-tsk?)" Ela: "I have had enough. Now cut it out!" Her cunt: "…! (ooh la-la?)" Ela: "It is too much, give me a break, keep quiet, take it easy, go to sleep, shh…" Her cunt: "…! (mrrhhghh?)" Ela: "I don't see why you're at it again, all this repetition drains me, it's not worth it after a while, aren't you ever bored?" Her cunt: "…! (whoosh?)" Ela: "I said no! I refuse to give in! I am not going to cooperate. SHUT UP!" She shrieks. She rocks back and forth wildly, blindly throws her cunt against any random surfaces around her and buries her hands into her thighs to block that entrance. Her cunt raises its pitch into a sharp hot ache that pierces Ela's abdomen and sucks her airtight. Ela can't breathe from the hunger. But she strains to control her cunt, oblivious to her past defeats. She wants the power to switch her cunt's awareness off and on at will. It is her natural right.

What possesses my cunt? Who takes responsibility for it? Ela often asks herself.

So Ela sits on her horny cunt, presses it down with all her strength and refuses to open her legs. The pain for pleasure mounts. Ela thrusts her cunt outward, upward, downward, against the wall, into the mirror. She drags it on the cold tiles, slaps it, pinches it, pulls at it, snaps it shut. She takes it into the shower. On the toilet. To the fridge for a snack. Out for a walk. Under the bedcovers. Her despair excites it further.

Ela's cunt is her perfect and terrifying burden. It penetrates her life like a siren, or an alarm, turned on into eternity.

Finally Ela succumbs. If she is alone, she grabs any object in her reach to fill up her cunt. In such an emergency, she can't plan a strategy or delay her surrender. She shakes and comes time after time, without even touching herself: the thought of her abandonment into the clutches of her cunt makes her come. She spends hours masturbating it to contentment, but masturbation increases her cunt's greed out of bounds: whereas it might be satisfied by five hours of straight fucking, it requires weeks of continual masturbation when each new orgasm intensifies its lust. After some days, her pleasure is so quick and sharp that she starts over every fifteen minutes. During these vicious cycles, she must postpone her other physical needs, as she is compelled to masturbate even on the toilet. Her ties with the world become dangerously severed. Her orgasms and fantasies stop only when a persistent and desperate enough man-in-love manages to break into her apartment and to cut through that charmed circle of self-fucking which otherwise, Ela is convinced, would go on forever.

In short, Ela's cunt is a beast.

A beast that Ela is doomed to lug around with her for life.

Men never understand that struggle. Most often it takes place in their presence, as a prelude to fucking, and they perceive it as an exotic manifestation of Ela's abundant, charismatic sexuality. After their initial awe, this fight turns them on.

Do all women feel this? Ela wonders sometimes. Do all women sail back and forth between Scylla and Charybdis forever?

Ela presents her cunt to men with great abandon, as if it were John the Baptist's silver-tongued head on a platter, gives them license to do anything to it, to try their luck and not spare it.

If a man is on the premises during Ela's resistance to her cunt's appetites, he first stares at her nervously, then wants to help her, so he grabs her cunt by the labia and tries to extinguish it. Although he appears to be Ela's ally, in fact he gives her cunt exactly what it has been asking for.

"Do not mistake my cunt for the *kudos*," Ela warns men at times, hoping to tip the scales. "My cunt calls for blood like a vampire," she adds, "enter it at your own risk." They break into a cocky laugh. Soon her cunt will swallow them.

No matter how often and hard the man-at-hand applies himself, the task of taming Ela's cunt is Sisyphean. Eventually the two lovers succumb to physical exhaustion: they speechlessly gather up their dead limbs, count up the losses on both sides, perform quick last rites, retract their smoking weapons and fall fast asleep. But her cunt, the beacon, the glutton, the epicure, stays fresh. Orgasms rejuvenate it. It immediately strikes out for new prey. In her sleep, Ela can feel it contract in waves of desire. Once again I lie wounded in my own camp, she thinks.

I am chained to it as to a dancing bear, Ela thinks and laughs.

Feeding her cunt is Ela's never-ending chore. When she watches it eat, she can't help admiring its carefree voracious appetite.

Men come to Ela raving "I love your cunt! A real cunt! There's a taste! I love how it's shaved. It's so light. It expands! Like a balmy dream…" "…Bright too! And it swells so much! It gets a hard-on, it stays soft like a fruit, and so dynamic! It pulsates!" "It's like slipping into the tentacles of a squid, like you are swimming nude and suddenly the entire ocean is condensed into this little powerful solicitous fist, it has a rhythm, a double spasm!" "It smells so fresh, like moist earth, wet paint, cucumber, thunder." "It's a delicacy!" "It's smart!" "It never breaks down! It even glows in the dark!" "It's so beautiful! You should be really proud of your cunt!"

What inspires these metaphors? Ela wonders. How can I be proud of something I don't control? Ela responds to men's endless linguistic exertion with equanimity: "Sorry, I wouldn't know"; or "It is outside my control"; or "It is independent of me." But men crack up at the joke and assess that she, too, is good with metaphor.

Her cunt tears Ela from the world and carries her to a continuous burst of herself, beyond moderation, obscenity, or kindness.

"I've never felt so wanted, I am at home in it, it's where I was meant to lie, meaning has come to my life! It calls out to me: Come! both when I am in it and far from it. I feel it wrapped around me all the time," men exult.

Ela makes annoyed "Don't exaggerate" or "I've heard it before" faces in response to all the spirited commentary, flutters her lashes and rolls her eyes in exasperation, while her hidden cunt plucks and sucks in and blows out its lips and contracts its muscles, swimming or nuzzling in satisfaction, then eagerly lunges at the nearest flesh. "Will you ever shut up?" Ela charges back.

"You have a lyrical idyllic cunt," corny men rave, "your cunt contains in it all the nostalgia of the world." Men speak of her cunt with the enthusiasm of adventurers setting foot on a new continent. They assume that if they dig far and deep enough, they will strike gold. "Well, I am blowed! God's gift to man! It's not oblong but round, fits like a glove and swells up like a sponge! And it moves! What suction! What a fit! It is the perfect size! We are built for each other! I can't let you go!" they explain.

"Let me describe your cunt: your cunt is endless. Your cunt is a rose petal in a glass of rosewater. Your cunt is green valley at dawn. Your cunt is a dense forest with woodcutters and wolves running loose in it. Your cunt is a dark bar crowded with loud merchants, drunks, sailors. Your cunt is a cathedral with a big bronze bell ringing in its belfry. Your cunt is a great nation's fleet with submarines and warships; anchors are pulled up, waves splash on deck, a cabin-boy jumps from the mast into the sea, the captain lights his pipe, the figurehead at the prow laughs, a game of dice is heating up. Your cunt is a transparent lake, and at its bottom lies a white sunken city, a colossal octopus rises out of the city palace and glides down the brightly-lit avenues mangling under its sucking tentacles thousands of fresh flowers which were used that very afternoon for the funeral of the emperor. Your cunt is a famous brothel buzzing with wily whores being painted with greasy powders and hard pencils, acned boys and panting fat men. Your cunt is the hummingbird that sings in my ear cuntinuously."

Ela sticks her finger up inside her, trying to comprehend what it is that men try so hard to describe. But she touches nothing unusual. She holds a mirror up in front of her open legs and attempts to see what everyone else sees. A soft shade of pink that shimmers in the light; unassuming. No heliograph; no watchfire; no labarum; no Magna Carta; no funeral pyre; no playground; no deep freeze.

Men brag, brawl, bludgeon, butcher, bubble, bluster, belch, bark, bugle, bulge, brandish their brash tools, bang on her door, beg to be inside Ela. They vow to conquer her legendary cunt or die at its altar. Each seems eager to be the only man left on earth if that solidifies his position against the rush of competition. Their magic wands, their divining rods, their fine radars point at Ela: It is she! So they spin around her like burning moths and exclaim: "Your cunt is out of this world!" Ela wonders: Where is it then? In an obscure other world? What do men mean?

Men want to spend their lives in Ela's cunt; to obey its rules; to lose their memories and their souls inside it; to sink into it and die there as a result of having come. Ela considers these to be the sad sonorous symptoms of an unclassified deadly virus. Luckily, she herself doesn't catch the bug.

Every few months Ela flies to a different city or country to get away from men who will stick anything in sight into her tight cunt in their struggle to stuff it up: lit cigarettes, candles, dentures, watches, credit cards, coins (to make a wish), crosses, crystals, wedding or high-school rings, worrybeads, pens, pills, glasses, keys, gloves, batteries, photos of their mothers and sweethearts, lollipops, pacifiers, baby or beer bottles, sashimi, caviar, elk flambé, steak tartar, greasy chicken bones, garlic (to ward off evil spirits), prickly pears, oysters (with shells, cocktail sauce, or lemon), live snakes, snails, Steve's ice cream, silverware, light bulbs, tulip bulbs, torches, hammers, mufflers, plugs, cords, cattleprods, war medals, knives, guns, Molotov bombs, phone receivers, umbrellas, the legs of chairs, tables, and beds as far as they will go.

Ela's paradox: Despite the constant invasions, her cunt stays the world's tightest. (She can't even find a diaphragm small enough to fit her.) Yet no man's cock (or man-inserted object) is too big for her cunt. There is even room to wonder whether any cock is big enough.

Men give to Ela photos of her cunt with their assorted trinkets peeking out of it. Their intruding possessions become lucky or magical after lying in her cunt, men tell her, and also bring men back to the experience of being inside her. Those photos become men's weapons against memory and mortality.

Ela dislikes such follow-ups: men who are perfect strangers send her hot photos as if having had sex with her gives them the right to behave as though they know her. Familiarity disturbs Ela.

Ela disassociates from the world during sex and is not aware of what men insert into her cunt. So her deep sense of propriety and privacy feel severed at the sight of such stupid snapshots, but she quickly reminds herself that she asks men to use their imagination while fucking her and place their core in her cunt.

These photos could be a means of destroying me, Ela muses, at least symbolically. Like voodoo. The thought excites her.

Sometimes handmade puppets that look like Ela are couriered to her anonymously from various parts of the world or are left on her doorstep wrapped in newspaper or old lace. Those dolls have long silver hair, enormous kohl-lined eyes, big hard breasts bursting out of deep décolletages, a smirk on their sparkling pink lips, and a tiny cross, army pin, needle, or penknife nailed into their cunts or their left tits. Ela gives them away to children in parks.

Ela enjoys sleeping on clean children, high pillows, and crisp sheets. She invites children she meets in the parks to spend a night with her. She likes her huge bed strewn haphazardly with nude children; to rest her hand on a girl's pointy nipples, relax on their new bodies, kiss a boy's mouth as she wakes up, catch a small ass between her knees while changing sides in mid-sleep. "They are my pets, my butterflies; sex would ruin them," she sighs. Men protest: "We men are children, too, you know."

In Ela's striking face men see, unexorcised, their fear of life. But

Ela does not understand anyone else's identity or integrity. She understands unquestionable, verifiable, hard facts: like sex.

Ela's cunt seems to be blind as a bat: if it were up to it, Ela would fuck regardless of looks, voices, diseases, or any attributes other than sexual skills. But she tries to set some standards.

The statistics are surprising: Ela has fucked c. 500 men. A low sum, considering that she gets two dozen offers a day, by all sorts of men who hurl themselves at her, shouting for bliss.

Ela's cunt absorbs men indiscriminately. It joins men's minds and bodies in a common pursuit of its fold and sucks them clean of their contents; her cunt unites otherwise unrelated men in the popular lust and hunt for its possession. Ela's cunt is a universal common goal. A communal meeting ground.

Most of her lovers are men whom she would rather not fuck, to whom she is not attracted save for the urgent pangs of her cunt. Next come men she selects for their sensual beauty or expertise. She takes the daring, the inventive, the quiet, the pessimistic, androgynous, high-foreheaded, eye-lined, long-lashed, big-boned males, and any single-minded masters of seduction whose lives are dedicated to sampling the most coveted or inaccessible females worldwide.

"You come and everything else dies; you are endless magic, deep waves, the perfect eclipse. I worship you like a pagan. All my words are for you," men eulogize her. "The universe disappears under your gaze and you replace it. I am a slave of your love. The world is your bed and your temple," they orate.

Ela resents being loved. The world holds on to me in the name of love, she thinks; it uses love to claim me, to name me, to run my life. Generic love should be tabooed.

"The miracle is in her nightclothes," men whisper respectfully like wide-eyed monks entering the sanctuary for matins. "God is wearing black tights tonight." "God is in the next room coming."

The speed at which people love Ela is a sign of how little attention they deserve; the longer they resist, the more energy she lavishes on them: this is her social barometer.

On supply and demand: the more men want Ela, the less Ela wants men. When she is desired by everyone, she desires none: she feels repelled.

"Ela's face holds a hypnotic fleeting secret," men compose. "Her face is part of the sky, a cloud." "Her face is enveloped in an invisible cocoon. If you see it once, you can always summon it back like the image of a sea or fire or of the mirror."

Men search obsessively into Ela's eyes; for it is the goal of love to find what they each need in someone else's eyes; to open up before them and to burn in them. Ela's eyes are provocative, prominent, absorbent, forgetful. They induce the inexpiable desire for the finality of love.

"Ela is known for the supple cruelty of her Grecian profile, her warm mass of silver hair, her restless reptilian tongue, her gold impetuous eyes that teach dedication to a lying god," men gossip.

I should have been excused from lugging a self: the burden of the body was enough, Ela thinks.

Ela's body, enfolded in thin translucent skin, has been arranged for comfort like a space-saving amenity designed and built to the highest technological specifications. Her small, strong, frail-looking frame hints of hollow passageways, underground crypts, secret silos. An ingenious hiding place.

"Ela pulls her body out of the mirror whenever she needs it," men confirm, competing for the inside knowledge. "There is genius in the plotting of her flesh," they testify. "She is new substance."

No woman can call herself free who does not own and control her body, feminists argue. How does that apply to me? Ela wonders.

"Ela is a reflection in a clear mirror. She looks like a picture, an image seen through a lens. If her original exists, it is invisible to the naked eye," men theorize.

Countless portraits of Ela hang in men's bedrooms or lie in their suitcases and drawers, in the breast pockets of men's coats and in lockets on men's chests, as potent icons.

"Ela is the evocation of all that is forever impossible to put in words," men summarize, "and she lives as a conqueror."

Men squint, lean back, frame, measure, draw, and photograph Ela, but cannot penetrate her surface. There is a distance between their eyes and their visual images of her. If they reach out to touch her, she is farther than they calculated. They never know if she sees them. When she looks at them, she reflects them back looking at her; so they watch themselves looking into her face, unable to read it; it faithfully imitates their own expressions and, by doing that, ennobles and magnifies them. But when they look long enough, her face opens and they see a blank space like black leader on a screen: a gap.

Ela read recently that 66% of men believe in love at first sight; 67% feel that files are being kept on them for unknown reasons.

Men treat Ela like a two-way mirror. In front of Ela they feel self-conscious, foolish. Away from Ela they feel abandoned and in danger. When Ela hugs them from behind, surprising them in the mirror, they freeze. They mumble petrified: "I want you to be mean to me. Please break me. I would like to be raped."

Ela thinks love is a form of gangrene that settles in silently, moves fast like a bacillus loose in the blood and takes over one's entire body, causing excruciating agony or insanity. A while later the pain stops, and soon after death comes. An unmistakable putrid smell signals love's nasty presence.

When men speak, Ela's lips mutely repeat every word they utter. Her eyes focus on their lips as if her next breath depended on their next movement. She closely follows each inconsequential sign from their mouths as though it could reveal the secret of the universe. She does it mechanically. Men adore her talent for listening.

I am constantly falling asleep on others, Ela realizes with some disappointment. I have never felt satisfied. Never.

When Ela speaks, in her tone of impeccable breeding, words become immaterial; men listen to the music, the roar and hum coming from inside her body. They cannot believe that a brain and a will may be ticking behind her marvelous mouth. They suspect that some intricate mechanism hidden in her body is tirelessly taping every phrase in her proximity in order to spew it back out whenever she needs language. As a rule, Ela comes out with irrelevant speech. It usually starts with: "Don't tell anybody, but…," or: "This is a top secret, okay?" which makes men cozily unique. Honored that Ela has spoken in their presence and in their confidence, men break into blissful smiles at the sound of her infectious voice and deliver themselves to her as her faithful prisoners for life. She wonders: Why doesn't anyone rebel? Why don't these men kill me? It never occurs to them that I may be fallible.

"Your beauty intimidates me! Could I drug you before we fuck? When your big terrible eyes watch me, I don't dare breathe. I am afraid that you will paralyze me," men admit to Ela.

"Is this overwhelming beauty or is my cock governing my mind or is my world deceiving me?" men wonder when they see Ela. She looks so complete that they cannot mentally undress her. She shines into their eyes so that they cannot describe her in any detail after she is gone. "She is the Virgin," they conclude.

Ela realizes that by being in love, men feel alive. They feel incomplete and free from the traps of identity. They don't want an insulated safe space where she would always be available and responsive; what crushes them is what enchants them: the loss rather than the domination, the confusion instead of the certainty.

Love always seeks unrecognizable, unfinished, and indefinable objects. So Ela is a prime target.

Ela has only contempt for men who lose their wits over her. How can she respect people who don't have the pride and the decency to hide their insides? She does not know how to use their love. Should she bathe in their hot innards like Gilles de Rais? Or preserve her beauty by immersing herself in her lovers' blood? Love remains too intangible to arouse Ela. So she drags their flared hearts carelessly behind her. "To play it basic, I can take your heart," she warns men, "I cannot quarrel and I cannot love." "I will build a fortress for you, a castle away from the world, where I can comfortably worship you," men ejaculate. "Man is alone until the moment he looks his death in the face," Ela clarifies. "If you saw your eyes," men interrupt, "you'd understand."

"What's-his-name was a pest, so I had to kill him," she tells her Mommie on the phone long-distance. "This week I killed a chubby sweet Iranian who could recite obscure seventeenth-century French poetry and whose calm heart-shaped face belonged in old Arab portraits; a lanky Indian with eerie yellow eyes, bony legs, and striking pink (not purple or maroon) lips like swollen labia; a small Irish boxer with a thin bitter mouth, a sexy mole, and hard eyes who asked if I saw him as a sex object; and an abstract painter who claimed his mind controlled his body and then protested: 'This is wrestling, you don't even remember my name, I can't keep up' with feminine breasts and pastel nipples, a bit droopy. Just a few hasty notes from the battlefield of love."

Ela suspects that she might also possess the world's tightest heart;

she thinks there must be a direct proportional relation between a woman's cunt and heart.

When men divulge: "I dream of dying from love and for love, for you," "Why does love make me long with all my heart for death?" "You love me as no one has ever loved me," "I love you as no one has ever loved you," "Let us die together!" Ela infers: these are creatures without mirrors. She answers abruptly to the men she favors: "I am hungry." If the love-stricken have no chance of success, she replies more sympathetically: "You'll dream of me."

Ela is disconcerted by any conjunction of herself with others. She cannot imagine merging or identifying with them. Recognizing another's face shocks her. She disdains the farces of good fellowship: pictures in wallets, address books, car pools, ready-to-wear clothes, horoscopes, pop charts, parades, organizations, gyms, shrinks. She prefers to sell off the other survivors. For Ela any temptation to love involves a betrayal of the mirror.

When she is loved, Ela reasons: I favor myself and hurt men, or I favor men and hurt them. Whether I give myself to them or not, they will suffer. Love always backfires. In the clash of love, the heartless win. But the masses have maldigested the Christian method: man can achieve anything, they believe, through love; the spirit of love will prevail victorious if only man has the faith and the courage to persist. They think that their smothering love is omniscient. They assume that, because they love me, they have every right over me, that love is a weighty gift which they can impose on to me and come to sow its seed. They love as easily as they shit: regularly, usually once a day. It escapes them that:

1. Their love has no intrinsic value.

2. Their love is not a diversion or an entertainment; it is boring.

3. Loving back is not an obligation or a civility.

4. Their love is a vulgarity, as base as luck or hate.

5. Their love shares nothing in common with flight or laughter.

Compassion, that Christian motto, is incomprehensible to Ela; she doesn't know how to help; she cannot distinguish destruction from salvation, for herself or for anyone else; she cannot understand herself or others; she tries to minimize her effect by passing to them the responsibility of all the definitions. Men love it.

Love is a male inheritance, like Adam's missing rib, Ela thinks. I don't have, passed on to me, half of a seashell—Plato's symbol—to search for its organic match. Instead, I have a bloody beast, Ela thinks.

Ela does not fuck if she feels involved. She also refuses to speak in her mother tongue, for it hangs loaded with meaning, emotion, memory and respect. She notices: When I am a myth, a dream, a representation, I fuck well. I soar through open space.

Men who are sexually overwhelmed by Ela try to explain and prolong their enslavement by falling desperately in love with her.

Love blinds people to their blemishes and violences, and to the inadequacy of the world. It chains them to their fantasies of others. It breeds sacrifice, stagnation, suffering, humiliation, Ela has observed.

Men insist on associating good sex with love. Men exorcise their sexual pleasure by falling in love; otherwise they feel guilty, insensitive, diminished, exposed. They need promises of possessive tomorrows.

Men use love as an aphrodisiac. When they love, the stakes are high; they feel anger, frustration, hope, and they serve a noble cause when they fuck, so their senses are heightened.

Love can make even miserable lovers seem sublime: those in love must persuade themselves that the object of their love is better than anyone who came before or who could come tomorrow, so they overlook the shortcomings of the beloved to protect their love-investment. That delusion, a strict limitation of the future, is impossible for Ela. Habit kills good sex. She would rather face the daily dread of life.

"Your eyes hold unfathomable tenderness. I am surrounded by your unconditional love. You give me all that you possess," men assure Ela. "I possess nothing," Ela protests. "You are perfect, but I am part of you," they add, "we are connected as one."

Love is perishable: every love plays out and in time becomes meaningless. Why must I watch the reruns? Ela wonders.

"A lifelong shadow lifts from my heart: my vague search is over. In you I have found eternal shelter. I am weak, Ela, take me, make me a man!" men exclaim with an undying passion. Love is immaterial and insubstantial and impermanent: Once they have it, men don't know how to handle it, how to be consumed by it, or how to preserve it. It gives them great confusion.

"In Ela's face shines the ancient light of the mood in which man comes face-to-face with God; she is the heir of past saints, the prophet of a new order of development," men extol.

Ela complains to people: "I wish people said that they love me because I can't love them back, because they want to be loved by one who can't love. I, for one, would like to be loved by someone who can't love. The impossibility of it. But no: they say: 'I love you because I want to be loved.'"

But being loved is Ela's character: No matter how many people love her, she relentlessly inspires more. She spends half of her life avoiding those who love her and half making them love her.

Ela wonders: Does the ocean love the men it drowns? Does it love their implacable purity, their soft malleable bodies, their pale fibrous lips, their sepulchral torsos, their fast-rotting cocks?

Ela thinks: People are a sea in which I lose myself. All men have come through a barroom door. When I fuck I am the void. The first penetration brings my death; I can't see, hear, think, I am all cunt. One pink slit through which shines a wet crimson beast. If I could fuck incessantly, I would be god, or vapor. I make a show of my orgasmic death, I burst in broad daylight, I die and come back from the dead to die again. I love dying.

Sex is my bath. What life takes from me the rest of the time in every way, I take back during sex; immune and impartial, distant from any violent wakefulness, I sense the world's overwhelming tenderness for me, its understirring of protective parental love.

Ela makes a point of having come in every public area she

frequents—groceries, boutiques, nightclubs, restaurants, parks, libraries, banks, classrooms, coffee shops, offices, subways, hallways—to feel familiar with it. If she is called in by an advisor, a lawyer, or an official, the memory of herself coming on that person's carpet, couch, or desk gives her a privileged comic viewpoint that allows her to sit through vacuous charades. Ela is unable to deal with the world professionally; she only strikes up morbidly personal relationships.

Generally Ela prefers public locations for sex because a good combination of lover, surprise, danger, and sacrilege brings out her best orgasms.

Besides, how can one know anything is real without outside witnesses?

Mixing their semen with that of previous and future lovers in one highly idealized cunt is aphrodisiacal: Ela's cunt is a homosocial mildly homosexual bond, a magical conduit that joins all men who come into it and also measures them up against one another.

Ela rates her orgasms by the cosmic sense they give her that she is God and she is boundless, not by their length or intensity: she doesn't value thirty consecutive spasms or three-minute-long explosions, but the few times when man, place, time and mind coincide to create an invincible new world.

Men run to me to have their illusions shattered, Ela tells men.

Jealousy is an aphrodisiac for men. Are you jealous? Ela asks them, referring to her other lovers. This heightens their sexual performance instantly. Do you want to join us tonight? she offers. The idea excites them. But they refuse.

Ela discourages any suggestion of prolonged male presence in her world. She doesn't know what to do with men, besides fuck them. Sex is the only way in which she can communicate with men.

The stories of men chasing Ela through thick and thin make other men chase her also. They discuss her orgasms and the past top achievers. They ask her to give them a chance. If she agrees, she says: "Let's have sex. It makes sense. If we fuck I will forget you." This frightens them. They blubber: "But you don't understand me." Ela: "We fuck and get it over with, or we don't see each other again. You choose." Most of all, Ela hates the sight of fear in men's eyes. So men rise to the task, eager to write history with their cocks; assured by some wife, mother, or whore in the background that they are high above average, they feel like pilgrims or crusaders setting out on a rocky course toward the great miracle awaiting them at the end.

She orders them: "Spread your body." She puts silver or pink lipstick on her festal cunt. "Get ready, go!" she calls and leads them into the nearest alley or onto the nearest table. If she likes them, she asks: "How shall I punish you?" If they boast: "Any way you want," she unfolds her whip. If they ask why, she winks: "For love." If they fib: "I can't think," she smiles and opens her body, changing from heat to ice and back to shatter their morale. She urges: "Do one for the mirror!" Soon she comes with a war cry.

Ela finds flagellation funny, sexy, and affectionate; whipping or being whipped produces a feeling of overcoming boundaries that is outside the realm of common sensations, free and exhilarating. When they relax, men enjoy it as the first sign of her love.

When she whips, she gives herself to it completely. She can only sustain the action for a short while. This does not diminish her pleasure. Ela prefers to whip fair innocent boys who grew up on big farms or in affluent suburbs. She enjoys their terror, their curiosity, their health, their determination to stifle their cries, their timidly offered white tender buttocks that turn red. And her own exhaustion. She never whips the same man twice.

She directs them to undress, grab the bed posters or lean against the wall or hug their knees, and be still. She admires their curves, moans, and lifts the hissing whip. She comes even before the first strike.

Later she lights her cigarette and commands: "Please stop that screaming. I need to rest. I feel a draught. Throw someone on the fire." When she is not played out, she is frank: "Is the show over already?" "Don't commoners have extraordinary sexual prowess?" Before entering her stupor, sometimes she comments: "It was fun," or "Well done," or even "I was surprised." "Did I abuse you?" men worry, "Did I arouse you?" "We don't use the same words. Be quiet, I am out of myself," Ela remarks.

Am I the opposite sex? Ela wonders. Or am I the sex?

After sex Ela sleeps with a lit cigarette between her lips. Men relate to her their unassorted childhoods, put out her cigarette before it sets the bed on fire and narrate till dawn. She goes off to sleep leaving them with their anguished consciousness and their vanquished dream of possessing her, converting her, hating her, banishing her. They peer into her post-orgasmic face that glows with heavenly peace and suddenly know that they can never be One with her. This thought torments them, and they interrupt their monotonous stories ("when I was nine, my father got drunk, pulled down my pants, and chuckled"), their voices crack, their blistered cocks fade and they exclaim to themselves: "How frightfully fulfilling love is!" and "She is a painting!"

But soon words spill forth from them again, for they still want her to know everything about them. It is as if an instinct for survival urges them to tell her about all their lovers, about the things that succeed in bringing some tenderness to their lives, the daughters they seldom see, siblings, jobs, books, hobbies, houses, idols, vacations, old nightmares, fantasies.

Their own prattle reassures men; their sexual performance alone leaves men threatened. They prefer the warmth of language.

Ela suspects that men use sex as an excuse for confession.

While men speak of their past, they feel equal and intimate with her. They feel that they are sensitive, that this is not a one-nighter. They open space for her to generate closeness. They are asking: Walk into my heart.

Ela thinks: I envy the stylites. I would love to live alone on a live pillar.

The morning after, the men shower, cook breakfast, smoke, pray, meditate, kneel by her, watch her cunt quietly rise and fall, develop hard-ons, break into rise-and-shine smiles, feel that the world is made of fresh light sperm, and wait. Ela lies in the same position in which she first went to sleep.

In her sleep Ela senses their proximity and pleads: Make them leave! Isn't it firmly understood from the start that whatever they place in me, I will betray?

When she wakes up, she asks: "Who are you? Have we met?"

For Ela a "one-night stand" provides an intensity created by the mystery of the stranger and the ensuing suspense, that transcends the individuals and that is impossible to sustain for long; any lasting relationship contains the seeds of its own pedestrianism. A flying fuck cannot be dominated. Anonymous sex is weightless.

"We should make love for a thousand years as the gods used to do," men exhort. "A child born from our embrace will be powerful enough to destroy all creation." Or: "This is the moment for which all life can be staked: Take me to your breast!"

Some days Ela puts on a long coat and flashes men in the street. The sight of a lovely translucent woman nude under a streetlamp like a succubus touches on the diabolical. They instinctively look away as if what they see could kill them. Their horror mystifies Ela, and mystification arouses her. Her common hunting formula of turning herself into an object to capture men, enslave them, kill them, and see for them, fails her. Her own failure arouses her. She likes to watch her power become her failure, to witness men in speechless flight from her exposed little body.

"You are the divine lover. Your love is excessive. You break down all resistance. You reward a life of devotion and discipline with release from constraints and precepts. You give permission for joy. Your lovers suffer amorous injuries by nails and teeth. If the pores of the body do not spill over with delight, if the mind does not dissolve, if tears of bliss do not begin to flow, if the mouth does not burst into loud song, then purification escapes your lover and the world," men praise Ela.

Ela likes to leave herself in scars. Things obtain value when they stand against a background of death. Wounds provide the contrast that highlights the life and beauty of flesh. She bites her lovers' nipples, draws blood and swallows it after rolling it in her mouth like a connoisseur. She memorizes the bouquet and the taste. She burns small dark holes into their palms with her cigarette as parting souvenirs of her lust. She carefully smells the sweaty charred flesh and sighs with pleasure.

Ela is an accomplished smoker: she can hold a cigarette between any of her fingers, inhale, and look with half-shut eyes through the smoke so irresistibly that her sight breaks men's hearts.

A blind fuck is courageous as any gamble. Blind love is cowardice, Ela differentiates.

Ela blindfolds herself during her minor everyday fucks to avoid the sight of men self-consciously stroking, kissing, and poking her with gummy love and reverence. "This is the real Test," men tell themselves, "the big time, I can't fuck up, my honor is on the line: Suppose I make a mistake, suppose I fuck like an actor or a secretary?" So Ela keeps her mocking eyes out of sight and exposes instead the pure eye of her buttocks which sends a bolt of ecstasy through men and loosens them up. She ties her panties over her eyes and fucks stark-blind. It is a joy to be faceless: a body with painted lips. She prefers not to see what she licks, what she desires. She dislikes the visions of human panic that surface during sex. After all, when they don't feel watched, men perform better. And with her eyes out, even if men fail, Ela can fantasize about them and come. She has never yet failed to come.

"My life up to now was spent with caution, and what happiness have I gained from distrusting women?" men confide in Ela. "Just now I saw you sitting on the bed and I thought you might have led me here…to kill me. Forgive me! I don't know what you are." Ela mistakes the tears on their dimly lit faces for sweat.

Ela is expressive in sex. Every night during the Great Performance, numerous consuming moods and designs appear on her face like ripples on water. Men can't tear their eyes from it.

Men feel grateful to be allowed in her. They think a cock is insensitive and crude. I must try not to become a hammerhead. Ela thinks: men are vulnerable inside a cunt, and at its mercy. They slide into something they have never seen. So both sides relish what they imagine to be the weakness of the other.

For that moment when they enter Ela, men feel in control, for it is their erection which excites her. That glory evaporates as they get busy deciding what tempo to follow, which parts of her body are most sensitive, how to use their muscles, weight, skin, and memory to satisfy her, how long it takes her to come, how to time their orgasm to coincide with hers. They blank out their pleasure to concentrate on hers. They delay their sensations and carefully plan to start with a bit of finger and tongue.

But Ela plunges into sex like a gleeful dolphin. She dives into the flesh head-on. She gyrates her groin, strains her neck, shakes her limbs from side to side like a tribal dancer, doubles up into loops, rises into a pyramid, unravels like a flowing ribbon, contorts into yogic formations. She moans, grunts, gurgles, gulps, giggles, twitters, squeals, sobs, shrieks, laughs, whistles, mews, clucks, crows, claps, chants, and wheezes until she is hoarse. She twitches, quivers, kicks, ruffles, nods, rises, and thumps onto the ground like a dying queen. She sings tremulous Egyptian pitches like a muezzin's call, and produces endless combinations of vowels, foreign euphoric sounds that compose an indecipherable discourse of hedonism. It is rumored that she speaks in phrases from a forgotten holy tongue.

"Why should I plan? Why should I work? Things come and go without my planning, in spite of my plans. Behind my work was ambition, behind my love was personality, behind my discipline was fear, behind my empathy was thirst for power; so I come, into you, Ela, wherever you take me, into the voiceless wonderland, I come as a spectator, not an actor; peace is upon me," men avow.

She grabs on to men, pushes them off, ravages them, rakes their skin into tiny pink furrows, sucks in their breath, buries her tongue in their ears, masticates their faces, traps their fingers in her mouth until there is no sensation left in their bodies, only the red cock that rams inside her. She rolls off the table or the bench or the ledge and, holding them tightly in her, drags them along on the floor, or on the ground, leaving behind a phosphorescent trail of cum like a crawling slug.

Ela's sexuality is not directed toward the world of objects, but toward itself; she responds to the sensations in her body, not to what causes them. So she appears both chaste and erotic.

She slaps, caresses, tickles, hugs, relishes, sucks, and excites herself, in an impetuous rage of joy, licks her cracked lips, gasps, notices nothing outside her spinning expanding body, drowns in a solitary madness that confounds her lovers.

Ela believes that St. Theresa came when she was visited by God; and so did St. Catherine, who argued against fifty philosophers and won, refused to marry the Roman Emperor and to be worshipped with him as God, and so the torture wheel was invented for her.

Am I causing all this ecstasy? men wonder. They think it is her love that gives to their embraces this potency and a meaning they never dreamed of before, so they hug her madly and believe: she loves me so much she can die; I am more than a transient cock.

Ela finds little difference from man to man. There is always a variety in fit, a distinct smell, a memorable taste, a rhythm.

Transported by her rapture into the highest echelons of manhood, secure in their sexual genius, feeling as finalists of the world championship for Master Lover, tremblingly alive and intoxicated, men now want Ela to focus her eyes and acknowledge them; to tell them that she loves them.

Strangely, men never sit back and wonder: Is she faking it?

"Don't you see," men grapple, pounding themselves into Ela, "Don't you know me?" "I am your slave, I am here!" they pant. "I am your prehistoric lover, I am back!" "Say yes!" "Yes, yes!" "Am I making you happy?" "Do you like it?" "Do you love it?" "Have you ever had bliss like this?" "Do you love me? Say it!"

Every man who finds himself inside Ela wonders: How is she rating me? Men fuck in the terror that another man has surpassed them; they fuck as if they were being judged by God.

Her lovers blow, puff, gush, fret, thrash, reel, grope, climb, and heave as if struggling with the ocean after jumping ship, they shove their flustered cocks from side to side into her last niche, agonize to hold on to the rudder and steer, to bear the brunt of her lust, break her trance, force open her heart and shackle it; they clutch their eyes to escape from the sights of her flame that bring them to the verge of coming, lights flash in their brains, they turn black in the face, blinded by sweat, but refuse to go down. They maneuver her body, twist her waist, rearrange her limbs, knead, rotate, swing, ride, plough, smother, sling, and manipulate her like a rodeo horse or a rubber puppet or a Chinese gymnast. Their breaths whistle through clenched teeth, their tongues bloat with the pounding blood, their overjoyed baguettes sail on lost to them for ever, but they cling to Ela even more tightly, and can still blubber: "I am planted in you," "I am a sword piercing you," or again, "Call me: my love!" They storm the fortress of her cunt for days, pound the breath out of her, beat ugly grunts from her throat, press for what now they live for: to reach her very center, her inaccessible soul, to hear Ela bleat: "This has never happened to me before!"

Ela thinks: Being owned and being fucked are opposites; possession is erotic only for that second when I hold a man tightly in me; the annihilation of the self is not itself erotic. Orgasm is the outcome of a vague deadly danger that forces me to reach beyond my capacities. A crime against the mind.

Sooner or later the men smell the pungent stench of a duel taking place, the foul odor of their own burning nerves: they are being devoured by her, and they become enraged; they envision every man whose marks have been effaced from the walls of her flesh, every fanatic who played deadly games with Ela with his cock in flames till he drowned in his cum and it dawns on them that no man has broken into her, she is voluptuous death. They feel exuberant like men who face a doomed struggle. They blurt out: "This will kill me. Do you want a corpse in you?"

Loss comes naturally to Ela. She loses or abandons anything she owns. It gives her freedom. Good sex is sex she cannot control.

They refuse to give up. This is their time in the lights, their only chance on stage, when they must break her into recognition. They fight against hope. They implore God to send them nine more cocks, to put one in her mouth, one in her ass, two in her ears, teams of new cocks always to replace the tired players with fresh ones. They feel fear. For they know that her cunt could open under them at any moment and hell will show through.

Sex is apocalyptic. An orgasm is a shocked stunned recognition: "God exists!" Each orgasm is a divine unmasking, Ela believes.

All these hours Ela rises and falls and laughs with awe at every nerve making itself known, at the pandemonium of her flesh, the whipping maelstrom in her cunt. She gives men everything but the words they need. She comes, faints, comes to, comes and faints again, and keeps fainting for longer periods till she loses consciousness for so long that she could be declared legally dead, and she no longer feels even through her cunt.

Men are suddenly shocked to feel their own pleasure: it comes over them as a quick, sharp, deep, joy that is out and gone. Then they have come to the edge of the cliff. They lie spent. Some jump off. Some calculate how far they must go for it to happen again. Some want to talk about it. Some ask to be held.

So when only gusts of air come out of Ela and her pupils have not been seen for hours, her pulse has long stopped and her body is jerked by spasms from head to toe, and men no longer know where their cocks end and her cunt starts, when they have cried enough tears and have poured into her their last life-drops, men groan with stunned paralytic grief, dash forward in paroxysm and shrink inside her. But they refuse to withdraw and face the deflated world outside of her. Instantly her wondrous snug cunt swells and grows around them, so that even after they shrivel and droop garish and wrinkled and dizzy from defeat, they still fit very tightly in that cunt, they feel it consoling and resurrecting them, and hear her deep reverberant laugh.

Ela suggests the key to her power: "I mean nothing I say. I never lie, for there is no truth to tell. If there is any truth, it can't be said. I speak in order to stay comfortable. I make a sensational laughing widow."

Ela lacks common sense; she needs friends or servants to look after her. So Ela lives as an honored guest. But being served by people who love her is exhausting and keeping those who serve her from loving her is impossible. That is the deadlock of Ela's quotidian existence. This explains the high turnover of all the persons connected to her.

People behave outrageously when they meet Ela, for they need to give themselves to her, but also to find a respectable reason for their spontaneous subjugation. So they arbitrarily treat one of her everyday actions as proof of her love for them and undertake to persuade her that she loves them. "Don't be afraid of your love! You love me because you trust me! You can fool yourself, but you can't fool me!" they claim.

Ela wishes she were lonely and tries to put people off, but her efforts go unheeded. She counsels her followers: "I have no information to give: the questions ask themselves, the answers reply themselves, I speak the way you'd vomit. I am not necessary to you. I am the light from a thigh suddenly revealed under a lifted dress."

Ela can be seen marching in the streets like Mother Goose nodding to a flock of pushy chicks that run behind her clucking: "Me! Look at me!" Some geese question her: "Why do you let people suck off you like leeches? They take life away from you, for they have none of their own." They point to one another with exasperation: "Who is he to be your friend?" In reply, Ela turns on her conversational auto-pilot: "Snails are hermaphrodites; they give birth with the first rains; they suck and chew on greens; they need humidity and wetness; they have no bones."

When Ela tells her followers that they stifle her, they offer to take her away from this world that drains her. The idea of her rescue, of saving her from others, is the center of their lives.

Men don't consider Ela subject to anything as vulgar as need, disease, or even physical growth; they don't believe that she has a past, or that she had a childhood. It mystifies them that she even has a body. She is so unreal that the workings of love lose their power in her presence; words become cumbersome, rough; meanings fall apart. She seems temporary, a vision that will vanish before their eyes at any moment; they fear that she will shatter like glass. They predict: "You are long past your dying time." Some console her: "You'll go through three lives before I finish one."

Ela's freedom is mere indifference. She lives well on her indifference, for people love her freely and easily because her own affections are not involved. They feel proud to possess her unpossessed spirit and buy her all that she can do without.

Ela hears the tick-tack of other people's lives, but they exist as fiction for her. The world is a second language for Ela. She contemplates: People can't see that I am normal. No one presumes that I am a subject. I need a sign on me. Something in me makes me an ideal amulet or wife. I look as though I should be owned.

Men blab: "Women like you turn up only in literature, they can't sit across the table eating dinner with me!" Ela provides them with every advantage: they see her naked, on the toilet, dead-from-orgasm. But she has a tenacious dignity. "I recognize you from books, it's so marvelous to meet you in life," they mutter. "You are life to me, but it's strange to be near you," they add.

No one knows who Ela is. So everyone wants her. She signifies the real world. "This is the real thing," men think when they meet her and immediately want to rise up to her standards, meet her expectations, fulfill her idea of a man and a human being. Ela has no personal ideas, so she accommodates everyone. She embodies everyone's ideals and pretenses, for she doesn't think she is someone specific. Her name, age, family, nationality, taste, change from person to person and from place to place. She is a series of evasions and digressions, an artifice blurry at the edges. She is arbitrary: a transmogrification, like a dream-condensation; that is her freedom.

Men place their hands on their chests and laud her: "I am only this being that must come to you. I am subject to you, profane, idolatrous. I must seek the secret from you." Ela steers her big eyes covered by an unseeing film upon men and retorts: "How sad that I am everything to you."

Ela feels uneasy believing in anything. When she formulates a doubt, she experiences a curious well-being. It is easier to live without a trace of belief So she cannot listen to men with any interest. She can discern the inanity of all points of view.

Men develop florid theories about Ela. They quickly judge that she contains more than meets the eye and undertake to unveil her. "She is a good woman misled by fate, and taken advantage of all the time," men formulate. "She comes from another land and does not know how we do things here." "Behind Ela's confidence beats a heart wounded by a great fatal love for a man," they resolve.

Ela thinks: Love is a curse. Don't be loved and you'll be happy.

"Oh, Ela," men babble, "I would be happy if I could just look at you across the table for the rest of my life!" "Marry me, I only ask of you one week per year; keep your freedom; I will support you and stay faithful to you." "I need you, I become you," they discharge and feel the tickle-in-the-spine truth of what they utter.

In the midst of such emoting, Ela's life would be terribly trite if she didn't have the mirror. As it is, she looks into it and thinks: I live in a playground and I have a clown's face! What fun!

"If you solve me," Ela contends, "I am not a mystery. If I am a mystery, do not solve me; make up your mind." "I have seen you before," strangers salute her, "I am worried about you. I can't think how you'll be if I am not around. Only I can help you." Every man Ela runs into advises her: "You must become the real you. No one knows you as I do. You must get to know yourself. The real you is sensitive, sweet, insecure. You need to take care of yourself. Let me impregnate you." They repeat: "Your cunt gives what only God can give: unconditional love and acceptance. I want to fuck you until I die. Ah, to expire in you! Now life has meaning."

In fact Ela has a past and it seems to her quite predictable:

Ela grew up in an affluent secluded mansion among seventy adoring servants. Her family owned many villages and villagers, animals, cottages, and acres of land. It took pride in nine centuries of pure blood, but inbreeding took its toll. Ela's first cousin had pink-eyed bald quadruplets by his sister, her other cousin took summer for winter and had a hill strewn with white sand on which he was drawn by sleigh in July, her third cousin was roasted alive on a spit by African mobs, her great-grandfather was a Coptic saint hanged by Arabs and venerated for curing the blind, whose grave became a shrine visited by thousands of Christians drawn by the fame of his miracles and his fragrant relics. Her male relatives were homosexuals and war deserters and there were very few females being born. Many of her family members suffered schizophrenic seizures and almost all died by their own hands.

Thus at the time of Ela's birth that celebrated family was reduced to only nine members: the brother-sister couple who bought a small Greek island and went to live on it, the pedophiliac cousin who, confused by the change of seasons, decided to move to a northern climate and to buy a castle in Siberia, two alcoholic homosexuals living in the city's brothels and five-star hotels, and Ela's immediate family of four.

Her maternal grandfather was the High Priest of the Orthodox Church, both bishop and godhead, reputedly the most handsome man in the nation, magnificent in his flowing red-and-gold robes and golden beard. He had large piercing eyes, pale fleshy lips, long soft fingers, a tall powerful body and a talent with words of any kind. Before God called him to His path in a macabre vision, he was a narcissist, a playboy, and a bisexual. As proof of his conversion he married his cousin Andromache, a meek, fair, God-fearing creature who bore him nine children, all of whom died but the last, a tiny girl whose birth finally killed the mother. He played the organ in church so divinely that tears flowed from the eyes of all who listened. Crowds flocked to hear him sing holy hymns in the voice of the old Sirens. He discovered a miraculous icon of the Virgin in a hot spring on the day Ela was born after another blinding dream and built a cathedral on that spot in Her honor.

Pilgrims came daily to ask Her help and offer Her mounds of silver and gold votive puppets. His portrait done in mosaic decorated the entrance wall of the cathedral. Ela had posed for the baby Jesus held in his arms.

Ela's paternal grandmother was the elder sister of her dead grandmother. She had sold her soul to a moneylender and then stole the contract, married, and murdered nine rich men of various nationalities, amassed a fortune, led the Resistance during both wars, fought with guerrillas, traveled extensively, took thousands of lovers, took part in the national elections on her own ticket and, if it hadn't been for the Muslim peasant majority, she would have won. She was famous for her charity, for her alarming moods and terrifying tantrums, and was known as the Queen's confidante and as the most sexually active woman of her class. She had green frightening eyes, a biting tongue, a sharp mind, a tremendous hunger for everything, an iron will, and disarming charisma. Ela was named after her.

Ela's father, her son, was a passionate irresponsible artist who sacrificed a promising career and a famous string of lovers in Europe, to live in isolation with the wife his mother arranged for him in order to preserve the familial purity and longevity. He wore torn overalls, drank wine and cognac all day, loved to eat, folkdance, crack jokes, ride, swim, and play soccer. He was hairy, tanned, muscular, bare-chested, affectionate, curious, and spent his time in the stables or in his studio making wooden carvings, stone sculptures, metal furniture, or developing photographs.

Ela's mother was a hauntingly beautiful, otherworldly, self-contained, impossibly innocent girl who had no interest in the world outside her garden and house and no activities other than reading poetry, singing opera, strolling, and resting. She wore exquisite silk gowns every day, took a two-hour bath and two-hour massage in the morning, was never out in the sun, had impeccable intricate manners, ate sparingly, spoke rarely, and fainted daily. She had died after birth and was resurrected in her coffin at her funeral three days later, after her father locked himself in his church to pray and threatened the Virgin that he would set himself on fire if she did not deliver a miracle for him.

Ela was given absolute and total gratification at birth. At her father's request, no rules or demands were put upon her. She abstained from play and worldly pleasures and spent her days in the seclusion of the dank dark empty mud basement of their ancestral mansion dreaming awake, certain that she inhabited the best possible world: life happened in her head.

She had no patience for the surrounding forests and gardens, the orchards, the streams, the purebred horses, the wolf-dogs, the Himalayan cats, the villagers' wild children, the books in the library, or her idolizing tutors. Daily life revolved around her as stark comedy. She was lauded by all as the gift of heaven. The family was convinced that Ela was chosen to fulfill a superior destiny. They agreed she had to remain an only child. Dad called her a jewel, a miracle, his life's joy, his only hope, the family's raison-d'être. She suspected a grand elaborate trap hid behind his words. The trap was the world. The bait was love.

Had she believed in their words, she would have become a mere idol prey to masochism and softness. But she resisted and gave in to a hard haughtiness by making herself into the most lonely of creatures: a creator. She chose for herself a useless heroism that would not be shared by many. She withdrew from the world into fantasy. From early on, the stupidity and passion of other people bewildered her. Their endless fussing over her and her own caressed and protected little body displeased her. She received hundreds of servants, workers, and peasants who came from the fields to offer her gifts, perform ritual blessings for her, predict her fate, bury her in flowers, wish her happiness, and kiss her feet once a month. Her birthday was celebrated with exorbitant fiestas for miles and the locals were so honest in their joyous mirth and worship that she felt convinced that they expressed the sentiments of all humanity.

Ela never knew that she was a child. She was considered an adult. Her wishes were instantly obeyed, she had the final word in major family decisions and gave orders when her relatives felt unequipped to act. She was a tiny well-dressed girl with burning eyes and tangled hair who was prone to ecstasies and who asked those she met if they had seen God's face and if they really knew how to fuck. She was impatient to have sex by the age of two, but, despite her demands, no servant dared humor her, for fear of God. She recited Browning and Coleridge at four. At seven she fell in love with Rimbaud. At nine with Beckett and Gertrude Stein. After that, she lost all interest in words. The servants said that she was a spirit of the sea. A fairy. She could steal away one's voice.

Squatting in the dark for hours she created a world more exciting than the one outside her: the crowds watched her fly across the sky, her suitors hanged themselves from trees in despair of winning her favor, islands, rocks, and seas called out her name in need and she emerged out of nowhere in flowing gold veils and huge scarlet scarves and killed in a blinding blow one hundred savages. She thought with elation: "I am All and I am Nothing; I am the Fear of fear, the fearless, secondless One, the Ruler of destiny, the Destroyer of fact! I require no one else for my happiness. I am alone through eternity, for I remain free for ever. If the universe tumbles down around my ears, what is that to me? I am the peace."

When Ela was nine, her family was forced to move to Europe,

persecuted by one of those blind fits of nationalism to which Arabs are especially prone. They fled for their lives in secret, leaving nine hundred years of history behind to be confiscated by the mob. No longer the center of a vast fortune, a venerable name and tradition, and an adoring population, Ela suddenly became an anonymous foreign entity who had to compete and survive in a vulgar world. She was only trained in the exercises of the imagination. She now required pedestrian skills, secular weapons. She quickly learned to use her vices and talents. She learned to speak in many foreign languages.

It was painful to meet other children and to join them. Ela abhorred their primitive groups that shared the same jokes, games, preoccupations, enemies, and methods. The democratic chaos of school—with smart, stupid, clean, dirty, big, small, meek, mean, pretty, ugly, rich, and poor students piled together and subjected to common rules struck her as ludicrous and incomprehensible. In the past Ela had treated her tutors affectionately because they loved her; but now she had to pretend to love them in order to gain their affection. Alienation, Ela's family heritage and her natural mode of being, was an insult if it was imposed from the outside; so she had to abandon it.

Ela's humiliation: on her first day her school went on excursion to an olive grove on a rocky hill. Her classmates played cops and robbers. Ela was surprised at being treated as one of them. During tag-and-freeze the ugliest, most stupid boy chased her. She ran fast, cursing her untrained pampered body. He reached her and with a dumb smirk, his thick fingers and dirty fingernails touched her on the left shoulder. According to the rules, Ela froze on the spot under a deformed obese olive tree.

She realized the world was full of nonsensical regulations and vowed never again to be subjected to the laws of the masses.

Aware of a burning hole between her legs, she spent the hot dead afternoon as a human statue, exposing her defeat, obeying orders, punished like a fallible pillar of salt.

She ran home to the mirror and made faces into it. Her mirror showed her that she was a monster, that she did not exist. A gap reigned in her. The mirror showed that she was a surprised abyss who to everyone else was a surprised angel; that she would never jump at the sight of her shadow; that she needed no excuse; was an art. She wrote with her lipstick on it: "The world will never know me," "The world is smaller than I am," "I will fool the world, and it will make me a saint." That day she switched from thumb-sucking to a mature addiction: masturbation. It was her way of making love with the mirror, her new act of freedom.

The next day in school she lurched into speech as a woman dying of thirst dives into the mirage of an oasis. She overflowed with perishable brilliance. The correct words came out of her mouth without hesitation or zeal. Her public moments were inspired delaying tactics for self-preservation, comic maneuvers designed to stay her terror as she rebelled against the needy new world. She prevailed over it by her innate cockiness as an heir apparent. She invited all eyes to be nailed on her and suffered like any actress. She used words to gain advantage, but she discarded any system of reference, robbed objects of their naive identities, and liberated the world of reality.

Ela's spoiled body betrayed her in school: she caught colds, children's diseases, strep throats; she did not run, jump, kick, aim adequately; after she rolled down the slide or around the gym bars she had to vomit. Her body was a burden she dragged along, an obstacle that rose before her at every step. Her frailty separated her from the others: she felt trapped in a crystal ball, like a message locked in a bottle at sea.

She quickly persuaded her classmates that their physical activities were ridiculous in the eyes of any logical outsider who might watch them hang like chimpanzees from bars or run senselessly after a plastic ball or jump again and again into a rectangle of sand; as a result, her class failed physical education en masse. She organized a boycott of the national holiday parade on the grounds that the prime minister whose refusal to the Nazis was celebrated was himself a fascist responsible for the torture and murder of thousands of democrats. That successful protest became an annual tradition for all the schools in the capital even though Ela's initiative sprang from her unwillingness to march last in line because of her miniature size.

Her male teachers fell in love with her even though she was just ten. They fought to have her in their homeroom, held her hand, cried on her lap, speculated on her origin, told her their secrets, offered to run away with her and begged her to come back to them in five years. The female teachers tried to pass to her the wisdom of lives wasted as good daughters, wives, mothers, and patriots. The other girls imitated Ela faithfully and ruthlessly competed to serve her. The boys followed her in troops, spent the night on her doorstep, accused and injured one another or themselves in desperate macho feats meant to impress her, carved her name on trees and desks, drew on the board big hearts torn out of boys' breasts and placed into Ela's starlike palm with tears of blood dripping through her eager fingers. The high school boys next door scrawled "Ela I love you" on their arms with knives and showed her the bleeding incisions. They wrote on the city walls in huge black letters: I LOVE ELA and ELA: I AM YOURS!

The admiration of the crowd did not penetrate Ela. Someone or other ran up to her at all times to confess: I love you. They love me, she thought, feeling nothing of it. They know that it won't come to any good, but still they give themselves over to me. There is more of me than this, she thought as she saw them coming. She enjoyed the freedom of complete isolation. She saw no image of herself in the world. So at ten, Ela had already formulated her basic approach to people:

1. Show them love, appear open, and remain opaque.
2. Never trust them (Never even trust myself).
3. Never believe what they say (I don't know how to believe).
4. Have contempt for them for being such easy victims.

For fun, she daily practiced hallucination: she saw a rowdy brothel in the place of a sober Byzantine church, an immense phallus held by screeching griffins in the park, a family of fat hermaphrodites involved in a complex orgy during class, muscular centaurs galloping on the city highways with their manes loose in the wind, a busy pink bubbly parlor at the bottom of her teacup; colorful horrors rose before her eyes and blended into her surroundings, constant transfigurations of beings and objects. As long as life was not real it gave her joy and solace.

Late at night she crossed alone the wide silent boulevards, inhaling deep breaths of freedom and libido, feeling that she was probably the maker of everything she saw. She squeezed through the wire fence into the ancient marketplace and lay on the hot old lively stones. She peered into every lit window, bent on her hands and knees to look into the basements of the poor at distant working class districts. She watched grim sailors argue in bars, wild gypsies bellydance around fires in their camps, rude drag queens bargain their asses in the central square, tired whores sit with fat open thighs on top of steep staircases, ghostly nightclub singers eat lamb soup at dawn, wise opium users share a pipe in circles at the outskirts of the forest and, deep in the forest, young couples perform rape or love. She hid from cops, cab drivers, and kind-hearted men who thought she was lost and insisted on taking her home. She learned to move silently, see and hear sharply, judge fast. Those she saw became characters in her ongoing fantasies. She felt her "subjects" love her in the mist and the openness of her imagination: a love that gave her plenty of space and let her stay alone.

She guessed what her subjects thought, desired, concealed, forgot. Their own actions gave unpredictable directions to her musings. Now her fantasies were live! She didn't distinguish what she felt from what she pretended. She saw pretty girls give birth to stones, snakes, chickens, and hogs, a massive underground plant that churned out and sent up fake humans, and surveillance insects patrolling the sky. She warned no one of all that.

Ela became a familiar figure of the night, greeted by men exposing themselves behind the bushes, their eyes glowing in the shadows with triumph, lust, and fear; dozens waited for her in the parks to jerk off; as she stopped to watch their plight, they bowed to her with respect. She befriended thin transvestites who were beggars by day, prostitutes by night, and hustled with them for tickets to gay conventions, fled with them from cops and the red sirens and strolled with them around the harbor where burly-muscled soccer-playing youths whistled and ran shouting behind them through winding cobbled streets about all the tight upright tits, round tough cheeks, hard protruding hips, little bursting dresses, platinum wigs, long lashes, bright lips, red nails, wavy gaits they saw; the queens offered her their shaved asses with girlish timidity, like pastries.

She joined anarchist activists and leftist parties, spied on nuclear arms and political prisoners, covered the city monuments with illegal slogans and posters, wrote soul-searching songs with old men drinking grappa beyond the curfew hours till dawn. She enjoyed the meaninglessness of politics, the endless labyrinths of words that were never penetrated by the light of the outside world. She was so young and polite that all the cops jailed her halfheartedly, even though she loved the handcuffs, the bloated guards, the orange uniforms, and the forlorn parasites who for some reason stay in prison forever.

When Ela was twelve and had just been elected school president, she first discovered that dancers, acrobats, and construction workers could give her profound physical pleasure. She spent the next months developing her cunt. It was the most exciting, fast-paced time of her life. She changed partners like underwear, or rather like the way people move from sentence to sentence as they speak. Every time the lights went on, she found herself with a new lover trying out a new position. She was swept away by the restless hunger of that cunt and did not suspect that its sensations might ever become redundant. She loved her new rootlessness. Her clitoris was a boil on the face of the world. Her cunt was a canker in the heart of the world. The world was street theatre, a live show produced for her delight. Life was not different from dreaming awake. Let the waters part, she winked at the mirror. She moved from country to country in search of...

How She Lost It

Ela is walking up and down the street, lost in herself. A black man comes towards her and expertly thrusts his hand under her long dress between her thighs. Ela thinks that this has happened to her before. What is he holding now? She looks up at the world with quick indignation, even though she is uncertain of the correct components of such an outmoded and unfamiliar facial expression. Should she frown? Gape? Wouldn't that be coarse? Is there a customary cry of irritation or horror that she should utter? Ela feels ridiculous being possessive of her cunt, but she tries to perform the motions hoping to portray that she is appalled, that she disapproves, that the stranger does not have her permission for his endeavor. *Andante*, she tells herself.

Her face displays: How can he barge in without asking? What

does he take me for? An object? Public property? Even so, it is common knowledge that most objects already belong to someone else. Whom does my cunt belong to after all? I'm such a thief, Ela thinks, feeling herself act as if she has made up or as if she owns her gestures, feigning surprise at the flaming doves flying out of her sleeve. Nothing of me that others see belongs to me. I reveal what I have stolen.

It is a pleasure for any passing disinterested spectator at this moment to look into Ela's eyes as they mirror the daylight with liquid fear, exaggerated amazement, and an undercurrent of coquetry. Falseness becomes her. The spectacle tantalizes the passersby who turn and stare with incredulity and satisfaction.

Ela is wearing a headdress of silver ostrich feathers that rise high above her head and fall down the back of her voluminous black gown of a tight crêpe-de-chine tunic sheathed in iridescent veils with pointy sleeves trailing from her wrists. She rises so majestic in her labyrinthine dress that her head seems to touch the sky; so elegant that she makes everyone around her feel anxious and inadequate.

The first passerby to stop dead in his tracks is a scrubby goggle-eyed idler; his mouth hangs open, eager to egg the black man on or pass him instructions or take bets on the developing fight; for despite her unadvantageous circumstances and wondrous whiteness, Ela looks as though she is the one who gives the orders. This small man at the back of every crowd, the *hoc genus omne*, who obviously sees himself as a stagehand, sends grave nervous glares at other approaching men, as if cautioning them not to trust their eyes. His face of a gargoyle brings to Ela's mind the faces of her men when they come.

Ela herself is in the dark. She, like the little man, is only a spectator, though hers is a more limited angle of vision. Like the proverbial cuckold, she thinks, I will be the last one to find out the doings of my cunt. If I knew this would happen, I might at least have worn something appropriate like a dress of fishscales. It is the old trouble with this cunt. It inspires this senseless behavior on its own; I can't be held responsible for what happens to it. Yesterday Ela had worn a latex mask of a drippy-nosed aged horned satyr with a frightening expression of shocked grief and a tuft of hair on the chin like a lonely pubic mount, and her tight bodysuit of goatskin. Why couldn't I have been attacked then? she thinks; it would have looked better. Now looking at the naive mob standing around like a class of students impatient to learn, Ela entertains a prophetic thought: Are we preparing ourselves to escape from the principle of identity?

The gargoyle has now disappeared behind more sightseers; they glance at one another for an explanation before they can trust the authenticity of the assault. Does anyone know what is going on? The silence indicates the absence of any official understanding. Once they ascertain that this is a bonafide mystery, the spectators take up their positions to wait for the rising action. They resemble people who have assured themselves of a good view in a triumphal procession by arriving early or camping out since the night before.

Ela secretly knows that she has only her cunt to blame for her present crisis. Minutes ago as she took it for a stroll trying to distract its hunger, she felt it open and shut its rims, draw its lips inward and quiver rapidly like a telegraph wire sending out an urgent code. She now recalls an aging eye surgeon who slept with her last week and then ran home and killed his son with a kitchen knife, because he wanted no ties outside her cunt. Ela wonders: I don't speak or think with my cunt; but my cunt writes my story. What gives it such power? Where does it come from?

"Did he who made the lamb make thee?" Who is in control? This cunt or I? If it is not mine, whose is it?

Meanwhile a black man has now come grasping a shiny gut-wrenching knife in his big primitive hand that is now groping between her thighs. He does not look up or around him. He is busy facing down toward her cunt, oblivious to Ela, bent over with a grimace of single-minded concentration that distorts his face into countless thin dry lines. He squints like a surgeon performing a delicate dangerous operation. He may be holding a surgical tool. He bites his lip solemnly, like a boy peeling his first apple or dissecting a fly or making a helicopter of a live cicada by inserting a piece of straw into its butt. The rest of Ela's body becomes numb from his lack of attention. She feels her big proud breasts sag sadly. She regrets that they always have to compete with her autocratic godless cunt. *Largo.*

In suit and tie, tall, clean-shaven, impeccably manicured, smelling of Ivory soap, Ela's violator seems to have come from a conservative paneled masculine world with bottled ships on spacious desks and leather-bound encyclopedias. Ela has a soft spot for this sort of male: feline preppy shy molten dark Muslims from North Africa. She feels the hankering tingle of her cunt. For the benefit of her audience, her face displays the electric pallor of a storm, her eyes the dimness of breathed-on glass. Her hair, loosened by the initial violence, looks like a nest of unknown insensitive birds or an eccentric architectural design or an alien who naps in mid-air; it forms two silver wings that rise upward and back. She holds herself peacefully: only the laughing quiver of her lips betrays the incessant machinations and present hullabaloo of her cunt. *Moderato.*

The black man locks his long fingers on the rims of Ela's cunt and pulls at it with force as if in a desire to detach it. As if it were just glued on to her. As if it were an optional attachment. A gadget. She thinks: *Affetuoso.*

This violent episode reminds Ela of her first public sexual experience. Dressed in riding pants and a burned T-shirt torn above her navel, Italian men's shoes with Maoist mottoes scribbled on them, and a Cretan knife hanging from her belt, which was her outfit for that year, her hands plastered with Band-Aids® and her arms wrapped in hospital gauzes to escape phys. ed., ten-year-old Ela was walking up the dark avenue of Democracy once when she felt something live on her cunt. An adolescent primate with feverish eyes, a new moustache, and an "available for mass consumption" look on his macho face, one of the leisured men called "fish hooks" because they hook on to anything female, wearing the trademark tailored shirt open low to expose an abundance of curly chest hair and a fat gold pendant, had expertly unzipped her pants while she wasn't looking, and his cold fingertips which, she imagined with pleasure, reeked of tobacco and sweat, scratched the rims of her cunt.

Ela was amazed by the transformation on the boy's face as he probed: he became gentle, grateful, almost intelligent. He shut his eyes, fell on his knees as in prayer and said: "Where did you get this gem?" Was this an epiphany? His eyes looked wet and unfocused. Her cunt became wet. He begged: "Let me have a peek" and, encouraged by her smirk, hardly believing his luck, rummaged in her tiny cunt with his fat fingers and then his tongue which felt like a homemade sausage or a mouse, and gave her a miniature orgasm. Afterwards, Ela tasted his fingers with curiosity.

He fell onto the ground in an extravagant show of pleasure. Ela thanked him with a courteous dip of her head which could have meant a further permission, pulled up her pants and walked off.

At the top of the knoll she turned back and saw him still sitting on the curb in stupefaction. She realized then that her greatest desire was to become God, so that boys, girls, and round black-clad women would kneel and kiss icons of her forever after.

It is autumn. Things are dying. The colors are changing, turning red. It is a time of indecision, emasculation, warmth. It is the perfect time for Ela who feels neither alive nor dead.

Ela isn't certain if she owes it to her audience to make up her mind and put up a fight. Is she losing immediacy? Should she call loudly for help? Some observers look perplexed; they seem to wonder if this is a lovers' quarrel and therefore not as entertaining as it appears on the surface, even though Ela and her grim mate make an unusual interracial couple. The audience also needs to decide whether to interfere to save her at the risk of being slashed by the psychotic Negro or sit back and enjoy the free show and the guilt, with a spicy hot dog or pretzel purchased from the mustached Mediterranean vendor who stands prominent among them in his stained white apron and oversized sneakers. Ela's initiative for self-defense would add to the macabre unfolding drama and she would command more attention.

But her protest might deflate her enraptured attacker who is now quivering undisturbed between her legs, and it might force him to retreat before she or the audience have a clearer notion of his motives and aspirations. And wouldn't the audience prefer to see the enigma prolonged? Aren't they favorably disposed to a further buildup of this dark suspense? After all, it is September the perfect month for the consumption of detective mysteries in the Philip Marlowe and Continental Op category. She wonders: What kind of animal is he? What does he strive for? Does this puzzle torture the spectators' minds or do they just think: What the fuck? Is the Slav pizzamaker who rolls his dough at a nearby window with his eyes on me thinking: Boy, could I plow her apart? Split her open? If only they let me? *Vivace*.

At this stage Ela might lower her eyes and raise her arms in distress to please her public and not antagonize, threaten, or disgust them. She takes off her cat's-eye reflective sunglasses decorated with bronze lizards mating on the frame, exposes her immense brilliant eyes to the world, and stretches out her thin neck sideways like Mallarmé's faun imploring in an alien dead tongue. In a pose that drives Draculas and executioners crazy, her gaze startles and unnerves the crowd. The eyewitnesses shift about, look away, hold their breaths, and touch their chests.

Ela feels the familiar sense that she is outside of life, an onlooker, that the spectators are the actual partakers of life. Her whorish and fragmented nature intrigues her curiosity: what do I have of my own that is not a response? Nothing but my cunt. My intellect is a result of being harassed. What seduces me into action? Is life a mute expression of the incomprehensible?

A sudden light flashes in her eyes, reminiscent of her effulgent cunt when it is stimulated, for now Ela notices the ritualistic shuddering and waving rhythms between her and this black Goth, writhing together as if under the influence of an unidentifiable hypnotic powerful will. Ela watches the man's rise and fall as if to record the world's maladroit struggles.

The light changes. Ela is bleeding now. The blood has attracted a bigger motley crowd of shopowners and shoppers, bag ladies, actors, petty thieves, insurance salesmen, executives. They all feel nostalgic for an old genuine crime of passion to take place between two clean well-dressed dignified persons, an irrational romantic mystical act from the heart. Alienation is transparent, Ela thinks, watching them. *Mezzoforte*.

With these great expectations the crowd grows so extensively that people arriving now at the back crane their necks expecting an aerialist, a stand-up comic, a preacher, or a pantomime and wait for the round of applause at the end of the routine when the audience disperses and they can move closer. Those who think ahead search their pockets for change.

Crowds always love to pry into Ela's secrets, to gape at her movements so deft and sufficient unto themselves that it is impossible to imagine her doing anything accidentally. Latent in even her most stagey gesture is an indifference to consequences: she has no interest in running from Herod's knife or Diogenes' lamp. Her insolence cuts through everyone's cocoon. She gives the spectators the impression that they are watching a sight so rare that it makes them worthy of being themselves watched by another audience; she enables the world to feel watched, and needed, like a celebrity. *Forte.*

The cunt, the main attraction, lying behind the curtain of Ela's dress, is wet, aroused by its attacker's impenetrability as much as by his groping. He doesn't strut or fret. He files away at Ela's cunt as a prisoner patiently saws at his cell bars. She senses his long muscular thighs pushing against the thin material of his pants, ready to run off into wilderness. She leans closer to his hand, cunt first, head next, chest last.

Ela recognizes again the excitement she felt a few days ago when one of the pug-faced, red-eyed, excessively salivating, Down's-syndrome dwarfs who usually appear in groups came speeding toward her, staring intently at her cunt, his brows joined in an effort to focus, his forehead wrinkled with a "now or never, gotta give it my all" look; he stopped dead before her with open legs and mouth and tense outstretched fingers, stuck his groin out and up as if to shake her hand with it and exhibited the most ominous and determined peak Ela had ever witnessed; he shook as if he were being electrocuted and his crotch continued to bulge into a vivid pyramid. The chosen cunt was dying to test that immense dumb cock. But his attendants came by before Ela had time to grab him aside and strip him. She imagined that he would have screeched and pounded her frantically until an unkind soul pulled him out of her months later; for Ela believes that the retarded can produce the most awesome fuck-sounds, shrieks of life's panic and that they fuck nonstop, for ever after, unable or untrained to withdraw without outside intervention.

For now Ela's inspiring cunt is being butchered. The Vandal seems resolved to get to the root of it. Seconds pass. He stabs around her cunt, screaming: "You fucking white cunt!" Ela is intrigued by his misinterpretation. Can he be mistaking her for someone else? Should she ask? Should she be polite and condescending or direct and righteous? Is this a racial episode? Is it not obvious that she is outside all race? She could say: "Sorry, but I am a foreigner." Or: "In my country we never had black slaves. We first saw blacks in World War II. At fourteen, I was clubbed by a black Los Angeles cop while protesting the death of a black worker. I fear I don't meet your expectations. I don't want you to waste your time here." But she keeps quiet, eager to see what comes next. Aware of the intimidating effect of her husky voice and vowel-stressing accent, she refrains from speech until she can better appreciate the scene. She thinks: my cunt is my gag; it prevents any other communication. He is still groaning: "You fucking white cunt." He sounds firm. *Sforzando*.

The sky lowers perceptibly. Ela feels herself enlarging. But as a typical Mediterranean she is less interested in her own precarious fate than in the intimate affairs of the strangers near her. She can't help wondering: What role is he playing? Why did he choose me? Is he an old victim of my cunt? Is he a new fan? Am

I the representative of all women in his eyes or is it specifically my cunt that he is punishing? Is he a chauvinist pig? Is he an archetype? Is he a sex freak? Is he serious? How long will he keep this up? Is he satisfied with the way it is going so far? Is this an experiment? A parody? A morality play? A necessity? A law of nature? Is this common practice? Is he an expert? A neophyte? Is he learning on me? Is there a proper name for this activity? Is there a bigger picture, a plot, a guild, a family, a sect, a pact behind it?

Is this the opposite of body building? Is he trying to tell me who he is? Is he trying to tell me who I am? Does he want to be pitied? Feared? Punished? Admired? Loved? Famous? Does he have an erection? I can't see. He must! Why else would he be involved with my cunt? Can the crowd see? But he bends with his back to the audience, so that only the blind cunt has a frontal view of his crotch. *Capriccioso.*

Ela leans closer over him like a wide-spreading black eagle, a vampire opening up to swallow him. He shudders visibly. She wants to laugh at that but stops herself; laughter would break the frail silence and she might never reach the climax as a result. Then she notices: I am in a shaking black-and-white movie. The bright cars moving behind him seem part of another world; they are probably rolling on a 3-D videoscreen in the background, zapping in and out of focus. Is it a B-movie? A kitsch buddy movie, in the tradition of the Trojan war? A low-budget cult film? A sappy splatter?

She thinks: Do I take this madman for granted? Is that my defense? Is that my flaw? Even the audience is a little afraid of me: they must suspect I am not entirely serious. The black man attacks me thirty seconds ago and I am already falling into a routine. Nothing new under the sun. For I can see him fucking: sad, raping the lock, treating his cock as a key. Everybody comes:

death—little or big—is the first and final argument. My cunt is nothing to me. *Allegro.*

The onlookers push forward inquisitively with glittering eyes and thick wool sports jackets reminding Ela of a cluster of sturdy fleecy cattle that now claim East Seventieth Street as their territory. She thinks: so this is what happens when there is no Face Control at the entrance. Ela wants an orgasm in front of this herd, provoked by the drifting and ebbing of her cunt clutched in a sexy tossing rhythm at the humid shadowy hands of the black man.

The crowd thinks: Is this a rehearsal? Have they done this number many times before? Is it a business? Is she paying him for this? Is she getting paid for this? Is it a nine-to-five job? Are there season tickets on sale? Can I bring my friends to the show sometime? Is it publicity for an off-off-Broadway play? Is it an A.C.L.U. protest? Why is it for free?

At this instant, bleeding and feeling faint, Ela is finally experiencing the so-called joy of life: something is happening! Perhaps she was made for this world after all! Perhaps there is a reason for her life! She suddenly feels toward this man the soft affection that she feels for an old faithful mirror which could be her crystal ancestor, the mirror that is her link to herself and represents her only worldly attachment. *Spiritoso.*

"She sees something," a New York University student gushes. Dozens of eyes open widely. The masses crave a religious experience. Ela dilates her gold pupils, rolls them up into her skull, parts her lips, drops back her head as if to swallow a precious lifedrop falling from heaven, shivers, slumps, grins, and then looks at the multitude compassionately. She gazes directly at them one by one until they feel certain, as if a chasm is opening around each one of them, that they are alone, fraudulent, facing their ice-cold mirror. Some look around them for a fast escape; maybe food or a beer. "What was it?" they twitter, turning to each other for help, moving closer together. She thinks: They'll do anything I ask of them now. It's happening. *Vivere pericolosamente.*

It all suddenly makes sense to her: the black man has pride. He prefers to kill than be killed. Her experienced cunt is now being penetrated in places it was never touched before. Her proud cunt that recognizes no one is now permanently marked by this man. He is planting himself inside her like a tree.

She senses the knife, the main device, hot and mechanical slicing into her. Her inflamed cunt chirps and sizzles like stirred and drenched embers. She thinks: this is the man as originally scripted, big and hard; he doesn't beg, flatter, whine, trick; he trespasses; this man can kill my parents, my past, my image. He doesn't seek refuge in metaphors; when he must have my cunt, he doesn't say: "I'll rip your cunt off"; he does it. Right in front of the Frick. *Con brio.*

Last night a lover read to her an article about a young Japanese couple: the man ate his girlfriend and the cops found left-over steaks of her in his fridge; the man said it was the ultimate consummation of their love, that she had consented to it. Did he tell her: "I want to eat you"? Did she demand: "Eat me"? This is the sort of reality Ela can understand without feeling stupid. *Rallentado.*

Bending forward with her black dress unfolding like a stage backdrop of a clouded sky, Ela's primary awareness now deserts her audience. She loses interest in the periphery and fixes her attention upon her morose slasher. She presses on his tense shoulders with her small hands reassuringly. *Crescendo.*

Attuned to his jabs, alert to the moment, Ela feels that she is living at last! The black man senses her careless generosity that grants him without argument everything he is struggling for. Ela senses his blazing effort, the risk of their public coming together to a release. Together they are learning the secrets of the knife. Together they are doing irreparable damage: they establish the anarchy of her cunt.

She thinks: I am not imagining this.

The sky is coming down on them. She stands relaxed and takes each sure-handed thrust with a deep inhale. A low deferential silver cloud spreads about her.

With the world's tightest cunt, Ela thought she should have been entitled to severe pains from sexual penetration. But she never before bled or hurt because of a broken hymen and assumed that she was born with no virginity, and ready for intercourse, or else that she had not been adequately pierced yet. Now the vaginal pain shoots through her as if to wake her up, and she thinks: I am a virgin at last. The conclusion of this act can't possibly reconfirm that men are inadequate.

Now Ela finally understands what men mean when they ooze deep in her ear: "My cock is a knife cutting through you, coming out of your mouth, opening you up!" She had never felt any such knife going into her, despite men's warnings. But she no longer lives in metaphor: this man's knife makes a difference. It makes her feel. *Veloce.*

Shreds of flesh and clots of blood splatter Ela's thighs. Tiny pink streams slither down her legs. In her brain a child soprano sings: "Blood has flowed, honor is saved..." *Anoso.*

The crowd does not have to look up to see the sky, for it now envelops the action like a narrator's voice. The clouds drift through Ela's legs in circles. Everyone present is startled by this stark intimacy between the elements.

Ela thinks: I have been a mistress of disguise, I have been limitless, and at this moment I am finally being discovered. I open like a bud.

It is an experience she is not to attain again: Ela feels loved. For an overburdened instant, she knows in her bones that he loves her. She can believe it: someone loves her! This new awkward emotion spreads out like carbon monoxide inhaled by everyone present; it gives her a migraine immediately.

Are these, then, the dreaded symptoms of reciprocal love? Is some unavoidable incomprehensible putrid-smelling gangrene spreading through Ela's body? Love flutters in her lungs, swells up against her diaphragm, burns and upsets her stomach: an arrogant, self-sufficient feeling, a secretive impersonal fatal force pushing at her insides and choking her. Her body cannot digest her toxic love. Her organs resist. Her virginal heart falters. She wants to puke. The clouds continue to dance around her. Her heart is a black clay pot forgotten on the fire.

On this gray New York City corner Ela stands lovestruck, looking like a lost ghost, trapped in a confusing respect for another being which pressures and floods her unprepared chest. I will now die of love, she feels, out in the open, in public. I am whirling in the midst of the unadulterated butchery of love! She relishes the blows of her love, as St. Barbara must have relished the infidels' tortures, with a divine exuberance.

Ela does not know how to receive and can only hope that she is doing it correctly. Love is my rite of passage, she thinks, I must now face it. If I love, I am no longer trapped in being me. This is my chance to be taken, to be possessed. To belong. To die. For a deceptive instant she no longer sees death as her reason-to-live but as the mirror: a vulnerable-looking blonde vamp with long gilded eyelashes, naked, and garbed in gold dust who smokes through antique cigarette holders, sways her lazy hips forward and sideways and is so civilized that she has done away with all language, down to the one last word: Come.

At Ela's first sigh of love, the whole world feels lighter and dizzy, as it does during take-off aboard a plane. Death has come.

At that same instant the man wavers and falls to his knees, exhausted and panting. Yet he persists with the cunt-chopping like a starved woodpecker or a Cuisinart® gone berserk. Ela faces thin white fumes coming out of her thighs and clouding her eyes. It is an old eccentric characteristic of her cunt that happened only in private till now. Whenever Ela glanced at her cunt in repose, while sitting for instance on the toilet reading *The Unnamable*, white smoke or steam was rising from it, as if her cunt contained a miniature pool of boiling acid. Her thighs were permanently fogged. She supposed that it overheated, resolved to tell a doctor, then dropped her skirts over it and forgot it. She usually concluded: My cunt is civilized: it smokes. To Ela smoking is a major sign of civilization: "Animals eat, sleep, fuck, shit, but they don't smoke," she explains. *Sostenuto*.

The fallen man grabs her knees for support. She is seized by sympathy. The sky has dropped so low that she is shrouded in moving ominous clouds, and if she were claustrophobic she would be unable to bear that closeness. In the present amber light her tired offender looks older, apprehensive, restrained, and old-fashioned. His breath smells putrid. He exhales cold gusts of air. He wheezes like a dying man. *Tremolo*.

He keeps cutting. She runs her pale fingers through his hair tenderly, as if to encourage or even cherish him, but her ring gets caught in his wiry tufts. She tries to pull it off by jerking her finger away from his head a few times, but she only manages to uproot a handful of hard gray hairs and increase his discomfort.

The knots around her ring become so complex that she finally has to use both her hands to disentangle and free her fingers one after the other. This takes a few seconds. In the course of that affectionate moment she hears his faint sobs, a sad blend of muffled whimpering and suffocation. She is also struck by:

1. The eyeball of her large silver ring, a glass eye of the kind that blind people insert in their empty wrinkled sockets in order to appear to see, which has the color of her eyes against the sun and was made especially for her as an amulet years ago by a very long-nailed albino witch on MacDougal Street who strangled herself with her own hands because Ela could not love her back, is suddenly staring up at her, intensely questioning her actions;

2. A novel written some years before by her third-best lover ever, Ares, dedicated to her, titled *When It Rains And You Wear White Penny Loafers* which he wore when they first met; in the book Ela—as one of the two characters—transforms into an all-seeing knife; the narrator lives, or perhaps is imprisoned, in an empty mansion with his unpredictable tireless sharp knife that, suspended in mid-air and flying around him from room to room, imposes a long list of irrational prohibitions and punishments on him; when he tries to speak, or disobey any of its numerous other orders which he does not know about in advance, or when he mildly misperforms any one of his moves during its complex choreography of sexual love, the knife cuts deep merciless but careful and quick incisions in his body, into his lips, his eyes, his cock, slowly mutilating him; so that one or another part of him is always bleeding; but it never kills him and it never abandons him; he refers to it as "The Blind Knife," a term that Ela did not understand then, but had not revealed her interest or her weakness of perception by asking

the writer to enlighten her; the story comes back to her now, out of the caves of her memory, and strikes her as suddenly relevant.

A vainglorious twilight is setting in. Things turn red, bloody, before they disappear. Death comes closer to everyone and the cell of life becomes so tight that for a split second Ela has to think of wet poppies or a girl's panties left on an old wooden table or fat mothers smiling on sunlit balconies in order to open up some space for herself to breathe in. The sky sits on her head lightly, as if to avoid waking her up. At this breathless alarming hour the world seems hanging by a thread, like a lover just about to come.

The crowd pales and shivers with anticipation.

Ela moves her palm to the stranger's chin and gently pulls up his face. She lifts it toward her and studies it closely. She looks at it upside down, chin on top. Her formidable gown billows. She sees his huge pouting purple lips, his swollen carved brown gums, his pointed stained ochre teeth, his overflowing clotted saliva; then, lower, his streaked sunken cheeks, his thick ashen stubble, his white empty eyes; then his bushy connected brows, his narrow wrinkled forehead, and back to his sockets. A slimy milky spotty film like rancid cum covers his eyeballs. Ela's first thought: This man has cum coming out of his eyes!

Looking into this despondent face, or masque, she does not need to restrain the disdainful look which is naturally hers. She needs to vomit. So he did not have the guts to show her his dead eyes! She thinks: a blind wimp. In close-up he looks decapitated; ancient; slow-witted. His frozen grimace expresses a distant hope to be relieved of his pain. He wears the tacky permanently imploring expression of those Christ-being-taken-off- the-cross idols that are sold in massive quantities outside places of pilgrimage. He has the broken flaccid nauseating beauty of Christ-in-a-Pietá. *Diminuendo.*

She lets go of his head. It drops heavy on his chest. The knife, the senseless prop, stays busy. Even now this crouched maniac keeps working! Ela thinks: a blind man is destroying my cunt. What a sublime waste! Was it all an innocent mistake? A misunderstanding? A farce? Should I hold my breath and break it all up as if it never happened? So this was a random act! I was not chosen! What a buffoon! How would he even know I wasn't black myself? Did someone point me out? Is he following orders? What if I had spoken? I still do not see why he is cutting me. Is it a duty for him? A torment? A loathsome perversity? A hobby? How many men do I know who would kill in order to take his place? I thought he would unmask me, but it is himself he unmasks; that always happens. It is the basis of all relations. So I find myself back in burlesque comedy. She feels a restless skin-tight disgrace. She feels her cunt in her mouth. She looks out across the avenue and swallows hard.

Suddenly Ela hears her grandmother's hiss in her ear: "Stay away from blind people, for they see in the dark. They can see us. Nothing works on them: they are comfortable with the dark. I am not allowed to say any more about it. The rest you must find out on your own. Beware!" So her grandmother had warned Ela years ago at one of the times she had thought she was dying. Despite her expectations, Ela never ran into anyone blind until today and she had assumed that the advice was metaphorical. Now she thinks: it is too late. I can't prescribe what happens next: I don't see the overall picture; I don't make this collage. I have been fooled. I let myself be part of someone else's plot.

By now the gloomy affected sky lies on her feet disemboweled.

Out of courtesy to her audience, Ela resists her impulse to faint. The crowd! she remembers, the crowd I am forever fleeing from and fleeing to: the big inarticulate stimulant. She thinks: I still pitch to the crowd. I still defy the realities I invent. I am still a hoax. It's okay.

She thinks: He is not a murderer.

She catches the eye of the store mirror across the street.

She thinks: I haven't lost it yet. I could sew it up.

The mirror thinks: What was blind Homer's relation to Helen? What was his reward? How could he live on, unable to see her?

She thinks: My core is now being cored.

The mirror thinks: Did Homer invent Helen's beauty? Was Helen actually a hag? Was his manipulation of men's vision his revenge upon the seeing?

Ela thinks: Was this a game of blind man's buff?

The mirror thinks: Is it my fate to never be seen?

The cuts come softer, sloppier, inside her. The blind man gasps like a maitre d' sniffing over a spoiled meat dish or a rookie cop who must alone disassemble a ticking bomb.

Once again Ela falls prey to herself: this man wanders in the streets with dead eyes, she thinks. So do I, in fact. What distinguishes me from someone blind is a miracle; a conjuring trick, I can pretend to see. It is expected that my eyes are connected with my brain, as it is expected that only one girl lies in the coffin and is sawn in half during the magic shows. This man wants to conquer my cunt. So do I. He is willing to take the risk and pay the price. So am I. It is possible that he came to it with his eyes open and he was blinded by it in the process: staring at my cunt so intently could certainly blind him. It blinds me all the time. We are in this together. Partners. Bonded. A team. A duet.

She tells herself: Here lies a man who can't see me; a man I can see without being seen; a man I see not seeing me. A man I do not pose for. His blank eyes, like the mirror, show me that I do not exist. In his eyes I face the opposite of a camera; I am in a reversed exposure. Free from human gravity. Here lies a man who may never have looked in the mirror. A man that pure!

Ela performs the most instinctive blind act of her life: she leans over protectively and rests her palms on the backs of the blind man's hands, rough, wet, with monstrous hard knuckles. Following the rhythmic movements of the man under her, she adds all her strength to the thrusts. The knife goes berserk. She closes her eyes and notices how expertly each return of the blade stabs at the contours of her cunt in the quickest, deepest, and least painful way possible. *Staccato*.

The two pairs of hands busily rise and fall under her dress that is by now pulled far above her naked thighs, though not far enough, but perhaps in another minute, the audience hopes, an arm may jerk clumsily and reveal what is consuming this couple so gravely. Everyone is concentrating on what lurks under the big black dress. Will flames, pink fluffy rabbits, or chubby white doves leap out of there? Or will the rabbits come out strangled and skinned, the doves carved and skewered, the flames liquid like blood?

The knife hits Ela's rich central vein. She smiles.

The crowd waits, quietly breathing through their mouths.

Ela realizes she is in a sense masturbating in front of the mob. Her eyes glitter with nasty challenge. Her rapacious cunt quivers like a fish on land, or like a scorpion's tail. Its high seductive death-rattle spreads through her nerves. She hums.

The speechless crowd imagines tall gallows being set up for her on the avenue, and a capital letter—*A for Assaulted*—getting branded on her chest with fire irons. The crowd thinks: At one or another age or culture, this woman would no doubt have paid with her life for this appalling frivolous act, whatever it is, that happens before our very eyes.

Raw, tiny gasps come out of Ela's mouth. She thinks: he tries to blind me; to steal my sight; to cut me off from my cunt—my beacon; to make me unreal. *Vibrato.*

The crowd now starts to suspect it is watching an MTV video performed live. That means they have all been cast to play the involved energetic onlookers gathered at the background of the main action to fill the screen. They have been chosen in advance unbeknownst to them and were intrigued to stay by the central number, which was also tested on them for its effectiveness. They will be approached at the end with a release form to sign and a thank-you note or even a token payment. It will come as a surprise. Some begin to shake their shoulders and bob their heads to the beat of the stabs. All try not to appear self-conscious, as they are not supposed to know they are being shot. That is the tough part. Luckily, the show—hard to say if it is a two-character play or a one-woman show—is gripping. If they could afford to take their eyes from the spectacle, they feel sure they would see cameras hovering over and behind everyone.

The two protagonists push and pull obsessively. Fast. In ecstasy. The scarlet early evening light flares on their faces as if they were standing in epic battle. As their fingers graze, she can feel the coldness of her hand. Will she come?

Suddenly Ela thinks: Jesus, this takes long! This incongruous thought echoes through her mind until she laughs out loud revealing her gleaming teeth. It is the same snappy laughing fit that Ela has sometimes during sex: an uncontrollable chuckle at the defeat of logic, a hearty cheer at the ridicule of reality that grows into a demented roaring peal of laughter. Now she giggles, flushed and elated, and fights her urge to dance, skip, clap, chirp, crow, cackle, sing, scream, fling up her headdress, hug herself, hold her sides and fall on the ground "cracking up." Her body shakes with laughter, her eyes bulge, tears tickle her lowered eyes as she tries to suppress her mirth in vain. *Obbligato*.

The crowd does not react. They see her sensitive eyes brimming with shiny tears and think that she could be crying. They watch her fierce convulsions and sympathize with her plight. The blind man, however, who must be oversensitive to mocking sounds and who has no sight to fool him, winces and collapses at once. He drops like a spent arrow, head first, hands next, with sad self-acknowledgment. *Con dolore*.

She averts her eyes and invites sterile thoughts to run through her head, knowing that laughter in this context is sacrilege, like laughing in church when the priest raises the host. Has he come, she thinks, or is this the fall of a man? Is this his tragedy or his triumph? Is he a martyr? How he has aged! she ponders. No Mack the Knife here. But if he can sing like L. Armstrong! I'll ask him to call out: "Good evening everybody!" in that thick ruined voice and burst into "That's My Desire" to cleanse my head of any thought. Her body quakes. She repeats: I core my core.

The old man hangs on to Ela's frame, his ashen head rests against her knees, his limp arms hug her calves, his tired face is raised toward her like a suppliant's; he has curled up into a fetal position. His withdrawal has pushed up her dress, exposing her entire pale thigh to the viewers: short, slender, muscular, glowing. But the cunt, the cynosure of all eyes, is still waiting in the wings. Ela draws the heated knife out of his fist with one hand as she strokes her stinging carved cunt with the other. *Legato*.

Has her blind accomplice died in her arms? It would be lovely: the unalterable outcome of a divine love; the closing of the circle. To stand with a corpse in her hands is always a powerful experience, an image of grandeur that would not be lost on the audience.

Besides, he can't take the plot much further.

The crowd is concerned and confused. Who is the victim now? Hesitant simultaneous whispers come out, dying as they are being uttered: "Get him help." "Get her a chair." "Get her a hot bath." "Get him under a cold shower." "Get an ambulance." "Hug him," a woman urges her. Then, as abruptly as they emerged, the whispers expire. The audience moves closer, out of an impulse to embrace the two victims, protect them and contain them, drawn to them as to two innocent creatures that have fallen from heaven.

Ela holds the outer edge of the mouth of her cunt and runs the knife once around its slashed borders with new admiration—expressed by raising her eyebrows—for the clean unobtrusive vertical incisions that surround it. She cuts herself as if she were simply tearing out a page from a diary, or peeling a kiwi. Again she feels death rest on her like a cloud. She swoons. She closes her eyes and smoothly slices around the main vaginal walls along the crescent shape of the existing incisions, uniting them all into one slow continuous circular confident carving.

As she pares her cunt out, Ela hears herself chant: Isolate it: I want the inside information, the source, I want to know what happens to the things that melt around me and disappear like snow flakes, but around everyone else stand solid like monuments. I want to be able to look at it and laugh. *Presto.*

Someone has cut off my strings. I smirk. Or my cunt smirks. I cannot tell which.

I might as well finish this off and see what comes next.

The bystanders on East Seventieth are presented with a memorable sight: a crumpled middle-aged Negro in a light gray cashmere suit, cobalt shirt, black tie, and a Panama hat lies prostrate on the curb loose-limbed and knocked out, in disordered bodily angles typical of retarded people, embracing the naked thighs of a very young woman with tall silver plumes flowing from the top of her head and long silver disheveled hair that caresses her radiant face as the wind blows it into sweaty *S*'s, who cuts a proud stately figure circled as she is unto herself as if in an attempt to grasp and unite or rearrange her own—perhaps removed or even spilling—insides.

And as Ela's cunt drops off, falling with a tiny "slomp" on the ground, the grotesque, nebulous, and curious faces crowding around her are possessed by pity and fear, which erase all their individual differences into a unified expression of awe. They sense that they see something which was never meant to be seen.

The disembodied cunt on the old cracked pavement produces a dreamlike effect on the witnesses of its epiphany: it appears through a haze or fog. It emits a thin white fume as if it were burning without being burnt, like Moses' bush. It imparts light.

So it is beauty, Ela acknowledges. The sight of her cunt spreads a white fire through her nerves. It gives her a pang of nostalgia. It should not hide all the time, she thinks, there is more to life than pouncing and hunting. Illumination becomes it.

In the limelight the shining cunt lies simple and complete. looks indescribably perfect, like an exquisite hothouse flower, a tossed stemless lily. It has elegant understated lines in the shape of two curves coming together. Its delicate frail form gleams like a big dewdrop, an open vibrant gem in the shape of a circle or a zero. An iridescent viscous film like rose oil covers its skin. Its hue changes endlessly from sea-silver to light pearly pink. It catches the eye so irresistibly that one is inclined to search its depths for larger signs of fate, and treasure it like an ancient crystal ball. It possesses a texture of inviting furtive softness, and many overlapping porous curves and rich folds reminiscent of trendy highlighted photos of canyons and layered sand dunes taken with a 4x5 camera.

There is no trace of blood or mark of violence on it. It is miraculously unbruised, even untouched. Possibly due to its muscle memory, it is lightly pulsing or breathing.

No one present can distinguish which exact parts have been carved out, but the result looks excellent: both swollen outer labia are included, the complete erect clitoris, the restless inner labia, a thin layer of vaginal walls that rises into a cylindrical semi-transparent membrane, a piece of the horizontal P.C. muscle; no tubes, no uterus, no rectum, no anus, no cervix, not a single pubic hair; the Grafenberg spot is probably hidden among the other removed organs of the independent cunt, but it is, as usual, very hard to locate.

Ela looks at her mutilated cunt and, for the first time, she feels proud of it. Her dress rustles with delicious melancholy. Her skin itches aroused, her breasts wake up, her veins ripple. The cunt faces her, not mockingly, but curious and observant itself. It seems tenderly watchful, vigilant. It rises lightly and stirs as if looking her up and down from head to toe and appears genuinely surprised. Ela likes it. It does not resemble an animal at all. Despite its brilliant surface, it looks dry and bears no relation to a slug of any sort, nor to a dark trapdoor. It looks inexorable like any other supernatural being. She thinks: It was not deflowered, but enflowered. She feels death come on her again: a soft spill. *Dolce.*

Ela knows her cunt sheds the glow of underworld knowledge: she feels the mutual hellish recognition. There is a league between them, perhaps abhorrent to them both. Her incisive gaze makes it quiver. Is this false orchid what Ela offers to those who love her? Is this understanding? Is this seraphic yawning fruit really her old Quixotic fire-spitting cunt? No matter how it looks, it is still a beast, she thinks now, inhabiting the unthinkable pink ether beyond. If I ever love anyone, it will be this evanescent water plant. But the last ties between us have just been severed.

The dark red clouds have parted. Cars are loudly passing by, but no sound penetrates the awe of the transported audience. The star of the street show opens and shuts like a phosphorescent oyster. It could be a deity, Ela thinks, breathing in the center of an ornate temple, sovereign and benevolent; rituals, perfumes, colors, hopes, and hymns should eternally revolve around it.

Is this cunt still considered mine? Ela wonders. It surprises her that she doesn't want to leave it behind. Here's looking at you, kid, she toasts. Her mind becomes knotted and she misses the sharp closing and puckering of the labia that took place whenever something bothered her: I never expected that I might not die when stabbed in the cunt. What now, if I am not dying? How do I live?

She bleeds in thin but consistent torrents that drip into tiny pink pools on the pavement. As she bends down in slow motion to leave the blood-stained knife on the curb next to its attractive victim, she has a flashback of a similar street-orgasm years ago, but she resists that memory: not now, I have no leisure. Ela would very much like to sit back and think of this unusual act as a sacrifice, an immaculate birth, a miscarriage, a desecration, a sculpture, a liberation, a revolt, a farce on men, on biology, on Shiva's lingam, on fallen meteorites, but she doesn't have the time. Now when she can still entrance both her cunt and her audience, she must leave the stage unnoticed, before the glares of cameras, officers, history, and law catch up with her. She meticulously wipes her bloody fingers one by one on her large raised dress.

While the numb stillness lasts, slowly so as to not break the fragile balance, her eyes wide in an aura of dream-freedom, with the intact movement of a girl who tiptoes into her parents' bedroom during their sleep to search their pockets or gleans through the diary of a friend who left to get her a drink or slides out of another sticky tired body after hours of continuous soft sex, and with the physical abandon of one who is at home with her body, Ela bends, picks up the indomitable cunt between her thumb and middle finger, places it in her open palm with care, pulls up the strap of her large Goofy purse on her shoulder, stuffs her blinding loose hair under her tight headdress, pushes down her dress, gingerly lets the petrified blind man fall completely on the ground, and takes slow calculated steps backwards and off stage, avoiding any eye contact with the spellbound audience.

She walks away. She momentarily glances up at the whirling dark sky as into a mirrored ceiling, as if to check her face. A turbaned Sikh in a Jack-In-the-Box uniform, obviously cursed with a practical mind, walks out in front of the captivated crowd and hands her an empty glass, or rather a clean peanut butter jar, where she can keep her cunt. This act accelerates the confusion of the stupefied audience as to the nature of the fallen object.

To her amazement, Ela is fine. She writes to the world on a big banner in her mind: Sorry, I am okay. She places her hacked plant with reverent gentleness into the jar so as not to destroy the tender roots. Now she is striding down the street through the busy hustling evening crowds, leaving after her the lingering subversive aura of a closed system and hearing behind her an electrified commotion suddenly explode.

The impulse for violence inherent in every crowd is all at once free to come out. The abandoned spectators behave like freed slaves and helots gathering forces to break into the Coliseum. Everyone looks about with self-importance, makes extravagant gestures and impatient facial expressions and asks loud questions: "What the hell happened, man?" "Excuse me, sir?" "Did you see what I saw?" "What did you see?" "I don't get it! Do you get it?" "What was all that about?" "Where did she go?" "Don't let her go free!" "Follow her!" Everyone simultaneously searches for a leader and strives to become the leader. They have become a mettlesome, high flying, aggravated mob.

Ela slips into a lavender drugstore and buys a pack of Super Maxi New Freedom pads and silver-sparkle nail polish. The girl at the counter in a plaid mini comments: "What a bright pretty fetus you have there!" nodding at the jar as she gives Ela her change.

Ela then turns next door into a small Pakistani mom-and-pop restaurant and heads to the ladies room. The odor of burning grease chokes her. She coughs. A tall dark handsome woman makes an incredibly fast but graceful appearance between Ela and the bathroom door, points toward the empty dining-area and announces like an old cabaret waiter: "Right this way, Ma'am, your table is waiting." She bends forward with the assuring attitude of an old, dedicated, and honorable servant, and for an instant Ela is tempted to hide in her chest and refuse to be part to any sequel. The strong-boned olive-skinned waitress must be the daughter of the ancient-looking shock-white-haired cook in a white nurse's uniform now sticking his mummified head out of the foggy kitchen catacombs with a hospitable and mistrusting expression. She does not even glance at the luminous sprawled cunt in Ela's hand and doesn't take her almond-shaped caring eyes from Ela's face. Her big sensuous dark lips wait half open and Ela is moved to kiss her passionately and abandon herself in sex. The warmth from this waitress jolts her like a slap in the face. She loses all focus, trembles, her feet ache unsure of which direction to lean in. All trace of color leaves her eyes and she prepares to faint from desire. But the dignified waitress, her face suddenly deformed from maternal worry, hugs her free arm to steady her and, misinterpreting Ela's signs of sexual arousal, delivers her to a purple door marked w.c. The choice has thus been made.

Outside, the more perceptive and dynamic of the spectators are already leading the crowd toward *The Ironpants Express.* But most of them are still busy constructing and choosing theories about the event. Their voices fight to rise above the clamor: "The world is unclean!" "She had a temper tantrum." "He had to die." "They must be joking!" "Fixing after fixing." "Wrong, mister: he had a temper tantrum." "He had to pay for it." "She is definitely a right-brain person." "What? Pay with his life for that weird hole we saw on the street just now?" "Far out." "A vindication of the rights of men." "That makes no sense." "She double-crossed him flat out." "You mean to say he acted selflessly?" "She radiated with heavenly light." "Baloney." "Would you call this a happy end?" "They'll screw in rivers, in fields, among a herd of sheep, on the day's catch from the sea, on our very beds if they get the chance." "Wheels within wheels." "Sex is the elixir of life." "Eureka!" "Damned battle of the sexes." "We're all sleeping in a burning house!" "AIDS changed love for ever!" "Kill, pussycat, Kill!"

A woman who watched the terrible excision closely as she stood right behind Ela's feathers, now frantically asks around her: "Does he love her? Does he pity her? Did he save her? Did he hurt her? Does he hate her? Does he need her? Does he beat her? Will he marry her? He must love her. He must! I saw it in his eyes!" She is out of control and attracts the attention of two cops who come on the scene to calm her down. *Prestissimo.*

Inside the narrow one-person purple enclave, Ela looks in the smudged mirror and feels safe. Nothing can hurt her in front of the mirror. She stares into it for a long while and does not blink, until her eyes are so bright that they begin to hurt the mirror. It breaks out into tiny cracks, like struck ice. She looks away. Ela touches the mirror with her fingertips, and the sense of the cold skin against the warmer glass is soothing.

Ela fills the jar with water from the faucet and puts it on the soiled yellow tiles at her feet. She fans her aching torn cavity. Suddenly she faints. A few seconds later she finds herself kissing the filthy floor as she regains consciousness and manages to get on her knees and sit on the toilet. Her joints feel liquid. She cannot control her body. Her jaws rattle and she pushes her thumbs against her wrists to stop the circulation and feel numb. She loses any sense of reality. *Mezzo piano.*

A wave of nausea overtakes her. She takes off her clothes in a desperate fury and falls loudly on to the moldy cool tiles, abandoning herself to the sickness, washed in cold sweat, noisily flapping from one side to another like a fish on dry ground, as if she is trying to leave her body behind down on the floor and take off into thin air. Her insides clamor to come out and a taste of horror settles in her mouth. But after some minutes she is cold enough to feel nothing but the goosebumps on her skin. The hyperventilation in her heart has frozen. She sits up with chattering teeth, her skin paler than a vampire's and her gaping wound directly touching the cool grime. She needs to empty herself. She kneels down and hides her face in the fetid toilet bowl, writhing, grunting, making sounds of throwing up. She sticks her dainty childish finger into her dry throat. Nothing comes out. *Appassionato.*

There is noise in the restaurant and two men enter. Ela peeks through a door-crack: cops. They roar in unison: "Ma'am?" Ela instantly picks up her cunt in the jar with her right hand like a weapon, supports her frenzied head in her other hand, sits up on the toilet and tries to gather her straying wits. She thinks: I should have bought some bottled water for the cunt, it may get infected. Then she looks down and tells her floating cunt, as she has told many men before, in an intimate tone: "It was lovely being with you, like sitting on a leaf. But if you knew how hard it is to convince myself that I want you!" She also realizes:

1. When men ask "Give me your cunt, baby," she can now reply: *"voila"* and hand it over to them without becoming personally involved.

2. Men have no longer the right to declare in her presence: "You just can't get rid of that cunt."

3. Life is interesting only when metaphors become literal.

Now she is trapped in the aftermath: away from the audience, separate from her cunt, Ela feels the familiar structures crumble between her legs into a chasm. Looking for comfort in a cliché, she tells herself: all that was living now seems hollow. *Piano.*

The cops guarding the ladies' room are barking: "Ma'am are you all right? Can you tell us what happened?"

On the toilet Ela fiddles with the tender moist edges of her scissure absentmindedly. She imagines that her cunt was an imp, a rodent, a team of termites chewing at the root of her like the elf who saws at the tree of the world; she had always felt it down there tirelessly eating at her insides, working for the day it could force her to hover over Nothing. All this coring is getting to me, she realizes.

At the entrance of *The Ironpants Express*, people press their faces against the soiled glass door or stretch their necks and push angrily against those gathered in front of them. Some cops order the restaurant door locked.

Yet most onlookers still seem willing to wait peacefully. They compare notes, speak up as critics, call their stockbrokers, their press agents, their shrinks, their lawyers, Oprah, their congressmen, their chiropractors, call work to explain they are held up in an emergency, call for attention. They buy film, buy cameras, pass out business cards, exchange addresses, recommend professional women's or abused men's groups, discuss discount sales, and suffer secret pangs of stage fright.

A chubby black boy composes a rap about it on the spot. The petty thieves are terribly busy. Everyone feels like clapping. Everyone feels important and incisive, like a Miss Marple or an Inspector Clouseau at the scene of an old school chum's ghastly murder. They look sincerely worried, for they assume there is an ultimate matrix common to all people, which of course is why they are members of the crowd.

A cop: "Miss, are you okay?" Another cop: "We've called the paramedics." Ela realizes that she is still in front of the crowd. She thinks: Cops shouldn't be legal. A cop: "Can you understand me?" The other cop: "Do you speak English?" She thinks: I could always see a doctor about this. A cop: "Do you know what day it is?" She pees a single drop. She thinks: At least I can still do peepee! The other cop: "The twenty-first of what month?" The other cop: "Do you know who is the president of this country? Can you tell me his name?" Ela: "Rumpelstiltskin?"

She thinks: It's not much as personal tragedies go.

Out in the street, rumor has it that the colored criminal is a famous singer. Stevie Wonder or Ray Charles or Marcus Roberts. "Ray Charles, Stevie Wonder, love, are all blind," some of them reason. "They were cute once, but now their kids are cute," an old man grunts. No one knows if the assailant is still alive, for no one stayed behind to witness his end. He disappeared in the crowd. He now seems hard to describe but easy to identify if he can be seen again. He was not anyone's idea of a black activist, that is certain. Fat cops take notes. Rude reporters ask questions.

There was definitely blood, they are told, torn clothing, a small knife; and something fell on the ground in the end, still breathing. A cop goes to look for the abandoned weapon. It is also missing. Perhaps someone kept it as a souvenir.

Back in the familiar squalid bathroom, Ela shuts the cover of the toilet, sits on it, takes her bright Goofy purse on her lap and crosses her bloodstained legs.

Public excitement is growing. A widespread black woman throbs: "Soon this site will become a shrine." A girl in a stretch dress breaks into sobs: "I missed the whole crime because I had my Walkman on high volume. Just my luck!" A black vendor of old magazines mutters: "Wow, watch out man, what a woman, what do you do about it, what can you do with her, how much can you take, just one look at her, one look from her is all I'm asking for, a bright pussy, how can you not love her, I've never in my life seen a woman more beautiful!" An emaciated straw-haired man protests: "Fetuses are living human beings! It was murder! I saw it! What gall! A public abortion!" An enthusiastic Southerner exclaims: "I've waited thirty years for this!" The simmering bystanders perspire. They want to see her, to feel her, to hear her true story, to examine the fetching outcome of this unclear violent act. They want to touch her wound which, some remark, has already healed miraculously.

For suddenly a new word-of-mouth prevails: it was a miracle! A phenomenon of worldwide magnitude! The crowd experiences a raucous arrogant exultation. Some swear they see a pair of large slippery red lips like Mick Jagger's up in the sky beckoning to them. Perhaps the miracle was inspired as a promotional device.

Meanwhile Ela is doing her nails; she applies three new coats over the thick silver nail polish already on them, then gropes through her Goofy-faced bag, smears wet polish on her skin and purse, finds her pack and matches, lights a cigarette, all in order to concentrate and formulate a plan. *Maestoso*.

People coming out of nearby subways and stores press the others for information and, in their ignorance, deepen the mystery: "Where is the corpse?" "Who pulled the trigger?" "Did the victim levitate?" "Did she swim in a pool of blood?" "Was the crime self-inflicted?" The reporters call their tabloids: "Gory Posh Accident"—third-pager. Then the Geraldo troop arrives with movie cameras and Geraldo decides: "Black Magic at Frick in plain view of thousands going by." "Bloody Satanic Rite On Seventieth"—first-pager, the reporters quickly revise.

Inside the purple bathroom, Ela notices that she has no underwear on. How will she wear a pad to stop the blood trail? And was she wearing panties during the attack? Did the blind man cunningly remove them? Are they lying on the curb? She cannot remember. Can they be traced back to her? Well, she should have bought tampons, but she thought she might be too tender after the gutting. She does not want to look down there, into her gap. Yet she is curious. What has she done to herself? What sex is she now? Does she still have an identity, is she a "she"? She concludes: I wish I could dream of something.

Outside, the masses are getting impatient. Can the two cops flanking the mystifying bathroom door hold off the curious crowd much longer? Will the police force Ela to come out?

Her earlier flashback returns: a tall whiskered islander came out of the shadows on Equality square and ejaculated: "My dear, are you amphibian?" Ela thought: Fuck, let's fuck, what a line! She looked up sardonically, he grabbed her thin waist, she lifted her dress, he sat on the curb, she unbuttoned his pants, he pushed his pinkie in her buttocks, she sat on him, he gasped, she bit his hand to avoid screaming when she came, it bled, he took forever, she came again, then he groaned, called out for help, croaked in anguish: "My god, I am being killed!" stuck out a white tongue, bit it, and came, choking and gurgling, jerked, his head fell back on the ground with an echoing thump as if it had broken, and he lay prostrate, obviously dead.

Ela stood up and bent over his limp body between her open legs, her hands on her hips, her ass glowing in the darkness under the streetlamp, to examine the results: his shrunk cock lay covered in blood, his abdomen splashed with blood and sperm. Ela suspected that her cunt had cut this huge mountainous man to pieces. Then three "fish hooks" walked by, saw her pale ass sticking out higher and brighter than anything else in sight and shouted with joy; she slipped away to avoid them and never solved the mystery of the bleeding cock. Now she thinks: These stubborn memories add to the confusion. *Pizzicato.*

The cops: "Ma'am, we have to see you." Ela: "I look fine. Contrary to popular belief, I am just sitting here constipated."

Her soft voice caresses the vowels; it sensualizes the cold efficient English, giving it curves. Ela thinks: Worse comes to worse, I can push down the shoulders to make this dress strapless and walk out of here singing, "Put the Blame On Mame, Boys," with open knees and arms, my head thrown back; no one would touch me then; but I don't have a glove.

The other cop: "Ma'am, we have to take you away." Ela: "A cop's job is to defile." Both cops: "Ma'am, we arrested the guy. He won't talk. We need your testimony. We're here to help you."

Ela tickles the loose shreds of her abdomen again, absentmindedly. She wonders if she could grow a new cunt. Would it sprout by itself? Could she have her old one transplanted? Does she want to? It occurs to her that now she can wear it at will, remove it before sleep, carry it in her purse, lock it in a safe, hang it on the wall, put it in the freezer, use it to unscrew the tight caps of bottles, heat it up, and, best of all, forget it.

In the jar, now that Ela examines it closer, her cunt looks irregular, almost grotesque: both the labia are oversized and colorless and seem covered by holiday sparkles; they are layered haphazardly, one starting before the other ends, not parallel but crisscrossed, and they move in the water like the suckers of an amoeba; the small thin elegant clitoris, situated far too low, points upward and sways like a steep vertical sail or an itchy nose or an antenna. Seen horizontally, the silver cunt wears an annoying conceited smirk, a roguish smile that reminds her of Iago or of a prophet. Seen vertically it pouts like the sexy glossy mouth of a vamp. The whole creature looks like an awesome adornment, an overdone embellishment from a different culture. She takes it out and rests it on her palm. She gets gooseflesh.

She suddenly has a craving for figs, grapes, mangos, papayas, as if to feed her frightening gap. Can she go grocery shopping now? She wants the tangy tears of boys to drop in her hot soup and their acrid urine to water her cactus plant. She must go at once to a park and a fruit market. She can't wait. Her palm is burning where it touches her cunt. Then she feels a tight pull and movement on her palm and jumps up with fright, almost throwing the frolicking cunt on the germ-ridden tiles in disgust. The severed cunt just made a leap. Yes. It moves. Ela calls out in a high pitch: "Mommie, it's alive!" *Fortissimo*.

Both cops trill: "Ma'am, we have to break the door." Ela replies: "Snails are sensitive to cold; yet their main enemy is heat. If they dry out, they die. They close their mouths with a thick white membrane and hibernate. They slide on their saliva." She switches on the recorder inside her to replay overheard words whose referents confuse and delay her detractors. This method is most effective with the more intelligent invaders; it can't hold cops off for long. She puts her cunt back in its jar. Now it looks like a slippery water spider flashing an eerie spectral light. Ela says: "That's creepy." She thinks: Why don't I make my winter's resolutions now, I will feel much better. Ela's commandments for a pleasant tomorrow:

1. Create a new grand illusion.
2. Buy a Romeo Gigli hooded coat with the Byzantine twin-headed eagle embroidered on it in pearls and gold.
3. Hear Mozart's *Requiem* in a long black silk robe and satin slippers first thing every morning.
4. Hear John Abercrombie live once a week.
5. Eat flying fish roe and *toro* sashimi once a day.
6. Fuck obese cardinals, ascetic monks, famous criminals, shapeless retards, and no one else.
7. See no human being whom I recognize: lose myself in short ecstatic crowds in the East, for instance.
8. Behave not as a lady, but as a mute empress.
9. Accept and befriend this accursed alien I have cut out of my body so that I don't end up like St. Augustine running all my life from temptation to civilization and back.
10. Move to an unreal space, such as a cloud or a window-case, for instance, where I can be in the world but not of it.

Both cops: "Ma'am, you don't leave us room to do our job." Ela: "I am a foreign national. I saw nothing, heard nothing, understood nothing. Haitians have a saying: 'A single cunt tows a fleet of ships.'" One cop: "Sorry Ma'am, the law is specific." Ela: "Wordy men leave me indifferent." The other cop: "Are you playing dumb in there? Open up." Ela: "Where is your ambition, your sense of noble rivalry, of style? Your discourse is lamentable." One cop: "Ma'am, everything will be all right, once you come out.

I promise." The other cop: "Do you have a weapon in there?" Ela: "You leave me no recourse but to surrender so that I may silence you. Our dialogue stinks."

She covers the mouth of the jar with her palm, flushes, fingers her vacancy to make sure that the bleeding has stopped, pulls her Goofy bag back up on her shoulder, returns the ostrich feathers to her head, thinks: I won't flinch, throws away her cigarette, puts on her sunglasses with the lizards mating on top of the plastic frame and announces to the world at large: "Okay, ragamuffin, I am leaving." One cop: "Drop your weapon if you have one, and walk out unarmed." The other cop: "We're aiming straight at the door. Don't try anything stupid."

Instantly Ela is attacked by her thoughts: How do I throw myself to the hungry crowd? Should I cry or sniff a bit? Let the people press my hand, pat my shoulder and say: "I know"? Do I hold my cunt in front of me like a shield or hide it behind my back or bury it in my cleavage to protect it from the barbarians? Should I wear it as a crown and walk out laureled with it? Intimations of royalty always keep people off. Should I hold it between my teeth like the coin the dead bite in order to bribe Charon with it for a safe boat journey from one world to the other, or like the half-dead prey a bitch proudly brings to show her owner? Should I carry it ceremoniously as a priestess in my raised hands like a sacred offering, a holy triangle, a chalice, the Gorgon's head? If I knew how to use it correctly, I would be safe. Isn't it my most magnetic aspect? Didn't it hold the masses dead in awe fifteen minutes ago? It put me in this precarious position and it better see me out.

Now Ela needs a grand Homeric exit. What can she give this starving crowd besides herself? She needs a trick. She thinks: I need to clear my head first; I need a cold shower; I need the silver sound of a chaotic fall rain to help me concentrate.

As if on cue, the sound of an enormous peal of thunder, growling, sustained, and hoarse, invades the toilet. The lights dim. The electric circuits hum. It chimes: Your eyes. I have had too much language for one day, now I hear words everywhere, Ela thinks; I breathe meaning into this hollow cunt and into this inadequate world and into this irritating storm. How much more meaning can I stand today? *Espressivo.*

But she feels befriended, a daughter of circumstance. She feels ready for anything: to tear up her precious cunt, to sell the universe. Ashes to ashes. She tells the world in her mind: When God comes, God will divide the world into toys and dolls.

Outside, the placid red afternoon turns suddenly black, and huge splashes of tropical rain fall like heavy menstrual blood from the sky. It is hard to imagine it ever not raining. The road churns like a frothing river. Fallen blue clouds swirl against the jagged serrations of the skyscrapers that loom like enormous jawbones. Violent streams tumble down the curious faces. But despite the deluge pouring from the skies, the inquisitive crowd stays on its drenched sentinels.

With her face and cunt uplifted, Ela greets politely the two cops who seem astounded by her elaborate get-up and her serene countenance: "I simply had to go to the bathroom. What's with this weather?" They tail her as she quickly reaches the door of *The Ironpants Express* with tiny dance-like steps and lifts her body up toward the crowd, as in a shamanistic rite. The cops behind her ask animated questions. But she steps outside, and her arms start to rise, fall, reach out, withdraw, and reach out again, her neck lifts up in a voluptuous ecstasy ready to be sacrificed, and she drifts into the mob, carried away in her own rapt trance, invulnerable. She thinks: They look like children who stand around hoping to be molested.

Her spellbinding surprise attack and the hard rain that is falling by the buckets, cooling their tempers and forcing them to look for shelter and to expect the worst, disarm the onlookers and cancel any sustained plans for a violent possession of the elusive duo. They duck imperceptibly, quench their hungry eyes and baptize themselves in the hypnotizing convulsion of her offering. Ela feels the mob so close around her that the electric pulse from their breasts burns through her veins. She can touch them. Her graceful unexpected bravery enchants them as a matador's reckless scientific dance charms the bull. A shiver of fear and pleasure runs through them. They drip heavily. The contrast between their outer wetness and their inner dry heat is comical.

Ela smiles a wide sweet greeting like a young genius who just completed a brilliant concert in theater and feels too embarrassed to bow. That sweet smile permeates everyone and brings out in them a helpless compulsion for expression, a need for sheer noise. The crowd murmurs and howls, and suddenly it looks like an inviting ocean where Ela can plunge in and be carried away and may even be reborn.

So Ela dives into the mob as into a cleansing bath, almost affectionately and with pleasure, without ducking her head. She welcomes the wet rumbling onslaught. She thinks: I am the clown, I take the pratfalls for them. They have come to watch me get devoured. They are here to strip me, tie a chain around my neck, bind me, drag me through the muddy streets, throw me in the flames, then jump in the flames with me; they want to impale me: I too want to be killed in public, to be savored, gored by crowds; to come on the stake. The crowd is waiting with stones in their hands, aiming at my eye, my mouth, my breast, my cunt. She chastises herself: The plot won't thicken.

She remembers being stoned once before like St. Stephen:

she had met a shy appetizing Arcadian male on a remote island plateau and led him into a nearby abandoned chapel; a chance witness had run to inform the nearest village, the outraged natives decided to get their guns and teach foreigners not to come and corrupt the local youth as if the island was their backyard, and hearing the angry mob outside, Ela had grabbed the boy, he silently crossed himself and they rushed out into a rain of rocks, around the back of the church, rolled down a steep cliff, bleeding and cursing, and a biblical virility overtook them, and they fucked on scree and thorns, screaming with pain whenever they touched.

The crowd hesitates. It begs her: "Don't leave." It wants her to start speaking in tongues. It stares and blinks, for out of context, her glittering cunt in the jar could be anything. They lick their lips as if they could be dry despite the rain. Their eyes stay transfixed, glazed, like children walking through the fair. No one dares ask: "Excuse me, Miss, what is it you're holding?" It is an uncomfortable scene; they want to know her inch-by-inch, to scratch her bare, to go arms and legs and head into her, and then to judge her. But they lack the necessary tools, the training. *Amabile*.

The crowd opens up, Ela walks on and crosses the street closely followed by the cops and the quick-moving roused wet horde. She thinks: This is not a retreat. The heavy rainy-day traffic slows down her followers. Anxious drivers rest on their horns and crane their heads out of their windows to ogle at the disturbance or come out to inspect the situation and ask the cops to keep the crowd off the street or start a fist fight. Some turn off their ignitions and wait. Cops run around, reporters shoot at random, cars are stalled bumper to bumper on the slippery avenue and the crowd is trapped tight in the solid sea of metal. Ela looks behind her satisfied, like a person whose epic mission has been accomplished. In the confusion she slides down the dirty steps of the nearest train station, buys a token, rides the subway for three stops, gets off and walks a block to her door, apparently unfollowed. Success! *Cantabile*.

But before she can cross her threshold, Ela must first walk through the line of irritable hopeful horny lovers, including the occasional kneeling adorants, who, having no idea of what has transpired, expect her to select one of them for the night. There are a dozen of them waiting. They all look alike, like Bruce Weber models. They wear Kouros, alain mikli sunglasses, Batman helmets, G. & shark handmade shoes, Boctok Komandirskie watches, Armani jackets, Levi's 501 pants. They smoke Silk Cut. They carry pastries from erotic bakeries, white chocolates, caviar, champagne, videotapes, cacti, or diamond rings. They are no cheap aspirants: they have Chanel boxers, Hennessy-washed mouths, rehearsed expressions and patiently saved month-long erections. Orchids have been sent anonymously in advance. Ela cuts through them like a promise. They call at her, quip, pose, Vogue, jitter, but they don't push. *Vivace*.

Once again she refrains from laughter knowing that it would spread confusion. She thinks instead: Are these my partisans, my patrons, my advocates, my friends in need? She inspects them gleefully. A familiar foul maggoty smell of love surrounds her. She chooses to speak to them in riddles like the Sphinx: "This is visual alchemy. I see the nymph Echo. Life is an ensemble of cloudy probabilities that candidly destroy us. I'd like to be alone. If you hear something late at night, some troublesome sound of fight, just don't ask me what it was." She points out to them the danger of the situation. She unlocks her door.

Once inside the loft Ela places her cunt next to the black blown-glass statues of voluptuous goddesses in curves and holes on the mantelpiece. She is suddenly greeted by one of the lovely children in finery she picks every autumn at the time of the first *eaux-de-vie*. She forgot about the child. Dorothea cries and carries on like any spoiled six-year-old, kicking the floor, howling, and whining: "You fuck everyone but me!" Ela gives her a bottle of essence oil to rub on herself tonight and sends her home in a haste, preoccupied as she is with her removed organ.

The loft is imbued with a heavy acrid odor, a mist reeking like oxidized apple: the rancid smell of love. It is submerged in a blue sylvan half-light, except for the white glimmering reflections of the streetlamps on the mirrors. Back to the decay, Ela thinks. *Scherzo*.

She lies on the shiny hardwood floor staring at the flowery moldings around the high ceiling that look like the wings of a blank stage and at the huge white walls decorated with a black-and-white George Weston photo of a vulva-like pepper, a black-and-white print of a Georgia O'Keeffe cactus flower and a collection of masks: feather masks, metal masks, stone masks, eyepatches.

The room is furnished entirely in black: black circular leather couch, crescent leather armchair, round rug, lacquered roll-top desk, round coffee table, birdlike lamps, canopy bed with wrinkled black-and-white zebra Perry Ellis sheets, marble counter, tiles, sink, and claw-foot bathtub under Fuseli's "Nightmare." They come in harmonious contrast with a collection of white bones: carcasses, a dinosaur jaw, bird skeletons, buffalo ribs, pelvic bones, skulls, sensuous, clean, and shining.

The most impressive presence is the mirror: one wall is covered entirely by mirror; on the opposite wall hangs a five-foot mirror in the shape of an 8, held up by two black angels suspended on a ruby-encrusted frame. She rests on it often by sitting on the lower cavity in contemplation. The third wall has the three arched windows which Ela also treats as mirrors. The fourth wall contains the main door, the closet door, the kitchen sink and counter, the bathroom door. The ceiling is inlaid with East Indian mirror-work, thousands of tiny mirrors that provide the most interesting fragments of herself. Her possessions are piled in a walk-in closet, a world redolent of old orchids and pleasant snobbery that resembles the backstage of a theater and betrays her sense of disorder. When the halcyon-cunt was hungry Ela thinks, looking about, this place used to throb with sweet fever as fresh bodies drifted in and out like rose petals blown in through the windows from the sea; now it is the hothouse for a strange thick-leaved plant that breathes in murky water.

Ela cannot deceive the mirror: something terrible, new, and more important than anything before in her life is taking place inside and outside her. *Scherzando.*

She wears panties and a pad. She pretends to herself that she is having her period. She has a migraine. She smokes and takes a nap. At first she can't sleep; she has visions of spurting blood, knives twisted into armpits or throats or cunts, arrows flying into her eyeballs. She sits up and tries to recall the empty face of the blind man. Can she laugh it off? Give me some time. Does she see the humor in this? Give me a break. Can she go back to bed? Yes. But first she gets up and puts the jar in her closet as if to hide it. Then she sees two short dreams:

A middle-aged emaciated Anglo-Saxon lies on his back in the middle of the desert on sand that looks dry and hard like cement. He breathes with difficulty, lifts his neck—he is seen in profile—slaps noisily his forehead, exclaims: "Shit! I forgot! I was supposed to become the governor of New York!" drops back with a sinister "dunk" of his skull and expires. Cut.

Ela stands in the middle of an enormous fluffy beige field. Her feet are cemented into the ground like the base of a street sign. A line of people in single file appears on the horizon coming toward her. As they approach, she notices that they are children, stern like Fanny or Alexander, of all different races and looks: white, black, Slavic, Hispanic, Indian, Scandinavian, Germanic, Oriental; they wear Ela's characteristic make-up: thick black liquid liner on both lids curved up at the edges in pseudo-Egyptian manner, wet frost-pink lipstick, silver sparkles under the eyes and on the brows; they have bleached silver hair with the roots grown out in their own natural color, long fake silver finger and toe nails, black unfamiliar dresses that hang too long on them, and pointed elfin boots. The application of the make-up has been inexpert, uneven and smudged, childish.

When the first boy reaches Ela, he stops abruptly in front of her, springs up on both feet and French kisses Ela, or in fact sticks a small raw tongue into her mouth forcefully, lands back on the ground, walks around and behind her and turns back toward the horizon, as the next child, a Dutch-looking girl—leaps, throws a long aggressive tongue into Ela's mouth in her turn, falls upright on her feet and marches behind the boy with the discipline of a soldier, as another wet malicious tongue invades and fills Ela's mouth which she can't close because the penetrations are continuous, so that she has no time to breathe and is suffocating.

The procession continues day in day out, in the dark, in the sunlight, in the rain, in the hail, tongue after tongue. At times a child's belly growls, she feels them spit in her, or burp, but the ritual continues in perpetual monotone. They look like birds who eat from the mother's mouth, but Ela knows that they are mocking her, that they actually stick their tongues out at her, from inside of her, which is ingenious. Two endless lines of these caricatures of herself alternatively dive into and emerge from the horizon, forever choking her. *Grave.*

Years later: Ela is cemented in the same field which is now white as if made of goose feathers. A couple who were recently her lovers—come out from the horizon, inflated like enormous balloons. Ela on her toes can only reach up to their huge knees. The giant doubles down, brings his blown-up but still recognizable Spaniard's face before her eyes hiding everything else from view, spreads out his usual tense smile, grabs Ela's tiny hand, pulls her toward him forcefully and shouts: "It's time to go home, Ela!" At that he walks away pulling her along, even though her feet are cemented into the ground. Her body stretches for a while and then cracks in half. The giantess looks back and smiles; she leans, covers Ela's ear with her basin-like mouth and whispers: "Adulthood is disappointing, isn't it?"

Ela takes off her clothes, squats in front of the mirror, decides not to look, wears her black panties again, unhooks one of the heads from the wall and wears it, a big feather owl mask. She pins Mommie's heavy gold and ruby brooch on the crotch of her panties, swallows two Percodan to sublimate the pain in her genitals, sits on the bed with her feet up, and smokes. She decides: It was a good experience. Now I must hide the evidence, tell no one, deny any rumors. She gets up to look for nail polish which will help her concentrate, thinks again, and walks into the closet that, overflowing with black shiny clothes, gapes like a cave. She takes out the precious jar and screams, despite the absence of a live audience: "Ow! Mama!"

The Unauthorized Section:

It seems that Ela's cunt has changed drastically. Was it water soluble? Did its exposure to dirty water distort it like this? She cries out: "Where is my fucking cunt?"

Now, finally, Ela begins to cry, in loud stubborn sobs and wails which, she seems to hope, will make everything stop and be solved or come back. Tears drip down her chin, her neck, and onto her nipples. It is comforting. She doubles up, clutches herself and crouches beside the mirror in the throes of a sudden piercing abdominal pain, as if suffering withdrawal symptoms. She convulses with cramps. This time she is certain that she is being stabbed.

During this intermission of Ela's anxiety fit, her eyes examine the new object inside the peanut butter jar: it is a shimmery transparent tube covered all around by tiny thorns or bumps of dark, perhaps protective, plastic, like gray erect pores or as if the pubic hair is growing back. It has the texture of rubber, like latex imitation flesh, or smooth wax. It can no longer be mistaken for a mushroom, a fungus, or a flower, afloat in the jar. Its manifold complex undulations are smoothed out, and it is compressed into a compact, closed, efficient-looking, as if man-made, object, a short cylinder, like a high-tech toy that toddlers can roll on the floor like marbles or throw into each other's palms for baseball practice or like a dollhouse miniature drum.

Ela does not go through further deliberations. She is not eager to discern the subtle peculiarities of this object that make it unlike anything familiar. She recognizes it at once through her tears: it is a wide-angle 35-mm lens.

Ela takes her two-inch medium-format Hasselblad from her purse and fits her ex-cunt on to it.

Ela now believes: Word traveled around, one of her ex-lovers found out about the separation, came during her sleep using one of the copies of her key which are in wide circulation among her suitors, stole her unprotected cunt, swapped it with an old lens as a nasty joke on her and he is happy at this moment, laughing at her, or screaming in the throes of ecstasy.

Did someone from the crowd follow her home? Was an old lover among the witnesses? Wouldn't he have come to her aid?

So as she sits here, her defenseless cunt is getting raped! And there is little she can do. She is at the end of her wits. How does she go about relocating it? And, assuming she finds it, is her loose cunt her possession and responsibility even after its removal? Would the charge of robbery and rape of her cunt stand in a court of law? Can Ela get its thief committed to jail? If her mind did not consent to the intercourse, does it matter that she wasn't physically connected with her cunt? Is it subject to her will? Is it a lost object? Does it lawfully belong to anyone who finds it? Couldn't anyone claim that it copulated willingly? She will have to prove the theft. She will have to prove it belongs to her. She would need a lawyer. She might have to go from court to higher court to highest court to establish a precedent. All this for a cunt she wanted to get rid of. She'd better write it off and settle for the unobtrusive lens.

She winces with shooting pain. She traverses the spacious room from door to windows and back with big strides, naked except for the jeweled panties, her hands folded against her ass, her head bowed, her heavy breasts jiggling, her silver hair flying at every abrupt full turn. She gestures to herself and shakes her head. She pictures headlines: STOLEN CUNT. NOT INSURED. FEARS OF MORE ASSAULTS. IS THERE A CUNT-THIEF RUNNING LOOSE? It is unimaginable.

She has forgotten again, as she sallies forth alone on a quest for her abducted cunt, the deranged fire, the raging mania and lunacy of her cunt rising and falling in its own froth. She imagines her cunt suddenly helpless, more exposed than a newborn baby, who could at least cry, completely unable to express itself. She feels protective: a sweet maternal exasperation at constantly having to run after an innocent and restless child.

So how can she discover the thief? Should she hire a detective? Under which pretense? How does she explain her suspicions in so many words? How does one get back, or claim, a lost cunt? Is there a governmental agency that deals with these complaints? A clearing house? Can she order a new one, through a catalog, let's say, giving a size, color, age, quantity, a credit card number and expiration date? Can she demand that such services be made available? Isn't the market made to meet any demand? Can she survive without it? Can she still screw? Who will she be without her cunt? If only her cunt was a pet or something nice, she could advertise it in the papers.

The best scenario for her would be that the thief would black-mail her. But what if he leases it out or makes plaster casts of it to sell to the tourists as they do in Hong Kong? The solution is to let go of it, not care about its adventures and not take it person-ally. Is she having a breakdown? Is she losing her last connections to the world? First her recalcitrant kidnapped cunt and now her bright logic? Have the lights failed her at the crucial moment? Then it occurs to her:

1. She herself looks for, and likes, transformation everywhere.
2. This lens is a materialized metaphor: e.g., "Women who have eyes between their legs." One more Word turned to Flesh.
3. The symbolism of seeing the world through one's cunt, and,

better yet, of shooting the world with one's cunt, is both fun
and appropriate.

4. It is not beyond her manipulative cunt to pull off such a
trick of metamorphosis on her.

5. Ovid gives her deep pleasure.

So after the failure of logic comes the mutation: the lens. Ela
is reluctant to see this at first, because it is a change she has not
brought on to herself. She would rather embark on a search for
her original cunt. She scowls: The world knows I can enjoy a
joke, but this? Or am I being tested as in a horror-movie? Is the
cunt testing me or is the world?

If the lens is my cunt, and I am not just tripping on bad junk,
this is a new reversed relationship for us. All this time I could
never see it directly, all I wanted was to look at it and now all I can
do is look into and through it. I can hold it now, do anything to
it except feel through it, except of course metaphorically. But I am
a dreamer. So a lens is useless to me. How ironic: We are finally
face-to-face, and I still know nothing about it. I feel more trapped
and more foolish than before. I like dreams to stay dreams, I like
following Ariadne's thread from room to room forever, I don't
want to face the Minotaur and then have to go home! That will
bring down the entire labyrinth. So I am just going to sit back and
enjoy the puzzle. No angst.

Ela also cannot overlook the possibility that she may enjoy
living by herself. Perhaps they contaminate one another. They
may both be calmer and happier alone. Without her to spoil it, it
may learn to control its appetites. Without it to lead her in and
out of trouble, she may learn to live with boredom like other
people. They will have to meet the hardships of life alone.

If, on the other hand, her old cunt is this lens, it will continue
to act as her companion and guide, a more considerate and

predictable one. She looks forward to the pleasures of solitude when she can live in her dream unfettered. If she breaks out of her sexual habit, she will be free of men, friends, leeches, dramas. She will not need to open her door, her mouth, or her legs to others. She can be truly detached. But she was so close to that felicitous cunt that it will be hard to forget.

Ela ransacks her monstrous closet looking for a soothing and comforting dress in which to rest her body, throws around dozens of hangers and fabrics and finds the perfect hiding nest: a long tight transparent dress made of stretchy silver net encrusted with multi-shaped gems that shine and catch the light in manifold reflections; it is very heavy in weight and attracts people to her in big numbers like moths, but it makes her feel protected and loved as if sliding into a womb of light. It also gives the mirror pleasure. She slips it over her head, and puts a gold diadem of entwined dolphins on her hair.

Her donut-shaped cunt, as she saw it on the pavement, brings to her mind now the image of false teeth: pink thick gums and the silver-and-white porcelain crowns. I must look just like a toothless mouth, she thinks with revulsion. But the term "false" strikes her as a new revelation: perhaps it was the wrong cunt for her. The cunt was rejected, expelled from her body like an unwanted tumor. Perhaps Ela was simply no longer the appropriate vehicle for it. She is no longer physically strong enough to support, feed, and look after such a cunt. She needs a lighter, quieter cunt, or even none at all, for a while. She needs to rest. She was fooled by habit into believing that a bodily part lasts forever.

She now knows how startled maimed soldiers or women with breast cancer must be when they wake up from the anesthesia to the sight of their legs or breasts or arms missing. The old shock of being expelled from Paradise. Maybe if this becomes known, she will have to parade on the fourth of July along with other veterans in wheelchairs and on crutches, planted on a slowly moving vehicle with her legs wide open to show her Lack. I am prime material for a Grand Victory Parade, she realizes, I can be the star of a carney, exhibited next to the Elephant Man, the Living Clam, the Four-Headed Turk, the Pea-Sized Emperor, the Hunger Artist, and the Fat Lady. In her mock-royalty dress and crown, her regal manners, her imposing voice, her shock of silver hair and long nails, she is ready to be the main attraction.

As she paints her eyes looking in a hand mirror, she decides once again that this is not a loss, but rather a monumental step of evolution and of progress. A historical breakthrough. It is not a product of her propensity for extravagant statements. She feels raised into a new peculiar fate. As if she speaks a language that no one else speaks. From now on her loneliness will be complete. She will literally see differently from anyone else. She turns to the big mirror for a reaction.

The mirror, unlike the men who love her, does not suffer from the Pygmalion complex; it does not see itself as a creator in love with the lifeless creation. It does not see itself. It does not see her as a single concrete person. It is hard and objective. The outcome of its inquiries leaves it cold. So Ela asks for its opinion, trusts its judgment, consults it daily. It asks for nothing in return. It is her relief, her abode, much as her cunt was reported to be for others. It is her archive. More explicitly: it is perceptive. As she wears her silver-net pumps, Ela reflects: Things are never what they are in front of our eyes. Even if I could be truthful, I cannot trust myself to say how I feel, or know how I feel. So the mirror must know what I think when I don't. It must undertake the role of the puppeteer.

Presently, the mirror strongly supports the metamorphosis

notion. After its fascinating development, the new cunt, the lens, becomes available to both Ela and the mirror, convenient, expedient. Ela looks at it closely and frowns: So this is it? Is this lens lying cool and wet inside her cold palm her pitiless torturer? Can it come? When Ela licks it, the taste is bland and sterile, almost plastic. It has the faint coppery smell of living flesh, a temperature as warm as her own, slightly below average, and she notices that the inner glass of the tube through which one sees is not glass but more like the spider's spittle that dries when it comes in contact with air but retains the transparent softness that resembles the secretion it originally was, thick as molasses, though not at all sticky.

Ela tries her best to feel moved, stand up to the grandeur of the occasion, appreciate nature's miracle, but the lens tastes like rubber or nylon full of germs and looks dull and uninspired compared to the radiant lotus that was throbbing on the curb and in that jar like a living heart some time earlier. She holds it inches from her eyes and asks: Is this my core?

Ela turns with a "What can I do?" nod in the mirror, and for that terrifying disorienting instant she does not recognize her own mirror. It looks lost in itself, caught up in its own complex activities of which, for that instant, she is not a part. Is it possible that it too has a separate self? That would kill her. What is happening today, why does everything she took for granted break up, why has she become a broken mosaic, a finished puzzle suddenly thrown into the air that falls back on the floor undone? Whose image will comfort her, whose support will she run to when feeling persecuted, if even her mirror now has its own separate needs to meet? Without her unflinching compass, she will certainly lose her bearings.

Ela refuses to pay further attention to this inconceivable

estrangement, or entertain the thought, or verify her original perception, ignores the disorder in her stomach, feels unequipped to face the new development, shrugs her shoulders and thinks: Maybe it needs to be washed. I always forget to do it and then I see shapes in it, which are only smudges and dust. Is there Ajax in this pit?

But the mirror looks excited: it ripples and unwinds itself as if to swallow an object of its fancy that sits on its center. The figure 8 breathes in and out furiously, undulating like lava, a flame, or a luminous air bubble, the ceiling is a shining waking boa of tiny asymmetrical shards reflecting the light from the lamps. The room is flooded with millions of sparkles that revolve in fast circles and hundreds of complex blinding rotating light effects that any D.J. would watch with deadly envy.

But many strange things have happened today, so Ela resolves to be patient and unintrusive. Love is ruthless. Two continents fought for Helen. She gives the mirror its privacy, which it deserves, since it has not had any before. She cannot after all chain it up like a man. She looks away, but she is encircled by it. Everywhere her eyes fall, she sees the mirror, mirroring itself from the opposite walls and ceiling demonically. Caught in a barrage of piercing rays darting back and forth around her and through her, Ela runs for the door. She steals a last glimpse of the exploding spectacle of light and of no sound, as she leaves the throbbing loft, and discerns a small silver circle breathing like an amoeba, a jellyfish, or a halo, under the surface of the mirror-wall, expanding and withdrawing as if gathering momentum to break through the pressure of the thin glass and out to the other— this—side. She does not interfere, and simply hopes that whatever her reflections may be doing, they will not set this damned rented loft on fire.

Out in the street, Ela is once again distraught about the meta-genesis of her cunt. She runs into the mobile bodies around her and feels disadvantaged, disarmed; she has again the sense of irreparable damage. She entertains herself with thoughts of writing to the Hasselblad company in Sweden and offering them the option to buy and patent the lens.

Should she withhold such an extraordinary machine from being put to good use for humanity? Why hide an invention that gives her no deadly personal pleasure? Resplendent in her bejeweled net, Ela walks and clicks her lens spasmodically, absent-mindedly, without looking through it. The meaninglessness of the activity consoles her.

Ela's father is an art photographer and, even though she refused his offer to show her the camera's secrets, she grew up surrounded by lights and lenses and feels secure holding one. She hates the manual labor of taking photographs, and the suspicion that she might imitate her exuberant dad. But she always carries a camera in her purse, as other women carry a revolver or a can of Mace: for protection. When she senses danger, she takes it out to stop potential criminals.

Ela was her dad's only model. When she left home he stopped taking photographs. He saw her in his dreams instead, or in daytime visions. He has developed the ability to close his eyes and see what she is doing at any moment. He keeps a meticulous diary of what he sees, and it corresponds correctly with Ela's specific gestures and actions at the time, down to the last detail of what she wears; it describes everything but her mute thoughts. For this latter reason, Ela does not feel invaded and considers his diversion inconsequential. She is open to the public. His documentation is precise and systematic, but lacks a thesis. And he has no alternative. He tells her on the phone long-distance:

"You are my God. I'll always see you."

People always comment: "Ela, the lens loves you." Ela's relationship with the camera is a mystery. It is an unqualified transformation. Photographs of Ela expose the necessity of asking whether it would be accurate to speak of her as a single person. In every picture she is unrecognizable; she resembles neither her live image nor any other photographs taken of her nor of anyone else. She reveals an absorption so intense it is more than indifference, it is an achievement, a historic complete nonbeing. In photographs, Ela functions as an obstacle.

Ela likes the camera, for it makes no demands. It uses no words and does not depend on communication. She loves to freeze herself, hold her breath, look at the lens without seeing herself in it. She feels that she truly does not exist then, for that moment. She feels an orgasm. She tells her lovers: "A camera is a woman's only friend. Would you like to shoot me?" She points the camera at them and notices with wonder: Men look in the camera as if it is a cunt, or as if they are contemplating suicide!

It is late evening now and the street is so full it gives Ela the impression of a riot. Ela finds that sexy. She thoughtlessly pushes the little soft pink button of her cunt and shoots at random. Something above her head creaks. She thinks: Heaven is just a floor above. Shooting with this lens gives her the same liberating maddening satisfaction she felt when flashing men in the street. She wonders why the same word is used for the light of a camera shooting in the dark and the light of a cunt exposed to men's public scrutiny and terror.

A girl in "wet" leotards runs up to Ela and screams in her face: "Don't be calling me a penis!" Ela thinks: Most people's goal in life is to make me feel guilty: how funny!

She turns into an alley and runs into a feminine Aryan boy

with exquisite bone structure who was recently her lover. She hates seeing old lovers again: it makes her feel old. He sits, or perhaps swims, in a big black cooking pot near some garbage bins. He appears to have difficulty keeping his head above the frothy dark water or soup or juice he is in. He may be drowning. Ela shoots first and then considers the possibilities:

  a. he is simmering while the savages have gone to buy veggies to add to the broth;

  b. he has been cooked and now he is getting cold after the aborigines abandoned their meal having found him sour or bland;

  c. he has made a moral choice to live in his pot, like an amphibian Diogenes;

  d. he is tripping and thinks he is on a Greek isle;

  e. he is taking a bath in public;

  f. she is seeing things.

She hears him call for help. She shrugs it off as just another scam.

Ela sits on a bench, holds her head in one hand and shoots with the other. An Italian-looking student comes in front of her. He grunts: "I don't like the way you're looking at her," and points to his big girlfriend who stands self-conscious and bright red by him. Ela points her lens at them, feeling like Atalanta shooting the beasts.

A young yellow-eyed man sleeping on the bench with his baby-like hands neatly crossed on his chest, now opens his eyes and delivers: "Your nearness resurrects me, makes me bold, happy, feverish. American women are bitches. I've thought about it because I've been studying Buddhism, see my…(unidentifiable word) beads here? I've been celibate for a year and I think to myself I'd like to have sex, I am good-looking, but I meet no women because I don't have anything and they all want something. They know you're lonely because women are smart, so they ask: Do you work? Do you go to school? What do you do? Women are after money. Don't you like money? Wouldn't you like a guy with a Porsche to take you back home and drive around in it? It's a competitive world. After studying for thirty-three years I've come to this conclusion." He shoots up. Ela shoots too.

A tremendously obese man with shaggy eyebrows, hairy hands, and a somber embarrassment sits on the bench and opens up: "My first impression is that you should be framed and raised up into a church window." Ela: "The dark doesn't get in the way, it is not bothersome. I need a film that does not respond to light; perhaps it could respond to movement or heat." The fat man: "My father is shy with girls. He drinks a bottle of whiskey whenever I bring one home for dinner." Ela: "Emotions exhaust me." The fat man: "I have a soul of rainwater." Ela: "Why do people want to get hurt by me? It's boring to make them suffer. At one time, not long ago, women weren't asked to be cruel; they were not even asked to speak." She thinks: This world is an infection, not a distraction. I can hear the projectionist behind me laughing; one more chuckle and I am leaving.

Ela gets up when a black man with a superfluous amount of muscles and dreadlocks comes toward her with a determined look on his face. She thinks: No, not again! There isn't much left down there! She shoots him on impulse, he smiles blankly and says: "See the looks you get, the alert that goes off, I read you." Ela: "Black people like me because I shine." The black man: "I must crack your cunt." She thinks: This is all foreign to me. This lack of polish. People ignore the details, the props, they don't make the spectacle worthwhile, and who cares if they are honest, the audience is snoring.

Ela enters a supermarket and asks to develop the film that was in her camera. The clerk recommends a thirty-minute photo lab next door where another clerk behind a counter explains: "You have a choice. You want them glossy or matte?" Ela: "Glossy pictures are vulgar. They look wet." Ela speaks in a low throaty steam that rises out of her lips and forces people to lean near her, smell the perfume from behind her ears, look down into her round passionate mouth, up to her gold liquid eyes, in order to hear her. Her voice is full of bright promises; she piles words one upon another breathlessly and haphazardly.

She goes to wait in a sushi den, but runs into a stringy-blond lanky optometrist she met in the Rockies who sermons: "How you feel is of overriding importance to me! No one can love you as I do. The best way to show you my love is to cancel myself. Presenting my heart is not enough!" Even the Japs are jolted on their seats by Ela's voice: "I hate muddled people: you die for me or you kill me, as far as I go." Looking like an apparition Ela turns to the extras, a role the customers embrace as gladly as any she might choose, and inquires: "What does he want?" The Japs watch Ela mesmerized. "Get the gentleman out of here," she orders. She orders saki. The Japs rise to do her bidding. The cowboy will not quit: "You make me feel like I'm free again!" They pick him up by his arms and legs and carry him out proudly.

The Sushi Q Den has run out of *toro*, so she can't use it to test if she can still get an orgasm from the pleasure of eating it. She wonders if she has lost her ability to come along with her cunt. She gulps down six pieces of flying fish roe.

On her way out, a small dark woman with a petulant face, upturned nose, and protruding lips, dressed in a bright orange business suit, follows her. She stops Ela at the traffic light and introduces herself in a confrontational urgent voice that momentarily catches Ela's interest: "How does it feel to have that face? Is it a burden? Do you feel blessed? What do you plan to do about it? Why don't you use American make-up to show off the bones? Have you had a screen test yet? How does it feel to stand out anywhere, to be immediately separated from everyone? Where can you look after a while?" Ela smiles with disinterest at the raving woman's Asian smooth black hair, small tired face, rough wrinkled hands that could belong to an octogenarian or a newborn and are unsuited for the two large emeralds that on them look cheap and childish, at her black eyes that sparkle intensely like lights on the surface of a lake. Ela: "I'd like to cover my head with jewels like your movie-star Rekha in the mythological roles." The filmmaker: "Your face needs the camera; it is made for camera use! Your face is a prism. The camera will go crazy on you, it won't know what to do! I must shoot you. What did your parents do when they first saw your face? Did you look like this at birth?" Ela: "Yes. If you see photos of Buster Keaton at birth, he looks as funny as always." The filmmaker: "Your face looks different every time it is seen, as if it is constantly distorted by some camera." Ela: "I could wear a black see-through sari with bits of mirrors on it. I want my breasts to fill the screen." The filmmaker "Your face contains all the possibilities. It is more pure than Garbo's." Ela: "I also like that woman Draupadi who married in a single wedding all five or fifty brothers, I don't remember which. If you are going to marry, that makes sense."

The filmmaker: "I know why you're in America: because of all places only here your face is not merely the most beautiful, but also the most cruel." Her pink upper lip and brown lower lip pull back as she speaks over huge gray teeth; her face is triangular and bony; her frantic eyes glare. Ela's voice trembles with a yawn: "I am here because Americans are gullible; I can live in a fairy tale." "No," the filmmaker cries with big quivering lips, trying to make her fever contagious, "Americans have no concept of a public self! They stay home with the TV, they live with their private selves. They never cultivate their public persona! You, on the other hand, come straight from the bowels of history!" Ela thinks: What a gory suggestion. Ela: "My earlier ancestor is Sikander, but some say I come from the sea or from the mirror." The filmmaker: "You have a conqueror's blood!" Ela thinks: This woman is hot in her head. With men, I function on automatic: I know one of us will die. Women are too verbal and too sensational. So they get carried away.

Ela nods to a young uncouth cop nearby and explains that this poor Indian filmmaker needs to be taken to the emergency ward. The cop breaks his back to protect Ela and empty the stage of the nuisance. He asks Ela for her name, address, phone number, and driver's license. She laughs. He brings the paramedics on the scene who put the woman in a straitjacket and take her away. He has to accompany them but promises to see Ela again. She goes to the all-night bank next to the lab to sit in the waiting area. She thinks: Fuck them, pump them, blow them, shove them in, do what they want, make love to them, but make them shut that mouth!

A dozen people are waiting. A Nordic hunk with the heavyset dumb eyes of a beast in heat, high cheekbones, and imposing pumped build struts in cockily in black tight parachute pants, red suspenders and a tiny ponytail over his long smooth sexy nape. He looks around, focuses on Ela with a fervent rush of recognition, sits across from her with his elbows on his round muscular knees that stretch out flat and bumpy like designer shelves, opens his thick legs in her direction and smiles crudely exposing a flat tongue. She looks away. He sighs: "Can I do it for you? I'd love to." He looks ready to implode. He must not know how to inhale, for he uses both his lips to breathe, pouting and making a show of it. Ela thinks: Shit, is this the mating season? He is almost popping out of his skin. He reminds her of a frog with a lit cigarette in its mouth that swells up with every breath it takes until it blows up, breaking into beige-green slimy chunks. Her loins tremble. Her lens heats up. She rubs it absentmindedly. My cunt, she thinks, is a mad machine.

He smiles his bright teeth and maneuvers his lips right and left as if they are executing the steps of a Bulgarian folkdance: "I have a forked tongue," he promises and waits for effect; "whatever sticks on it, comes. It's reptilian. No woman has left me." With this the pointed flat red specimen slides out of his mouth as a challenge. It has tiny white bubbles like gooseflesh on it and looks like a glistening clit. "Excuse me," Ela whispers, "just a moment," runs to the bathroom and vomits. She always throws up, repelled, when someone turns her on.

But remembering she no longer owns her merciless cunt that snapped and kissed itself uncontrollably on these occasions, Ela goes from the ladies' room to the lab. The acned clerk smiles apologetically: "The pictures didn't turn out well, so we won't charge you. If you leave them overnight, we'll have a technician take a look at them." Ela is not interested; she shoots to keep from thinking.

The sexy bullfrog follows her to the lab. He raises his arms to the ceiling and spills from his seams: "Lord, you who made this inexplicable woman, give her to me! Let her be my undoing!" Once again Ela has to appeal to the audience: "Now take him away." Her voice, rising from the mythic bowels the Indian filmmaker had mentioned, inspires everyone present, even obscure creatures working at the back in the dark, to come out of torpor and into action. They adopt menacing cut-ice expressions, take big forward strides, breathe deeply and surround the culprit. The insolent wooer retreats moaning: "Lead me astray!"

Ela looks at her helpers waiting for further instructions or for a reward and thinks: I must buy self-printing film first thing tomorrow, preferably infrared.

Now she relishes the immunity and novelty of her situation: men may no longer restore or destroy themselves in her; she does not go about bearing a gift. As she runs home, her arms and hips turn this way and that like crystals catching the light. Is this what people mean by happiness? she wonders. I could have tried it years ago. It's like swimming in space.

Sitting at her desk, Ela lights cigarette after cigarette, frowns, looks at the pictures and realizes that they complicate and possibly solve the mystery. But first she complains to the calm-looking mirror: "I looked in the mirror before and you were not there." Then she examines the prints: as if the lens had many surfaces to shoot with, each picture includes not only what Ela had seen through the lens, but everything around her in a full 360-degree circle. Ela herself appears in the middle of every picture as a dark shadow like a thin whirlwind, shooting out light sparkles or water drops in every direction.

The lens is seen in each print as well, not once but twice. It takes Ela some minutes to decipher everything:

a. there is a minuscule black hole in the whirling shadow's blurry hands—approximately where her hands would be, a tiny gap, like the mouth of a distant tunnel or vacuum that gapes ominously at the center of each picture and into which the circular visual structure of the entire photograph is slowly falling, or coming out of; for all the elements in every print are shot in slight movement, though not as a result of a shaky camera, but as if it were the outcome of some arduous experimental lab work, so that nothing appears accidental or out of focus, and every picture looks like an unusually successful abstract photograph; as if the camera itself contained a creative processing inner mechanism that can control and distort what the viewfinder sees;

b. a bright flighty white (or silver or even pink considering this is a black-and-white film) butterfly or amoeba, which Ela believes is the second appearance of her lens, appears sitting like a glowing alien on the body of the most highlighted and focused character in each photograph; it looks almost as luminous and florid as it appeared on the pavement this afternoon;

c. the gestures of all the persons photographed are exaggerated, made in grotesque angles, like mimes frozen in moments of overpowering emotion, struggling to reveal with their monstrous contortions what they cannot with words;

d. the non-human objects—trees, benches, signs, clothes—remain unclear and lost in a mud of gray.

Ela realizes the magnitude of what has happened today: not only did she for a short period manage to look at her mysterious cunt, face-to-face, and have a clear specific picture of it in her memory, but she can now see her lost cunt joined with others, with strangers in the street; it is restored to her, so that when Ela looks through the lens she still owns her cunt. It is a new indirect way of copulating. Her cunt can rest or rub itself on any passerby that it hungrily selects, and Ela can watch and even have a tangible proof of it in the photos. But she does not need to feel; she can simply imagine.

Ela checks the lens again and finds that it shuts at aperture f/32, the smallest opening in any lens, which explains why the lab gave her large 8x10 prints. She realizes that this must be related to the extreme tightness of her cunt. The lens must have an inconspicuous built-in flash that does not light up in warning when she shoots, for though she had not used a flash, her evening shots are carefully lit.

Ela quickly changes into a comfortable transparent pink harem outfit of loose pants and a small tight top, picks up her magic lens without the camera and leaves the room in a hurry. In her excitement she has hardly glanced at the mirror for its reaction. Of course, she thinks as she runs out, the mirror might disagree and advise that she should simply look through the lens more carefully when she shoots, and hold the camera straight and in front of her face rather than down in front of her womb or in her moving hand, that she should not use film that has been sitting in her dusty camera in her purse for months, clean the lens that had been submerged in the dirty water in the jar, and stop projecting. But Ela is both impatient to test her discoveries and happy with her theory.

This time she looks through the lens very carefully. She holds it in front of her right eye, closes the left, focuses on a sensuous part of a bystander's anatomy and immediately notices the familiar image of her insatiable cunt attached to it.

Ela remembers reading that during the Sand Creek massacre the white soldiers had scooped out Indian women's genitals and worn them on their worn-leather hats as trophies. It had left an indelible impression on her mind, as an outlandish image of sexual savagery. The sight of her snow-white cunt innocently posing, or imposing, on noses, hats, fingers, shoes, crotches of white men walking around unsuspectingly, offers her a similar, reverse, triumphal sensation; she gloats. Is this a dream? Can there be a foolproof method of knowing when a dream is real?

Ela sees the same world through her lens that she discovered in the photos. She sees behind her and all around her; she sees herself as a shadow seeing through the gaping lens; she sees her tight white winged cunt resting comfortably on whomever she zooms in. Ela concentrates and tries to sense what her cunt feels from its close encounter with a naked arm, mouth, cleavage: the texture of the various skins, the different temperatures, the moistness. She is exhilarated. She doesn't need to expose her face to plain public view again. She can hide it behind this soft trustworthy lens. She doesn't need to fuck again. She doesn't need to shoot again. She doesn't need the mirror.

I myself am overly excited; I never foresaw such a fantastic development! I wish I could relate the visuals on film. Mine is certainly the wrong medium. My intimacy with her allows me to see what no one else sees. In that sense, I have always fooled her. It makes me feel proud.

Suddenly, due to the exhausting excitement of the day no doubt, I doze off for two or three seconds, that is I shut off to the world, alone as I lie in the dark, and I see a vision; or else I have just had a visitation of some sort, which should not occur to creatures like me. I "see" a nightmare: I watch myself dive and ultimately crash into Ela's bed. Ela lies naked on her zebra sheets wearing a white feather dove mask. I glance into the mirror and face not my own blank reflection as I would expect, but that of the lens, hovering in plain air and winking at me, just once. I wake up soaking wet, wide-eyed, wondering: were my eyes open or shut? This has never happened before!

Ela has returned home. The large room is dark, and the glare from the streetlamps forms bright prison-cell bars on the wooden floor as it bursts in through the blinds and the mirrors. She lies on the bars and sees her body become a breathing shining game of tick-tack-toe.

She thinks that from now on she would rather not use her eyes, but see through her lens. She imagines that, if this peculiar chain of events continues, she will become a camera. She is ready for that exciting and perhaps last transformation. She will fit herself back on to her cunt and wear it as before.

She is in such a good mood that she jests with the mirror in mock-salespitch: "The new Quick Fatal Snap is a unique package of high-speed film which comes complete with its own f/32 lens and shutter. No setting is required: just press the pink button and shoot. You'll enter a new world of vision. With Quick Fatal Snap's minimum 1/100th-second shutter speed, you'll get great quality pictures, even on overcast days. When the twenty-four shots are taken, they will be self-developed automatically. Carry your Quick Fatal Snap in your purse, pocket, briefcase, brassiere."

She lifts her leg, rests her foot against the mirror and glances nervously at her wound with gleaming eyes: has it healed by any chance? No, it is in tatters. She reasons: I see a hole where I had a hole; a bigger, looser, darker hole instead of a smaller, tighter, brighter one; but a hole no less sensitive and perceptive. Sitting Indian-style in front of the mirror, she pushes the lens inside the gaping toothless mouth of her thighs.

It fits! It does not feel uncomfortable. The cool moist lens easily and contentedly nestles between her legs as if it naturally belonged there. She starts to touch it. She feels it soft and wet like a contact lens or like mucus. She feels how sensitive and attentive to her it is. Her gold pupils dilate with surprise, then slide off into her skull leaving behind white sparkling eyeballs. This is the most satisfying insertion Ela has experienced, for the lens takes the place of both her tight cunt and of a perfectly fitting hard cock. She caresses it.

The tip of her tongue comes in and out of her lips rapidly. She groans, rubs the lens, presses it with her middle finger, and it sinks in like stretched plastic foil. When it wrinkles deeper she moans louder. It is unclear to her if what causes her pleasure is the pressure of the lens on the sensitive nerves of her sore abdomen, or if she feels through the nerves of the lens.

Her thighs now lie open in a "split," forming a straight sensuous line from knee to knee. Her feet are curled under her ass for support, her pale pelvis flaps up and down like the wings of a desperate bird sweating in its attempts to take off, to disengage from gravity. Her veins rise out of her skin as though they were embroidered in green silk thread on her thighs.

In front of the mirror, in the unlit room, Ela rises and falls drenched with bars of light. She arches her back forward, curves it backward until her head touches the floor, and rocks, her hands busily rubbing her lens, and makes higher and higher and less civilized nasal calls and snorts, until she chokes and comes. At the instant of her most frightful inhuman shriek, when her big eyeballs shrink into thin slits of white light that gaze out at the world as if with reproach, the dark lens snaps shut once with a single sharp "click."

This is how the strange lens comes, with a wink in the direction of the mirror. Ela immediately dozes off into a peaceful void. The lens keeps smirking.

No! Did that merciless cunt contain film? Was I shot, suspended as I am everywhere here like a regular peeping Tom, utterly humiliated? Did it take a picture of its own inexorable orgasm? Has Ela now recovered her sexual connection to the world? If so,

I must now resume my post of the pathetic inactive seer. Lens fucking will be the death of me.

I recognized the fatal danger when I heard that "click" of utmost sensual pleasure. It was not only the intimidating shocking sound of a lens in orgasm. It was the sound of a gun being loaded. It was the sound of a toy being broken. It was the sound of a machine being turned on or off. Like the guillotine.

I watch her think of the men she will easily fool who won't notice the difference in her cunt in their excitement, their penises desperately fighting to break through the glass, that, although they will never pierce it, will stretch deeply enough so they will be held tightly inside it and will not suspect that they are being exposed to the world's eye, inside that castrating machine, that senseless shredder of cocks which snaps shut at the moment of its pleasure: Cut! and then freezes them in defeat and shoots their insubstantial members when they have no recourse but to withdraw and ask for a truce. No man will come out of this awesome "cunt" with his honor intact.

And what higher justice permits Ela to hold her cunt in her hands like a blazing emblem or torch and go about shooting people with it, without losing any of the pleasure it had afforded her before, without having to undergo any austere trials of initiation? Why did this ruthless wild cunt surrender its freedom to her when it had never given in to her all the years they were united as one?

I must not fall asleep, I must do my best to stay up, for throughout this day a disaster has happened every time I shut my eyes, Ela thinks, lost in her post-orgasmic stupor.

Throughout our co-dependence I kept the greatest possible distance. I stayed impersonal. Thus I ensnared her. I did not join the ranks of all the self-glorifying, needy humans. But in essence if I may use that word—I have been determined from the start to trot inside her like a conqueror. It is simple: she uses me to keep herself from disintegrating, and my goal is to extinguish her, absorb her, put her sight out, stop her sexual stampede; to tame her and ride into town on her, so to speak. I have the patience and time for it, and I will wait until she has eyes for no one else and no one else can see her.

She is slowly moving again. She indulgently removes the lens, fits it on her camera, looks into it and takes a picture of the mirror. She is glowing, blissful about her new snap-on snap-out cunt. She wears a short dress of steel and runs back to the all-night lab. She asks to develop the prints of her photo-masturbation. Does she come equipped with film at all times? Will there be a shot of the lens coming, in addition to the shot of the mirror? But that is truly terrifying!

As she strolls down the street, I realize that no mirror would ever dare to stop her or refuse her anything; she lowers her eyes and lifts her nose away from the misery around her, for beauty loves only danger and is unmoved by the fall of a small kingdom.

Now she, like myself, imagines with anticipation the small black and white dots that will compose the shadowy whirlwind whose hands will hold the dark hollow gap like a chalice, and the white winged cunt that will lie in repose on the most arousing part of her own naked body. Will she even recognize herself? Will she be, as usual, someone she has never seen before? A torrent of light enclosed in a sphere of mirrors?

Faster than I expected, the acned clerk calls Ela back. He tells her these prints also came out badly, worse than the others in fact, what kind of lens is she using, is it fish eye, is she focusing correctly? "You do something wrong," he adds, "when you shoot."

She winks at him, pays in a hurry and grabs the prints. She holds the lens tightly in one hand and leans against a lamppost to look at the prints under the streetlight. She apparently does not see anything she expected, for she frowns and squints with confusion. But she was alone in the room loft, and only my eyes showed through the walls, so I feel positive that Ela must be the main figure on the pictures.

She walks slowly home, lost in herself.

My curiosity is tremendous, but I must wait until we reach the loft. On the way back, we pass by the mirrors that flank the entrance of a funky boutique, and I suddenly notice that I cannot see Ela's reflection in them. I see her glimpse at the mirrors once absent-mindedly and keep walking, apparently unaware that she is not there, that one can only see reflected in them the other side of the street and the cars going by. Unless of course it is natural for her to see her absence. I am not sure if it is a product of my imagination, if it has happened now for the first time, on this day spent in constant wonder, or if it has always been the case; whenever I see her look in the mirror, and act as if she sees herself, I simply assume that she is there; yet I myself always look at her and not at her reflection. I must now remember to check out if any other mirrors reflect her. But I cannot dwell on it at this time. I must prioritize.

Resting on the 8-shaped mirror under the strong white light, smoking, Ela leans over the photos again. I now look closer and glimpse a flash of vague recognition in her huge black-lined eyes that frightens me because it is self-mocking. I immediately look at the picture in her hand and see not Ela, but only myself; I am portrayed naked, spotted, stiff, unglamorous, indecisive, incomplete, hovering off the ground as though hanging from an invisible noose, tense and shiny like a clammy worm caught on a silver hook. I seem incapable of gravity like an air-filled balloon and like a long thin figure painted by Chagall. I look as if I have just been found in a deserted concentration camp after a long horrendous war. I show a bare vertical stillness that is the image of death. I feel like scratching my own eyes out.

I tell myself that my portrait could be mistaken for an enlarged image of the lens; that Ela may never suspect it is I.

The charming relaxed white cunt is not on the print at all. What has happened? Is there no formula according to which this lens perceives after all? Will each series of shots differ drastically? How can anyone live this way?

The second print looks like the photograph of lightning; minimal, lucid, timeless. A course of light that strikes against a black background, as the light was too brilliant for anything else in the room to be picked up on film. High-contrast, fluid, poetic, abstract. The photo of the end of a blackout.

As we both stand breathless and very close to each other, looking into ourselves, at our shocking self-exposures, I wonder if this is not our great moment of consummation, the smooth mute union that I have dreamed of. We may never be closer than this.

Even in the midst of our intimacy, I cannot enjoy it before I explain how I was captured and framed in Ela's place when she shot herself in the mirror. This mystery takes me back to my earlier mystifying observation. Suddenly I remember what every young woman, usually named Mary or Marie, learns in the course of a film about Dracula: a vampire has no reflection. Have I missed the major clue to Ela's secret all these years?

This could explain her power, her magnetism, her sexual hunger, her restlessness, her indestructibility. She may have adjusted to the "sexual revolution" of our times by moving her canine teeth from her mouth to her cunt. That would make their detection practically impossible. She sleeps during the day, sucks dry her men at night, lives among bones, and smells of decay and love, feels neither hatred nor fear, only ennui, and fools even her own mirror. It could all be true.

I have heard Ela publicly divulge: *"Je suis de mon coeur le vampire."* But I take nothing of hers for granted, not her honor, her youth, her impulses, certainly not her words. I have always known that she has no concern for life. I know that she may kill me if I come into her orbit, without malice or any other feeling, that her selfless instinctive indifference kills. Besides, I believe that the female vampire is the symbol of the give-and-take of the world. That is what Ela represents to the multitudes who are drawn to her and recognize her: the craving for a final everlasting death and the inability to die; the fate of eternal youth; a hunger beyond words.

But those were metaphors I used to while away the time of my loneliness. Now I have seen proof! She is one without a second.

I always suspected that Ela's sexuality was a quest. Now I can safely assume that she is searching for the lover who will kill her, whose love will enable her to die after many centuries of redundant cities and crowds and long graceful throats and tired bloodstained teeth. And I am that virginal lover. Strong enough to receive and to dazzle her until I thrust the staff of light, the flaming cross, into her tiny hard-to-locate heart. Is that the self-realization I exist for? We will both expire in the expression of our love. It must be done. Now!

Ela looks into her new confusing photos with some boredom. She has had too much symbolism and exhilaration for a day and it's not even midnight yet. Her imagination is tired. She decides to save the excitement of deciphering these prints and uncovering their metaphors for the next day, which may be a dry uneventful day. For now she would rather hide that playful lens and go to bed, or better yet have sex. She can call in one of the perfumed men waiting outside. Her legend will blind them to the ruins that are her present vagina. She thinks: I need to fuck a slave; there aren't any left nowadays; I need to embrace and excite a big body scarred by the lash, to French-kiss a tremendous threat, to caress a centuries-old cruel suppression. The idea of children or clear-eyed Americans or empty lonely mirrors is revolting.

I confess the obvious: I admit I have loved her since the dawn she was born. Yet I have also forbidden myself to love her, and I shake as I see my own weakness. Life will be unbearable for me, if I must constantly face my love. I cannot escape it now that I have agreed to call it by its name. Yet I continue to feel I am a transposition of Ela; I add the logic, the cohesion. I am meant eventually to unite with her into a single character. That is my purpose. I have no way out. I love her as myself and I ask for nothing, but for her to look at me as she looks at herself. Take my kingdom, Ela, and reign! Here you will be free of rules and limits of body and mind and cunt. Nothing will possess you. Dig into my face. Show my eyes no mercy.

It is all useless now. When she took that photograph, she lifted the lid of my fragile world which, like an untreated film imprint, is distorted when exposed to the light, and she revealed my hidden worms: my honor is lost. Only the undead can kill the undead. I disappear, disintegrate. A broken eye drops on the floor. A crystal iris. I try to stay unnoticed. I keep quiet. She makes no sign of interest. She may not notice my absence for a long time, if ever. She will fill the gap with her own image. I feel that I am being dismembered as Orpheus was by Thracian maenads, only my murderer does not deign to tear me into four-ounce chunks, and I am forced to implode. My moment has come. I have seen myself. I hear a faint husky whisper: "Come."

I could still kill her. Isn't death the common denominator in all beings? Wouldn't death unite us? I should kill her, and take her with me. No one else can stop her. I know her better than anyone. She has something of the invention about her, a man-made quality, indefinable and inexpressible. She transcends the individual and so she threatens to destroy everyone. Blindly.

But I don't. Not because I can't kill what I love, quite the opposite in fact, I can't conceive letting what I love live; nor because I can't murder something so admirable as the organism that is Ela; nor because, once defeated, I hurry like a coward to retreat from a last showdown, but because I have seen myself.

I realize that everything I have done up to this moment has been in order to see myself. There is nothing obscure left of me, nothing mysterious or questionable enough to push me into any action. She has given me what I was looking for and did not know it. I too, it turns out, had looked for myself in her. So let those who follow pick up the banner. I am fortunate. Suicide, of any kind, translates the metaphors into reality. I am no longer in vain. Thus, I am no longer. Don't look!

II

?

How She Found It

Ela is going to the zoo. She has woken up today with an intuitive certainty that her long-lost wily cunt lies finally within her reach. She feels that she will soon use it again. She knows that she will find it in the zoo. Perhaps she dreamed it. She goes out at once and asks the pedestrians on fourteenth and seventh: "I'm sorry, I need to get to a zoo. Do you know where I might find one?" They stop at the sound of her otherworldly breathy voice. There is a big zoo in the Bronx; that's all her informers divulge.

In the subway to the Bronx Ela swings her large pink fan to and fro and strikes up a conversation with a Japanese waiter who serves her sushi at lunch in the same uniform of oversized black-rimmed glasses, oversized baggy black shorts, massive black shoes and big white cotton shirt he wears now; despite the stick-thin funny legs coming out of his huge shorts, he carries himself with high dignity. He sits next to Ela and chirps: "I've seen you come. I serve you *toro*. I watch you come every time you eat it. I couldn't imagine you taking the subway! I saw one of your lovers yesterday: he looked scared." Ela: "Affection is the means. What is the end?" The words rise and fall in her throat as if bouncing in a deep well. He informs her: "I study philosophy. The only difference between Plato and Aristotle is that Aristotle never masturbates." Ela thinks: How naive. He had young Alexander masturbate him instead. She thinks: Do animals masturbate? Is masturbation a sign of civilization? Ela: "Is reality the apparent absence of paradox?" The Japanese intellectual rolls his tiny eyes and trills: "At last I know you! You are the true untouchable! No one can give to you! No one knows what you need!" Ela thinks: sex. Ela: "Are the Japanese into pain?" She opens her enormous fan like a peacock's tail.

During the past six months Ela has been more or less celibate. Against all her expectations, unless drunk or stoned, even men who were not familiar with her authentic cunt have suspected during a regular fuck her lack of proper genitals. A few stopped midway in terror or assumed that she was a surgically re-formed man, a castrato. Most politely brought it up: "Do other men talk to you about your cunt when you have sex?" Or: "Help me find your clit, sweetie." One man got up half-done to read a medical encyclopedia, but found nothing relevant in it; another said it was a sign that she had a holy destiny to fulfill and should abstain like Joan of Arc; someone asked Ela if he could show her "cunt" to his shrink; and many men demanded to know the whereabouts of the rest of her cunt. They felt cheated.

Of course Ela succeeded in persuading men that they were

mistaken, nothing was missing from her body, and accepted their apologies with a certain indignation. The discovery of her lack did not prevent them from falling in eternal love with her and giving themselves to her on a platter. But it had become a painstaking verbal process that lasted a few hours each time and turned her off to sex in the end.

She made up stories; she told them in advance that she had a motorcycle accident and the Bultaco's brake had pierced her vagina; she had been fucking it while driving. She described how as a girl she had been bitten there by a shark and had narrowly escaped with her life. She explained that this was the shape and texture of foreign cunts; and so on until it all became redundant.

Besides, her orgasms suddenly bored her! They were not as exhilarating and liberating as before. She actually felt them now as her shackles to the real world. That led her to believe that for her freedom now meant freedom from habit, and to decide that all sexual ventures with men would be fruitless until she found her—or, at a last resort, someone else's, any, a—cunt.

So even though she is made for lethargy, Ela is willing to act for the sake of a new cunt. She has started searching for one quite diligently. She is tired of feeling wide like an airport hangar and no longer able to hold a man between her lower lips and shake him like a fish until he vomits saltwater.

Thanks to this adventure, Ela has learned that her cunt is useful. But she continues to ask herself daily: Why do I look for it? Do I need all that trouble? Do I want it back? I don't. I do, I can't, I won't, let it come after me instead. Let it make an effort. I'll take it back if it comes.

The Japanese philosopher: "I can't understand your presence, but your absence gives me excruciating pain. There is nothing natural about you, not a gesture, not a movement of your dress. You are a law unto yourself. You are the desire that crawls under everyone's skin." Ela: "Love is a paradox. What do I care that the earth is round?" Then he gives her explicit directions for the zoo and, before they part, he takes her picture and asks her for a last word of advice: "Shouldn't you be persecuted by the authorities, shunned by the people, damned by priests? How have you persuaded the world to let you be in all your stunning difference?" Ela: "Everywhere I look I am in the zoo; no matter whether I am caged behind the bars or whether I stand outside them, in either case all I can see are animals behind bars." She closes her fan, coughs and walks away windswept as the train goes by her, holding her neck with one hand, smoking with the other, dressed in a black sequined flapping cape with pink satin lining, a tiny tight transparent red lace dress, an usher's gold-braided hat, baroque pink velvet boots and austere black impenetrable sunglasses. She comes out of the subway crypt and slowly pulls herself along the way like a phantom dragging an invisible ball and chain from her ankles, but the world sees only her beauty.

Ela has never been to a zoo, but as she enters, she shudders with a sense of recognition, a distant memory threatening to seize her. She stops by the first cage and thinks: What are these animals staring at?

As usual Ela finds herself under public scrutiny. The animals turn around, stop everything abruptly, grunt, and stare at her in awe. It annoys her. Do they find her weird? Do they stare at every visitor as though they have never seen anything so interesting? Have they been trained to pay all this attention to people? Do they think they are human or that she belongs to their species? Who hides behind them? Who is responsible for them? Who came here to look at whom?

She takes off her glasses and tries to stare them down. But her gaze that pierces the feverish, glazed eyes of the crowd only helps to keep them fixed. The various animals seem fascinated. Ela wonders: Is it my clothes? I am glad I didn't wear my dress of emeralds. Spring is perfect for that dress.

Ela walks fast as if pursued, looking straight ahead, until she reaches the monkeys. Suddenly she stops. Every monkey is fucking, in mix-and-match couples. Monkeys without mates are jerking off. They look human sitting on their rings, staring at each other open-mouthed, drooling, reaching through the cages and helping each other come. They give out the chopped choked sounds of broken, running, tape recorders. Their pink, swollen, ripe asses open up like smashed watermelons. Those asses look like separate beings, with soft sexy skins and exaggerated pouts. The monkeys sit on them as if on scarlet round oversized cushions.

Ela watches them eagerly, without needing to hide—as they are a different species and thus under other codes—her natural, haughty, whimsical disdain. She leans on the bars, crosses her calves and smokes, smirking with glints of self-mockery in her naked eyes. Did she come here only to witness a vulgar sex show hoping to save herself from craving sex? But as with everything exciting in this world, the monkeys fucking is both repulsive and stimulating. She licks her lips. The monkeys cough and screech. She gasps. The monkeys notice her and turn to stare, breathlessly. One of them winks. She winks back.

Ela has changed her mind about what exactly happened to her cunt. Soon after the disappearance of the lens, she decided that the lens had not been her cunt, but an impostor strategically placed in a similar jar to fool her. Perhaps her cunt was stolen after she found the lens and devoted all her attention to it. The mystery lens was a foil to keep her occupied and unsuspicious for some days. Or else it was her post-separation hallucination.

Ela stands in front of another cage, watching baboons fuck. She feels an irrepressible certainty that her cunt will come here, attracted by the mad spring fever odor. But at this very instant she feels jealous of the baboons, of their bulging puckered soft assholes which remind her of enlarged cunts. She thinks: Can I participate in this miracle? Can I join?

Typically, the heated busy baboons interrupt their frantic loud fucks to stare at her dumbstruck from the ascetic enclaves. They become still and quiet. They can't take their beady horny eyes off Ela. What are they looking for? Then Ela recognizes that look. Love! Adventure! She knows these faces well.

I confess: I stole it to examine it further. I first took its temperature, measured its dimensions, analyzed its texture and consistency. Before dissecting it, I decided to fuck it first. It was an experience I could not deny myself or my science. I was eager to enter a cunt unshackled by the confines of a body. But at that point, I realized that the stupendous cunt was perhaps still alive. It was not cooperative by any means. It was slipping and sliding out of my hold like a snake. Initially it grew into what looked like a lens, long and thick as a limp penis. But I was not intimidated. I held on to it, though I was in shock. It split into writhing stems, like an octopus with tentacles. I grasped it tighter. It changed into a fleshy tulip, an arty sensual clay ashtray, a jerking red squid, a pink squirming mouse, a black cockroach, a prickly pear. I became determined to get to the bottom of it. When it eventually turned into its original shape again, it was still stretching itself into abstract shapes like silly putty, and its colors ranged from green to blue to pink to silver, like an angry face.

I persisted, more curious than ever. I played sexy watery music—Jarre's "Equinox"—on Ela's CD, and lowered the lights, hoping to seduce it. I set it up against some pillows and tried to penetrate it, but I encountered various acrobatic failures. I am one-dimensional when it comes to these things. I had to hold it steady under one hand and myself in the other, and it was not easy to position it correctly and keep it still under my control. The very second I put it down to attempt some further adjustments in the setup, the protean cunt took off.

It literally ran off; it did not slide or roll or hop or leap away, but ran upright as if on a couple of tiny invisible funny feet. It took countless quick ginger train-like steps, in the manner of an earth-worm. It looked like a tiny yelping dog whining and limping quickly away after having been hit by a car. I could not believe my own eyes. I watched it escape at an unbelievable speed. It hid under the bed in less than a second. Once it was out of sight, it proved impossible to locate in the room or outside. I searched thoroughly for two days before I opened the apartment door. I guessed it slipped through the air-conditioning duct or the bath-tub draining pipe.

So how does anyone find a single stray cunt in New York City? Now both Ela and I are searching for her footloose cunt.

Ela asks a big-bellied red-nosed crooked-legged fish-blue-eyed lemon-skinned middle-aged guard: "Have you had any unnatural incidents in the monkey cages lately? I am interested in strange unexplainable sights that people have actually witnessed. I look for a small but noticeable creature, silver or pink. Aren't you the man I am looking for?" She fans herself passionately. The guard slurps and warbles: "For twenty years now, Miss; yes, I am; I am Bob; I support the I.R.A. and enjoy sharing my gruesome experiences as a part-time paramedic, but now my heart beats like a bewildered bird as, sexy and comfortable, you smile at me from across the years, inviting me to screw you right here in front of the animals. But what is the use of what I say if the sounds finally touch your half-naked body?" He stops abruptly and resumes only when Ela gives him permission to answer her query. She thinks: I better not look again at the monkeys. If the light were any better, they would realize what I am and break through the cages roaring for pleasure.

Bob tells her a story: a beautiful shiny pink insect started bothering the animals recently. At first everyone thought it was an expensive wind-up toy that some child threw to the animals; it did not stop moving, especially around the mammals' peckers, and when they went to clean the cage, it cunningly slipped away, so the guards modified their conclusions. They decided it was a tiny pink slimy frog that had an unusual ability to twist its body into a circle, or else an exceptionally fast slug. But when Bob threw salt on it, it did not disintegrate as slugs do. Most of the zoo workers thought it was a Martian, an alien visitor studying earth life, but Bob did not believe in the supernatural. Bob was sure it was a tropical insect that came over on a boat from overseas and found its way to the zoo by instinct; it might be an unknown bug that had not yet been classified in any Western encyclopedias. He called the vet and the entomologist of the zoo, but they could not even recognize the overall species of that creature. Three days later, thanks to the guards' careful planning, the invader was removed from the cages before it did permanent damage. It took nine men to get it out. Bob and his friends succeeded only because they discovered its Achilles' heel; they had to hire nine gigolos to entice it away! The men groaned, sweated, stripped, walked out with it jumping all over them, got into a wagon, and drove off.

"Where can I find it? What is your guess?" Ela interrogates him. Her voice is anxious, childlike, deep. Bob would check out the prisons, these creatures usually end up in prison, he explains. He heard a rumor that it is being passed around in jail, causing a new agitation. "The men's jail?" Ela repeats with apprehension, thinking: What will be left of it after all this handling? "What do you expect? Don't look surprised, women are too sane to fall for its act. Besides, what could a woman do with that hollow thing? Wear it around her neck?" Bob replies.

Ela thinks: So from the zoo, I must go to the prison. What company it is keeping now that I am not there to hold the reins! It pushes itself too far. She takes the subway home to dress for prison. She likes to travel underground when she is depressed.

It is in the baboon cage, right now, I see it, spanking the monkeys, literally! It is jumping excitedly from baboon to baboon. It turns around. The minute it sees (?) me, it is gone. I must track it down! This is my chance to get the full scoop.

An awkward balding dumpy man in a loose white suit, pink tie, and beige detective's overcoat hanging sloppily on his hunched shoulders and Yorx SFI AM/FM stereo dark sunglasses around his eyes, that transform him into a monstrous fly, welcomes Ela into the train. He nods his head right and left continuously like a loosened jack-in-the-box, and interlocutes: "Hundreds have trusted you. You cost lives. Do you get carsick?" He looks her in the eyes for an answer and at the same time tries to balance his leather briefcase between his legs and lean against the metal pole for support in order to use a Pioneer portable mini-compact stereo-TV, a Zenith Supersport portable computer with a scanner, a MC50 Ricoh portable photocopier with IM.F portable fax, a Futrex 1000 that reads the body-fat content, a RC605 Denon pocket microscope, a Sony mini-recorder-digital diary-calculator-databank, one after the other; all of them hang from his arms limply in a most graceless and stiff way that reminds Ela of the British Queen carrying her purse in public; they clash, clatter, and clang in rude cacophony, as he rocks with the motion of the train. Every few seconds he feels his back pants pocket for his wallet.

Nevertheless, the energetic cramped yuppy offers Ela his assistance as she gingerly steps on the train and, dragging all his vulgar fetishes with him, sits next to her in order to show her the core of his life, that he calls "O": an Olympus camera with '50s design, old-fashioned flash and smooth aluminum body. "I use this," he confides producing an 8-mm micro-camera from a pocket, "but O is my great love!" "I know her story well," Ela assures him, "and I believe the woman is a male homosexual. It lacks class, but has a lovely sense of timing."

When Ela finally gets off the subway car, she runs into a puny dapper Chicano holding an enormous pink umbrella and accepts his pert offer to walk her in the rain: "Who are you, woman? I've been in a beer commercial. You're beautiful, my God. I am grateful for small favors. Eddie Gonzalez. Please touch me, I am young!" He has puffy lips, bulbous lids, a Travolta haircut, and his nervous thighs shake and kick continuously as if from a terrible itch. He stares at her mouth the entire time as though hypnotized but somehow also manages to see the street and stop her a few times from crossing into the heavy traffic. On her doorstep he French-kisses her like a high school sweetheart. Ela nods with empty eyes, knowing that he, like the rest of humanity, would torture her much more painfully if she showed him her boredom. Eddie gives her his resume, stapled on to an 8x10 black and white *retouched* head-shot of him, bows, and watches her go up.

Of course I wanted to bring myself into the picture, to be a protagonist, a hero: to be weak! Yes, it should have happened: I should have died; I would have preferred that. But as it is, the cunt took off and my mock-sacrifice went unnoticed. It was my fault. I did not change the cunt for an old lens—though the symbolism of it moved me deeply—on the day it was scooped out. I simply availed myself of the cunt; right after Ela's return from her assault, during her nap, I could not keep from seeing it more closely: I took it in. Ela saw the lens with as much surprise as I did, when she woke up; I had just stolen the authentic severed cunt and was sure that the jar was empty and that eventually she would see her cunt quivering in my hold and attempt to take it back or force me to return it, as I would sooner or later do, for I had no intention of causing any damage. I was not certain that this lens was not a new incarnation of the cunt, perhaps born in reaction to my imprisonment of it. Then Ela left with her trickster lens, and her cunt broke out of my hold and ran off. I watched it escape. Upon Ela's return I saw her unusual photos and began suspecting that the cunt could be in two places at once, or else what I had held or what Ela still had in her possession, one of the two, was the reflection.

Her apartment, replete with glass and bones, repels Ela. She needs the energy of a crowd, a quick charge. She covers her mouth in black *purdah* and, like the night, descends on the city in her little red dress. She stares at all the women in the street accusingly. She feels mistreated and vengeful. In her mind she pictures herself killing hundreds of women, strangling them one by one without spilling any blood, then stealing their cunts, cutting them out, collecting them, freezing them, pickling them, drying them, selling them, painting them, gilding them, using them for pots and wallets, wearing them each alternately, changing into two or three different cunts in the course of a fuck, and finally exchanging them—maybe ten for one?—for her own.

A towering hulky woman in blue velvet overalls, with breasts bulky and hard like grapefruit, curly red hair, and no fingers past her crumpled knuckles, takes her hand as a medieval knight would and calls to her: "Sister!" Ela drops her silver head in the stranger's stupendous cleavage and answers: "You bitch!" She wonders how she would manage to kill such a huge woman.

The fingerless lesbian hugs Ela until she is hidden inside her abundant chest. Her breasts smell like cayenne pepper, seaweed, and moist scouring pads. She wears nothing under her overalls, so that Ela can see, from where she is buried, only the big off-white pores and stretchmarks of those flabby long tits. Ela sneezes. The woman invites her to her house, and specifies: "You look like you need women. I hate talking about myself, believe it or not. I smoke all the time. I have two kids. They are nice accessories. I don't breast-feed. I design puppets. I am casual but avid about sex. I may be oversexed. Have you always been an exception?" Ela: "I am a congenital liar. It is true. I never say the truth." She speaks fast and breathlessly so that the listener is overtaken by the terror that Ela will suffocate at any minute, give out three tiny spasms, and expire. Her voice purls and scintillates, innocent of sense.

"You have the voice of a soothsayer," the big lesbian booms. Ela: "A seafarer?" "Call me any names you see fit. Every spring all the witches leave their homes," the lesbian now blares. "You may call me Desdemona. I am a symptom of nature. I will pass." Ela lies happily cuddled in the grandiose peppery tits and pays no attention. Desdemona: "They carry themselves like queens. They dress elegantly and raid this city, go to expensive department stores looking so beautiful that no one notices their gold blank eyes. They steal our children while lightning strikes outside one afternoon or a tired cashier makes a counting error in the candy aisle. They teach them to love horror; the horror of a belly that thinks, of a mind that only knows hunger, of an eye that reflects what it sees, of an ear that absorbs like memory. They swallow our children whole with the bones like game birds, after they dance with them in the light of old desires. Do not be fooled by their fresh tormenting smells and painted shy smiles every spring. These women eat our sons who are beautiful like daughters and our daughters who are strong like sons."

Ela is lulled. She follows the big fingerless lesbian home. The enormous unwieldy breasts, heavy like exotic giant mushrooms, bounce and slap Ela's tender face as she walks backwards with uncertain steps still hiding between them. They make a striking couple. She whispers: "I draw pleasure from sweet or wild fucks that are born away from men or against men; I like coming alone."

When Ela saw again the fatal photos of myself and her lens on the next day, she was disoriented by the absence of the lens which now followed the disappearance of the cunt creating a pattern, and even afraid that the rest of her body might start to disappear part after part with no further warning. Left empty-handed, she decided to get used to the gap and hid any evidence of the lens as if that part of the adventure had never occurred, for it was hard enough living with the memory of her lost cunt. She buried the photos in her closet and hardly gave them a second glance, for it seemed no longer relevant to understand the nature of a lens that was in her life for four hours. So she treated it like yesterday's lover. In fact she hoped gradually to wipe off all memory of her old tight cunt and assume that her new genitals, once they healed, were what she had always known.

Waking up after a mediocre night with an overly excited and wordy suitor, she reasoned that the precious lens had been temporary, a day-long device that self-destructed, for in its place on the closet floor she found a small pool of thick dark silverish unrecognizable liquid that vaguely reminded her of vomit or menstrual blood or acid. What was she to do with an ounce of silver-blackish secretion in the place of a cunt? So she assumed that it had dissolved after serving its obscure purpose. She licked the lens-fluid, just in case, unwilling to waste it or separate it from her body, and wiped the floor with Ajax. She gave it no more thought. Like her cunt, her lens had been a delusion; a snare; a cobweb. She was glad to be rid of it.

Ela lies on her back on a dark waterbed that swirls and swells and swishes and caves in like a sex-doll's rubber mouth opening up to swallow her. A tremendous strapping naked Aspasia pounces through the bedroom door: gone are the overalls, the high heels, the bobbed perm, the lipstick, and the tight girdle that made her look human. Hecuba now bursts in with her red hair pulled back, her puffy cheeks flushed, biting her bloated lips, looking like a hungry disheveled seamstress turned Jacobite rebel breaking into the Bastille or haunting Marat's home, a hefty Spanish butcheress who just killed her husband in a moment of bad temper, a mean chunky Nazi colonel in charge of a concentration camp with a fondness for heavy sweets and thin cocks, a female Sumo wrestler, or the robust runner in Picasso's painting *The Race*: big-footed, soft-assed, flop-titted, thick-waisted, red-faced, bulb-eyed, rough-hewn. She holds out her fleshy arms and doesn't care what happens.

Ela dives freely into that mountainous lumpy softness and sucks it at random, and is herself being sucked into endless freckled folds and creases and canyons as into the tentacles of a giant red squid or into the mouth of a mammoth clam, in full abandon. She feels the various parts of her body crumpled up, spread out, warped, separated, perhaps corrugated, certainly lost to her. Only an elfin foot here or a narrow bony shoulder there that spill out of the ample thumping female mass indicate Ela's drowning presence.

The cunt, not I, is the gap at the center where everything goes and disappears, sucked in and spewed out. In those few minutes it was with me, I held a candle under it and watched the flames eat at it. It was a heavenly sight. What frail harmony! Sex with fire is the perfect ending, I thought.

Hilda is endowed with the fattest longest clit Ela has ever seen or heard of, easily the largest in the world. A consummate mighty clit that fills Ela's field of vision and overflows beyond it. Ela bravely faces that quivering monster and wonders how she can ever affect the nerve centers buried in it. She notices that it looks exactly like a towering taut juicy cactus the color of an eggplant and wider than Ela's pinkie. She spends the next half-hour yanking at it, whacking it, biting it, chewing it, pinching it, kneading it, slapping it, spanking it, stretching it, twisting it, scratching it, hoping to pass sensation down through all that rugged muscle and fat. It probably owes its awesome dimensions to many hours of fingering and pulling, Ela thinks admiringly. So when Wanda yelps inhumanly like a dog fatally wounded, as if someone has found her heart and is presently piercing it on a spit and roasting it, Ela wipes her brow and falls exhausted on the red-carpeted floor with the image of a red demanding clit indelibly engraved in her memory. But she has no time to rest.

Immediately afterward, the Great Yolanda carries her in her arms like a new bride and drops her into a brimming hot bathtub. Magda flops herself on a nearby stool with her massive thighs wide open, rewarding Ela with a continued frontal viewing of her powerhouse-clit and of the sparse stringy red pubic hairs on her otherwise old boring purple labia. Ninja employs her hard mighty forearms of a mythic laundress, her vast shoulders and colossal swinging breasts, all to clean Ela. Her gnarled stubs clasp a dozen bristly brushes expertly. She scrubs Ela with loofahs and oils and aromatic beads until Ela, submerged in burning lather, cannot breathe from all the suds and steam that choke her mouth and nostrils, and her skin is white silk thinner than a newborn's. This passionate manic creature can only be a German Jew, Ela concludes, gasping and giddy. Sarah looks porky, happy, and out of breath. She obviously loves a thorough clean-up.

Back to the carnivorous waterbed for Ela's turn: Aglaia heaves and dips and perches herself like a fortress on top of Ela, breasts first and heaviest, and squashes her so that they can fuck face-to-face and clit-to-clit, like bulls. Aretha starts to rub down Ela's tiny neck and lick Ela's eyes, and her saliva burns them like astringent, when apparently she changes her mind, gets up, giving Ela some breathing time, puts on a record of the *Swan Lake* soundtrack, pulls up her imaginary sleeves like Mama Bear preparing to clean house and launches a full-blown attack on Ela's body. She uses her rough feline hard-as-a-worn-shoe-sole tongue, her broken pointy teeth and brutal fingerstubs that are each thicker than an erect cock and do not wither with wear, buries her hot red face between Ela's legs in a gross crass attempt at sixty-nine which she is far too long and big for, as Ela's mouth can reach just below Andana's breasts, and sucks hard like a vacuum cleaner. Squeezed between the whopping bulk of this gladiator and the wobbly wet mattress, suffocated in pain and pleasure, crammed and cracked by that triumphal lust, swooning under sexual overkill, as Sonya's immense mouth drills into her still-healing vaginal cavity and sucks all life from her, Ela realizes:

- a. her frame is too small and frail to withstand the coming abuse, and this may turn out to be her last fuck;
- b. without its previous elasticity, her gaping tender vagina will experience unspeakable tortures in the hands of this maenad and may even get chopped up again before she knows it;
- c. the waterbed is giving in under her.

So despite her bliss at being fucked by such a female beast, despite her urge to leave herself in the hands of this behemoth, Ela labors to rise from under Yalta's pressure and motion to her that the bed is leaking; but as she opens her mouth to shout, she starts coming from both mouth and cunt in profusion. It is her first full orgasm since her break-up and subsequent bereavement. It is such a joy to come, and to know that she can come! With the same brilliant liberating orgasm as she used to.

Wondering if this stark two-woman duel represents her new favorite sexual pattern, Ela screams on the top of her lungs to let Matilda know that she has come and now deserves a moment's rest. Belinda lifts her big open furious face, smiles proudly like a child who has pulled off a prank, notices the thin silver vomit trickling from Ela's mouth and frowns motheringly: "AIDS?" Ela: "I am sorry, I can't stop coming." Malta: "A funny thing happened to me as I was coming: I wanted to die for a noble cause." Ela: "Waterbeds make me seasick." Her post-orgasmic voice resounds sweet and heavy, like a priest's caress. Ida: "Strong feelings never bother me. Do you need to rest for a minute? Can I go on now? I am enjoying you tremendously. Like fucking my own cunt. Redemption does a lot for me."

Ela points to the torn shrinking mattress that is reduced to a wrinkled bluish plastic sheet sunk under a large pool of stale-smelling tubwater and cum, and then shakes her head emphatically. Splashing about, as they progress into the post-sex chat Ela initiates, moving cautiously on her hands and buttocks, Ela struggles to pull herself away from that slippery bed without breaking her bones. Paola, dripping streams of sweat that add to the wet mess, lights a Fidel cigar. Ela: "I politely take my leave." Luella: "Do you also intuit the absence of God?" Ela: "You know nothing about me!" Lucinda: "As I look at your beauty I want to sit on the curb or crawl into my bed and cry like a child, with snot running down my manly lips." Ela: "It does not pain me to hurt you." Helena: "After twenty-eight years in therapy, I have a right to say: I am not alone. Nor unloved. If I let you out of my hold it is only to get a better view of your short slender thighs, your tiny pale waist, and your hard round ass." Ela, making her escape from inside the wolf's belly as it were: "But you can crash me; you can put me in a crate and mail me to the Near East; you can crystallize me and drink me in your tea; you can cremate me and eat me in soups; you can crinkle me between the pages of your Bible or stretch me out on your roof to dry and then expose me in a fancy neon-lit glass case; you can start a collection." Fontana: "This dress makes you look like a fast-spreading fire. I can't catch you. Some things simply don't die. Little bonfire, be careful with yourself: is it windy out?"

Ela goes home and lights the fireplace. She crouches next to the mirror and hears a growl in her stomach: What makes her think it is worth anything to stay alive? Where does she think she is going? Why does she keep going? She thinks: I am not even a woman who bites her nails. The firelight flares in her eyes, and they flare in the mirror. She is stunned by the unworldly flower-like youth that looks back at her, animated with pleasure like a bright girl on a rollercoaster. She resembles her cunt; a thought blazes through her mind: Am I my cunt? The fire blazes up. Ela wants to jump in it.

Meanwhile, in the same city, her oblivious cunt is well on its way to getting famous.

Ela squats, opens her thighs, closes her eyes, opens them and looks at the wrong place—her mouth, not her vagina—and on reflex jumps back, even though she has seen nothing frightening, loses her balance, falls hard on her ass, and shouts: "Ouch!" She hates speaking aloud when she is alone; it makes her feel needy; it wounds her ears. That is the result of her effort to force herself to look into her mutilated vagina.

She thinks: Was my cunt just misplaced somewhere and I am making a fuss over nothing? Can it still lie in that omnivorous closet under the piles of clothes and appliances? I could search for it once, just to make sure. One day I will look through my junk. I need patience for such a chore. If only I had something down there, anything, a pea, not just an open empty space, I wouldn't feel so exposed.

With a quick plunge into the fathomless closet, Ela changes into a black leather cap, see-through lace Calvin Klein bodysuit, black leather Harley-Davidson vest and short Perfecto leather jacket, a long straight dress of Assyrian mesh that hugs her like a glistening metal net, black leather boots and shoulder-length earrings of two fat black-and-white alabaster cows with big pink crystal twinkling udders and round pink gems on the foreheads that remind Ela of her flamboyant cunt. She sprays her long hair with iridescent silver sparkles from a can. She asks the mirror in passing: "Do you think I am ugly?" The mirror: "Do you think I am ugly?" Ela: "You? No! I am ugly."

The mirror: "You? No! I am ugly." Ela: "Me too." The mirror: "Me too."

The phone rings in the closet. She lights a cigarette, coughs, and hears her recorded voice whisper as if in breathless panic: "Go away, keep quiet, don't make noise, leave me alone." After the beep, her dad says to the answering machine: "Ela, will you let me come? In my visions you are giving birth and your vagina slips out instead of a baby and it is crying, so I swaddle it. I don't know what to feed it. It is pestering me. I am losing weight. What can I do? I don't know its ways. It's cute! Why can't I just come and hug my daughter?"

Almost six months ago:

That first week Ela went into the intimidating closet and turned on the TV news, something she despised doing, and read even the small script of the most tiresome newspapers, hoping to get news of her cunt. She heard nothing and gave up.

Then, a month later, coming out of a sushi den, Ela noticed a disheveled reeking crusty wino who sat open-legged on the steps of the New York City Opera House, which was closed for renovation, had put her sparkling cunt in a rusty coffee can in front of his unzipped fly and strained to fuck it in the "armchair position" repeating with a high call: "It is my first hard-on ever!"

The unmistakable reflections of the light on its wet surface gave it away even to Ela who is most inattentive and unreflecting in the street, engrossed in flighty thought. The vapors exuded from it were so thick and the bum's body odor so putrid and stifling that she took a long breath and held her dress over her nose and mouth, before she walked into the affected zone around him as if she were going into tear gas. She wore a long tunic of rose petals and gold Roman sandals. When she was close enough for him to take notice, only inches from his oily face that reminded her of volcanic formations seen on distant islands, his dead eyes sparkled with thirst. Overtaken by her excitement at standing so near her lost cunt and by the heady earthiness of its physical circumstances, Ela found herself fainting into the bum's lap. She turned her neck up for air and fell. At that insidious moment, with the bum busy watching Ela, her cunt slipped out of the rusty can on its invisible mini feet and disappeared.

The bum was begging: "I am Homer. Today is my lucky day. I beseech you: hide yourself! Become invisible to everyone but me!" "Oh, invisible," Ela replied, practicing her latest style of conversation which consisted of repeating a word people said to her, usually the last, to give an impression of sophistication and interest. Her dazzling hair fell on his face and blinded him. Homer: "What is beauty?" Ela: "A jack-in-the-box?" She looked like the winning flower arrangement at a florists' show for the fourth of July. Homer felt a spasm of patriotism: "Ask me to go to war for you! Order me to kill for you! I am your victory! I am damned! *Maudit!*" This must be what they call Pyrrhic victory, Ela thought; "Victory," she shouted, speaking to her distant cunt. Homer wiped his brow, threw away the empty can and opened his arms above his open legs, rocking like a baby or an insect turned on its back: "Burn my heart, end my gallop, name my misery, extinguish my flame! Loot me!"

At first Ela thought she had rescued her endangered cunt. She felt proud and happy that her cunt was alive and about, even if it lived under such dire conditions and had lost its last dregs of discrimination. Knowing that it was not imprisoned or killed put her mind at ease. But Homer looked incapable of any serious hard-on even after being exposed to the combined effects of Ela and her cunt, so Ela realized that her cunt had only been testing its cock-teasing powers on him. It had not undergone great danger. It did not owe her anything more than a grin.

"I can hear the mythical spider coming! To wake us up, to chain us, to change us, to wash us in its supernatural light," Homer burst into an apocalyptic sermon addressed in general to pedestrians, panhandlers, gang members, cutthroats, muggers, pensioners, junkies, winos, and cops wandering outside the Opera House; the "great unwashed," Ela thought.

The subway that takes Ela to the men's prison is crowded: it is lunchtime rush hour in spring. The car reeks with syrupy perfumes, rebellious body odors, and dissatisfied hormones. The passengers sigh. Most wear motley uncoordinated combinations of cabbage green, orange, yellow, and red. Regardless of outfit, they wear tennis shoes. The women's skirts have back slits. They remind Ela of Mardi Gras on remote islands when the locals dress up and act like naive tourists of various nationalities.

Ela suffers herself to be gazed on by people who believe she is not looking at them and by dark men who seek her glance by loud gestures. An oily-haired, big-nostrilled, large-crotched, horny Puerto Rican sprawled on the seat across from her cups his groin with his palm as if to protect it and fixes his narrow eyes on her—missing—cunt. She thinks: Would he understand if I said there is nothing there to look at? He suddenly rises, pushes through the passengers who stand upright and uptight with their steaming bodies in rocking contact, reading best-sellers and tabloids watchfully and fantasizing about each other, and bends into Ela's ear, all the while piercingly looking at her cunt.

He tells her: "Your problem is you don't believe anyone hears you. Chiquita, do I hear it! Your feet have never touched the ground. You are a woman up for grabs." His skin color shows a sickly constitution. His lips seem shy. Ela: "Could you keep quiet?" The Puerto Rican: "I love music but I avoid it. It makes me aware of time, getting old, but I love it 'cause it says nothing. It's all looks!" He stands so close to Ela now that his crotch touches her mouth. Ela thinks: I am not into this. The Puerto Rican: "Yes, you are! Your pussy sings to me." Ela thinks: He is too hot; it bothers my skin. The Puerto Rican: "Does that make you feel all juicy?" Ela: "You smell like a baboon." The horny Puerto Rican, still looking where her cunt should be: "Nas...ty! How often do you score? Your voice is an aphrodisiac." He shouts in her ear to be heard over the noise of the train; his breath burns her cheek, his pelvis burns her chin.

She gets up and squeezes away from him through the crowd. She dashes forth using her elbows as rudders. Hands sneak on her breasts or buttocks and multiple breaths are exhaled into her nostrils. She keeps her mouth firmly shut. Bodies fidget, stir, and fuss and many feet step on hers and she steps on many feet. Her metal dress, heavy, cumbersome, and inflexible, pulls her down and yields the unbearable stench of sweaty rusty iron. It is ineffective as armor and, revealing more of her than the average eye can bear, attracts greedy glances, but it prevents direct contact with her skin. Her stylish cap falls off her head constantly, her Perfecto zippers are caught in soft clothes, her boots crackle and weigh her down. The sour animal odor of heated leather chokes her. Ela perseveres until she reaches the gap between cars where air can circulate, leans back on the rattling sliding door with her cheek against the graffiti and shuts her eyes. She still can't breathe. Then she feels a hot and soaked throbbing slug fall on her under-belly. It could be another Puerto Rican. At that she faints.

On the other end of town, at this very moment, her cunt plans to flood the market.

She comes to, lying on the filthy floor, her skull bouncing up and down on the metal, her feet held high up against a middle-aged unkempt bearded man and a thin bland woman in white plastic fur and caked Doctor Ruth blush, exposing Ela's naked open thighs to the curious occupants of the car. Ela often finds herself in this position in public. She thinks: Whenever I faint, people lift up my skirts and take a peek. My cunt attracts all the sympathy. I lose consciousness, they raise my legs. It must be instinct; a repressed necrophilia maybe? They must think it's my cunt that causes me to faint, so if they air it, I will be OK. Or that it feels suppressed. They insist that the blood needs to go back to my head.

Suddenly someone slaps her. Someone else drenches her with cold Coke. Someone else forces a jelly bean through her teeth. Someone fans her with a Harlequin romance. Someone sprays her with dime perfume. Her eyes blink, her pupils disappear, her mouth twitches, her lower lip feels swollen. She meekly raises her small hand to cover it. The women leaning over her with concern look like wilting greens, carrots, frozen vegetables. The disgusting taste in her mouth reminds Ela of old men's cum. A squash in orange lipstick, baby-blue eyeshadow, and Divine hairdo explains to all present: "She is having an epileptic fit; I teach elementary school and I have seen kids with these symptoms. You can buy medication now for this kind of thing." An over-dressed gray-faced bag-lady in a red flannel robe and old men's slippers, a tomato, nods: "I'm a kook. Ma'am, are you a kook too?" An okra with skeletal torso, anorexic limbs, hollow cheeks, xs-Levi's, and shoulderless top: "She isn't much of a cookie anymore. My father-in-law gets these spells from diabetes. She needs an insulin shot." A big potato in a lame business suit: "Maybe she is a Pentecostal." An antiquated shrunk artichoke with bright blond hair, black-penciled eyebrows, purple-colored wrinkled and plaited lips, a florid polyester dress and matching handbag pitches: "I read about it: a woman who just gave birth to nine monkeys had these symptoms during her pregnancy; it's a new thing; it was on the first page yesterday. We better warn this girl." A cucumber with very long legs and terry cloth dress from mail-order catalogs of the type who goes from Brooklyn to the Limelight on Saturdays in high pumps: "No, my grandfather has Parkinson's, like the woman in *On Golden Pond*, and he acts like this, shaking and falling down all the time. I can't stand being around him." This starts a conversation on the nature of assorted diseases and relatives.

Slowly Ela manages to lower her legs. She hugs the cold metal pole, wraps her legs around it and convulses. She faces the calves crowded around her, smells the assorted feet, feels an unnaturally hot breath in her ear, and hears from behind her: "You've got an electric stinging haunting pussy, not a magpie or any such thing. No respect for anyone. You put down a man's desire like it's offending. Your pussy sparkles as pretty as it is deadly. Nothing is sacred to you. I'd love you even as a dead carcass." The horny

Puerto Rican. He adds: "We'll sing in a tub, run nude on a beach, fingerpaint each other, I'll surprise you with *sauce à l'orange* on your nipples and pink ropes tied on the legs of the bed for you to use without wasting time or lust." Ela thinks: What ever happened to the crystal, the cognac, the pretty silent boys, the marble bathtubs, the orchids? To those gold-cased amber smelling bottles with Eros sculpted on both sides? She turns toward the kneeling boiling Puerto Rican and throws up. This creates a great uproar.

Five and a half months earlier:

It all began with a black man coming, a blind man coming, to be exact. If blind people speak with their gestures as they cannot mimic the rest of the world and so their actions reveal their thoughts, on that September afternoon the mystery man spoke to Ela. They had a talk, that's all.

The day he was released from jail, after no charges were pressed against him, I was in Times Square looking for Ela's cunt which had just run away. I figured that was where it would find refuge. It was the first snow of the season. The streets looked like a leper's skin, dotted with mud and ice falling off in big rotten chunks. The hot-dog vendors were freezing into chubby hairy icicles. The blind man who, according to various sources was already revered in certain Black Power New York circles, did not want to be released and felt discriminated against by the system that paroled him. Angered by the injustice that reflected on his race and his handicap, he had called for a press conference after having unsuccessfully begged his jailers to keep him behind bars. It was held out of the police station at Times Square. And so I came to witness his new performance.

This time he spoke unimaginatively, using trite regular words, to the reporters who held out their mini-recorders at his face: "Did I not confess to a crime? Am I not responsible for a violent attack against a defenseless fellow human being? Don't I have the right to a fair trial? Don't I deserve the strictest sentence under the law, as I do not have the excuse of being blinded by rage or circumstance or any of my victim's words or deeds? Am I not a public menace? Why am I discharged like a second-rate citizen, a worthless invalid, a miasma? Was mine not an imaginative unique unprecedented crime? Committed without logic, or monetary gain for myself, out of sheer raw badness, in cold blood, excision for the sake of excision? Isn't America outraged? I refuse to be a threat to society only because society is blinded to the danger I represent! I do not want to have to prove myself again! I did what I had to do, as a man, and now am ready to take what is coming to me. I challenge the Public Defender to shut me up."

He refused to answer questions about the crime—about the object, for instance, or the body part that had, or had not, fallen out of the girl onto the street, and which was later put in a glass of alcohol and carried away, in secret. He said he had no right to speak about the crime, that would be invading his victim's privacy, it would be too presumptuous, all he did was a clear-cut mutilation, he did not expect anything from the victim in return, he did not want to be rewarded or thanked, he made no claims on her or her story. He only wanted to pay his dues. If she wished, his victim could further illuminate the crime. So he spewed clichés at the press and ignored the pressing questions: Did that mean that he knew her? Where could she be contacted?

At first the crowd, attracted by the presence of microphones and cameras, kept combing their hair and staring toward the lenses, squeezing to get within camera range, silently hoping someone would point a lens at them, just like a handgun, invade their depressing privacy, and hoot at them in a Gallic voice: "You feel good... Very good... Give me your lips, your eyes... Now, sideways... I'm capturing your sensuous eyes, your flesh...come closer...you love it... I'm coming to you... That's it! Beautiful," preferably James Brown crouched over a Nikon F2.

By now the crowd had given up on its fantasies and was fed up. It knew an uninspired performance when it saw one live. There wouldn't be much of a story here after all. A respectable-looking man with thick cheekbones a sign of peasantry in his blood a smart long coat and Gucci briefcase protested: "This is an outrage! This country is just too permissive. We shouldn't give people the right to withhold the truth from the public. It is a crime against the mild-mannered citizen who wants to know what occurs in his community. Congress must enact a law that forces every-one to answer any questions we, the taxpayers, find fit!" The crowd had heard this rigorous speech many times and laughed or nodded tepidly but quickly dispersed. It left a gap.

The crowded passengers ask each other for paper towels to wipe their shoes or for help to step over the little pool of silver vomit; they balance cautiously on their neighbors, hang onto sleeves and purses and laps, spray more cologne, make grimaces of exag-gerated disgust, hold their noses although it is impossible to smell it amidst the perfumes and sweat. Even those who were only stealing glances at her before, in hopes of being themselves stared at, now face with fear Ela's light silverish vomit that rolls, diffuses, and slides around following the jerky movements of the train. They point to it wide-eyed and mutter plosives as if they stand in a low-budget '60s film staring out at the UFO on their lawn. Some space opens around her shiny excretion, the desired corridor via which Ela makes her way out.

She heads for the nearest booth out of which usually pokes the head of a black uniformed conductor who announces the names of approaching stations in an unintelligible jargon, and every so often stands outside his post to overlook the passengers with the pompous proprietary authority of a medieval landowner who inspects his live cargo. There she can be temporarily protected.

Soon an older fat black man in a blue uniform a few sizes too tight for him, with a sad face, strong jaw, and deep eyes, questions Ela in a guttural brutal city accent: "Who brought you here? Did God tear you out of heaven with his teeth and spit you out? Is there passion without an object?" Ela: "I can't breathe." The black conductor: "I am Wendell. I want to sit with you in a field of daisies. Give me the benefit of your unshrinking fresh immodest glance." Ela: "Can I sit here?" The black conductor: "You have dealt me a mortal wound." Ela: "Could you move over a bit?" The black conductor: "I didn't mean to crowd you. You blast me and leave me blind. I want to be blind, I want to be blasted, I don't want it to be any different; I love you! I must know: Where are you from? Where are you going? Where do you live? How old are you? Are you married? Are you straight? How long are you staying here? Do you have sisters? What is the perfume you wear? Do you want a cigarette? What is your brand? Have you ever been to a baseball game? Do you like blueberry pancakes for Sunday breakfast?"

I was slowly making my way through the sex arcades on a hunch, after my encounter with the black man, going from one peepshow to the next, looking at other cunts as if searching for some inspiration, when suddenly I saw it. I was stunned but certain. It was on top of the vagina of another woman, exposed for my eyes behind the filthy glass, in fact a two-way mirror, of a dingy booth on Times Square. I could never mistake its silver sheen, the incessant plucking of the lips that formed a circle exhaling and snipping again, or the dreamy fog that gave it the shifty appearance of a mirage. I even put in one more of those special fake-gold peepshow coins with a single eye engraved on them, to make sure. It was it!

Besides, an experienced eye like mine could distinguish the edges of the broader, darker, and flatter vagina that it was supposed to cover and replace showing around it like a dish on which it was being offered. There was no harmony at all between the fake overacted caresses the woman bestowed on her body and the fluid authentic electrified movements of "her" horny cunt. They were miles apart in quality and sensitivity.

What was the cunt doing there, taking over the place of other women's genitals, showing itself off shamelessly to any horny undersexed passerby? It was a fraud here, and besides, it had no right to throw itself so beneath its station! To see that special creature lounging between the ruined legs of a low-class black whore hired as a spectacle for a quarter! It was making a fool of me, that was certain: I couldn't have it, I could only look at it, for as long as I could stand it, for a silly price.

Just like old times, I thought. I got up from the lone metal chair and went looking for the pimp. I found no one around to let me into see the lucky whore in person. I put in a new coin every forty-five seconds to hold on to the view. The naked dried-out black woman didn't look particularly lascivious or erotic, but bored, overfucked, drugged, and terribly matter-of-fact, even businesslike. Why did the cunt ever choose her?

The walls of the viewing booth were covered with dull brown pantry wallpaper with small flowers on it, as if the owners had wanted to make the voyeurs feel at home. The only thing missing was a spraying of imitation scent of mother's cooking. Even the tall wastebasket, presumably there to receive any discharge, was lined with the agrarian wallpaper. A large decrepit sign read: SEXUAL ACTIVITY PROHIBITED. I knew it could not be accurate if the cunt was here. The slot held up to ninety-nine coins, but I could not withstand Tantalus' torment any longer. I grew impatient.

Knowing how close to me it was and yet how unavailable, I began to kick the glass with all my strength. I threw the wastebasket at it. I punched the screen repeatedly, screaming: "Give that cunt back to me!" It didn't break, but gave in a bit and then rebounded, and I was reminded of the soft glass of the lens; they were probably made of the same obscure modern plastic.

The whore suddenly vanished, replaced for half a minute by a mirror that reflected my desire and rage, and then by hissing static. Out of nowhere a sleek broad-shouldered Korean man jumped at me and hit me a few times in the groin, but I felt nothing of course. I was shouting, telling him the story of the cunt, how I would pay him as much as he asked if he helped me get that one cunt, which didn't belong to the woman inside the glass, but to humanity, and was running loose, and had to be captured, for the sake of science if nothing else. I might as well have been talking to a monkey, or to the cunt itself: no expression disturbed his dumb pudgy face; he threw me out. I went back there whenever I could, but the cunt was no longer around. I knew it wouldn't be found at the same spot twice. I needed a new plan of action.

Ela is chatting with a young pock-marked blond guard at the gate who wears a violet silk scarf around his neck under his uniform and a blue carnation in his chest pocket. He looks off into the distance as he inhales the smoke squinting with small Bogart-like eyes and muses: "Love for me is like sleep. After sex sometimes I ask: Must it be like this? I think I am afraid of it; I always lock the door before sex. Afterwards I eat like a Roman." To impress her further with his worldliness, he adds: "What is 'life' in Greek? I used to know it." Ela: "Pussy…" His eyes light up and he nods, yes, now he remembers it. She notices his soft thick tanned neck, beautiful like the neck of a strong woman. He tells her his name is Harlan and that she has struck the first blow at him and will also strike the last. She tells him she needs information about some-one who has recently been in this prison. She admits she doesn't have a name, she only knows that person is in prison for reasons of promiscuity, she doesn't exactly have a physical description, she is really doing this as a project for a branch of NOW, but she is certain the creature she must find is agile and sexually irrepress-ible, have they had any extreme instances of that kind lately? Her metal dress is cold and wet against her skin. He says of course, they always do, why, only yesterday a lifer got his cock chewed off, isn't that something, tsk, unimaginable, he doesn't know exactly how, but inmates go through those things all the time, they can pull anything off, they're maniacs in there, it is impossible to keep up with all the sex hysteria; but they know a good fuck better than anyone; but that bird is gone, and the lifer is in the hospi-tal unconscious. She asks to talk to the victim's cellmate, or any other prisoner who has been there long and knows all the gossip, the kind who never receive visitors, a Pete, a Harry, a Tom, a Dick. Harlan promises to bend some rules and pull some strings for her; all he wants in return is the light from her eyes, he says. She agrees. It is a deal.

For weeks I was running to massage parlors, sex clubs, porno-extravaganzas, S&M shows, bondage parades, swingers' groups, sex-aerobics classes; I peered into lewd aqua blowups in periodicals sold hermetically sealed in plastic, titled *Prude, Rapture, Squeeze, Shaved Pussy Special,* and into countless vaginas peeking through torn stretchlace undies or wrinkle-free explorer's garbs; like many Japanese businessmen, I placed fifty dollar bills into sweaty g-strings to have the dancers show me their costly dull vaginas at close range; I touched huge stone-like silicone breasts and bribed obnoxious pimps; I watched girls do all kinds of absurd things to themselves, lick their own nipples, suck their own mouths, rub a phone-receiver on their clits, push their own fingers up their asses, tie themselves on stakes, swing over the room in a glass cage and pretend they were two people fucking; I saw girls whose vaginal muscles were stronger than my pectorals play Ping-Pong with their vaginas and smoke with their vaginas; I saw girls fucking on stilts, in refrigerators, on chimneys, with Dobermans, with a clothesline, with a machine gun, hanging from chandeliers, both with chains and in chains; I saw hundreds of ropes, metal cages, metal cocks, nameless instruments of torture. And I patiently continued to go from porno show to porno film to porno shoot, anywhere I could locate an abundance of genitalia and audiences, thinking that the cunt could not resist that combination.

I ran into it when I least expected it of course. I was sitting in an XXX theater, exposed to the pervasive odors of sailors' cum and unwashed socks and to the prolonged discolored bleating on the screen. The moment that the soundtrack picked up as though the cavalry were coming and the porno stars repeated: "Yes," I saw the cunt. It was sitting a few seats in front of me! I wouldn't have perceived it in the dark if it weren't for its familiar eerie glow that made it look as if it were made of sparkles. I ducked at once so that it wouldn't spot me and lurked for a while in the shadows trying to form a plan.

I noticed then, to my astonishment, that it (or should I at this point say "she"?) was sitting next to someone who, after some more careful examination, proved to be nothing less than a substantial dick. Yes, loose in the theater, by itself, a dick out on its own! Where did she meet it? Did she abduct it from its owner? Did she severe it off to keep her company?

They were sharing the vinyl seat and were wildly imitating the fucking as it took place in the film, so that they would hurriedly change positions, and slow down or speed up or curve backwards in accordance to what was projected on the screen as if playing at being the mirror. The dick showed great talent: it performed the part of every changing uncontrollable stallion diligently and without for a moment losing its strong upward curve. The cunt, on the other hand, was clearly improvising, moving when the porno star's vagina remained still, changing rhythm and confusing its ambitious partner, probably feeling bored by the repetitive missionary positions and the stillness of its movie counterparts. She pirouetted in and out of the pounding dick, spun around it while it penetrated her and kept undulating its belly, or hole, flirtatiously like a luminous oriental dancer.

Even though I had looked at crass sexual imagery and stared at genitals for the past few weeks, I could not control a surge of revulsion that overtook me at the sight of this terrifying obscenity, of this mockery, as I sat witnessing two unaccompanied genitals slurp and slosh in a small pool of secretion, fucking blindly on a public plastic seat! I was surprised by how much the presence of legs, underbellies, waists, arms, and heads contributes to, and perhaps even justifies, our interest in, and our tolerance of, sexual conduct. Genitals, I realized, though necessary and even enjoyable, require some sort of seasoning, a few extra touches, to give them the appropriate look; otherwise they are petty, alien, and disgusting like obscure protozoa or wormy salivating mollusks that have crawled high up on someone's clean white wall unnoticed. This wasn't a sight of life!

It was now clear to me that the cunt had picked up this separated dick, and perhaps was planning to start a family of similar loose genitalia jerking themselves obliviously into eternity! This time I planned my next move, making certain I wouldn't overreact and lose it. If I ran towards it, throwing out my arms to grasp it, if I called to it, it would see (?) me and slither away. I slowly rose, walked in the aisle, stared only at the action on the screen as if absorbed by it, hid my face in my coat collar, until I reached their row and stepped sideways toward them as if to sit down next to the mating couple. They were rolling in and out of each other with abandon, and I lost no time: I abruptly sat on them with all my force.

Now I had them trapped! I could feel the romancing genitalia fumbling around under my coat, perhaps still unaware of their change of fate, the dick pushing toward the entrance of my buttocks and tickling me. I took off my coat sleeves, let them fall over my prey and stuck the sides first into the borders of the seat, and then, once I had made sure they were still there, slowly united my coat ends as a makeshift parcel. Quickly, joyfully, I got up, grabbed the struggling contents of my coat in my two hands, tied it more tightly around them, turned it upside down so the flat back was underneath and the tied openings in my hands, and ran out. Now I had her! She was under my bondage! They fought like live cats in a bag, about to be drowned.

I stormed into the dilapidated hotel next door, got myself a room, locked the shaky door, checked the opaque windows which luckily were not broken and threw my derelict package on the dirty unmade bed triumphantly, in ecstasy. I was ready to dance, swirl, shout a paean, blow up the place! How could I have imagined, after all my precautions, that the cunt had once again tricked me, that under the scarlet lining of my coat lay only a single erect dick? Yet that was the spectacle afforded to my eyes as I untied the knot. What could I do? I looked around the room even though I knew I wouldn't find her. Perhaps she had detected me all along and escaped at the very last instant just to enrage me more. Perhaps she had turned to liquid and trickled out of my trap. All I knew was that she had run off slipping through my hands again. I had it and yet I didn't have it.

Meanwhile, the excited dick seemed to have no consciousness of its new circumstances. It danced a lonely number on the bed, standing on its wider base, blindly reaching around with its head right and left and upward hoping to touch a penetrable surface. It had no idea where it was or what it looked like. I was so disappointed that my impulse was to take it out on this poor victim. I admit that I tried to strangle it for some seconds. I put my hands tightly around it and pressed as hard as I could to choke it. That was a mistake, for the immediate result was a forceful off-white arch of liquid squirting out of its mouth into my eyes. It occurred to me that I had given it pleasure instead! Irony upon irony, faux pas after faux pas! I was clearly not made for this plot! I considered, for a moment, giving up. I thought this wriggling writhing air-grasping fool was a sign. A mirror. What the hell. I could put it in a jar of water, take it to Ela and say: "Look, use this." I would insist: "Let's forget you were a woman. You and I both will start over. Be a man. With your singular looks you only need to screw this on and you'll be a perfect male too. At least try both sides. Like Tiresias; you'll be a seer. Blind perhaps, but the wisest seer!

You'll feel men's point of view, what they see inside a vagina, why they go mad, all those mysteries. Then you choose." I knew I could persuade her. I have that power. That, I was made for. Perhaps there was a moral lesson somewhere here.

Now Ela is shooting the breeze with burly red-headed hairy unshaven Harry in whispers about this and that through the visitors' window. Harry is six feet tall and wide like a truck. He wears an immense yellow scarf in the pocket of his uniform and a similar yellow tie over his collar. A lit cigar hangs forgotten between his huge fingers. She confesses to Harry that her brother George's cock was just bitten off, it was so embarrassing the family was keeping it a secret, they were hoping he could get an operation, like a sex-change but to get back his old sex because what is a man without his cock, he's useless, you understand, especially George, they didn't know how it happened, it was during his sleep, he didn't know what hit him, and George's penis was gone, it was a mystery who took it or where it had gone or how to find it, he woke up and it was missing you see, he was feverish and said a fairy took it but that's George for you, and she guesses these things do happen, obviously, seldom but they do, they don't get publicized of course because no one wants his name in the papers with that story out about him, naturally, but she heard something similar happened here not long ago, so she has come for a clue, to help out George, to find out who stole it, to catch that beast, did he know anything about it, or who might give her something specific.

Harry says she has the right person, he himself heard it get bitten off. He discloses: "It was a pink plastic dildo, what they call it, a jolly-jumping pocket-pussy, but high quality, a killer, man, exactly like the real thing, someone must have sneaked it in and it was doing the rounds; I've got a love doll called Sheena, it sells for $39.95 and has fleshlike extra-thick skin for a lasting relationship, said the label but that is nothing in comparison I mean totally high tech the guys were fighting over it and everything like it was a real broad. Dick asked the guards for a judge so he could get married to it, ho ho ho, he's nuts, so it finally reached Pete, who's the big man here and has got red tattoos on his chest that look exactly like that pocket pussy but a darker red, I mean true portraits of it which wasn't really a pocket pussy, it turns out, Pete said it was a real-life woman's cunt, on its own, what a find, and this was a real man's job so he'd keep it to himself he wanted to sleep with it every night because he said he'd never screwed anything so tight and right, this is the best fucking cunt in the world you jerks he said, and Pete's had pussy from all over from every town and country, said he'd let us watch and beat off but that was all, he punched Dick's eyes out for asking to borrow it, he ordered 'no talk with Rosie!' that was final, maybe they knew each other from before. Dick said to me secretly this thing will ruin Pete he'll fall, it's a man's calling to love one broad once and good and this was it for Pete, Dick is a smart little pig so Pete kept it on a string all day, a wire or rope or something, like a bird, a turkey chick, and said to us 'Rosie this' and 'Rosie that' and in the mornings he called out "I've got a live one here!" and then he laughed, he let it free at night to screw, he'd stick it in and start screaming crazy "fucking Hell, I'm God!" He kept the jail up, everyone was jerking off, I've never heard a man come so much and so long, we thought they'd have him removed to the madhouse or shoot him up to shut him up but I guess they liked to listen too, until the fourth night that he had it, it was weird, just dead silent all of a sudden, we couldn't get a peek because we were locked up but this guard says it was slipping out of Pete's fist

like a live eel, it wouldn't stay put, it shook and squirmed like
the devil but you don't know Pete, he held it hard and went in, we
heard nothing much but then it happened, blood and all, Pete bit
his tongue and didn't utter a sound but they found him knocked
out. The creepy thing went off on its own, just like that, carrying
old Pete's cock."

Ela looks at the other prisoners in the visiting room and realizes: No one here has playful eyes. Ela: "Where did it go?" Harry:
"The doc searched the toilets and they asked us all if we saw it but
Pete's cock vanished with Rosie. Who knows where! Reno, for all
my guess is worth ho ho ho. The two of them in love, Pete had
it coming. What could they do to such screwing genius? Arrest
it? My notion is, they should shoot it, or else it'll put a lot of our
guys out of use. If this puts your mind to ease, I make you a bet
they will soon. You can't grab a man's cock and run off with it like
nothing happened!" Ela: "Don't they want it alive? To make
heads or tails out of it?" Harry: "Who would trust it near them?
You've no idea how good it is! If they're dumb enough ho ho ho!
All I know is I don't think Pete will be back. It's not easy stuff.
How's your brother taking it? Will he live?" Ela: "I must find it.
Who is the guard who saw it? Where can I go next?" She notices
that Harry's ears are small and elegant like seashells and his gray
eyes look wet, as if he were ready to burst in to tears. He has
been still like a statue all this time. Harry: "The guard has been
off-duty since, maybe he's having nightmares or getting drunk or
whatever, it shook him up. My theory is, it could be anywhere. If
it doesn't get shot on the spot, it'll go to prison. The cops aren't
gonna let it run loose for long! Besides, it's killed a dick! Or two
with George's. Check out the women's. If it's a cunt, that's where
they'd take it, if they caught it, no? If they wait to fry it in the chair,
it'll do much damage yet. Once a cunt, always a cunt, I say. They

better not let it in back here, I'm telling you. Don't call me Dirty if we don't destroy it, lynch it like they used to, I say we'll give it what it deserves this time, we'll tear the witch apart. We'll fuck that sucker! George shouldn't worry about that, if we get our hands on the little shark again." Ela: "You're a nice man. I'll keep you posted. Call me if it comes back for more."

Ela is going to the women's prison. First she looks through her clown-faced snakeskin bag, takes out her nine-inch-long puppet earrings and wears them. From her left ear now dangles Carmen Miranda with big laughing red lips and surprised little eyes, pears, oranges, and bananas piled on her head, a red tube top and yellow straw skirt, loose brown legs and oversized red pumps moving in any which direction as if in a mad cancan, loosely held from four silver threads. From her right ear hangs Cher in a long black fur, black mini of chains, big white pumps, closed pouty mouth, bedroom eyes, and black frizzy hair jerking about precariously. Thus equipped, Ela leaves the criminals' abode. No Ariadne to greet me at the prison gate, she regrets.

She thinks: At least this time I'm dressed for it. Women have anthropocentric taste, I hope these earrings will do the trick. She considers changing into frills and flounces and knots of pale ribbons and taking her large pink parasol with the gold border to squeeze it romantically folded against her hip. But she is not informed on female criminal taste and it is now late afternoon, visiting hours are soon over, the wind is blowing hysterically, and she has began to glow already. She can't afford to wait another day, or hour, if her cunt is already in such serious trouble, with its life (?) in danger. She must catch up to it.

I am obsessed with finding that cunt. I see nothing but its wet smirk around me. The harder the search, the more excited I become. I entertain no more thought of a truce. I want an unconditional surrender.

I am bent on finding the lost treasure. The cunt is my nemesis. My failure only gives me more reason to look for it everywhere. For me, this is a pilgrim's progress.

That tragic night I threw away from me the miserable sticky dick that had shrunk in my vengeful hands to the size of an earthworm and decided to change direction. I had tried all I could in the hard-sex arena and here was the sad result. I left the seedy hotel and threw the dick into a Salvation Army collection basket. All dicks look incredibly old when limp, I noticed. Perhaps somebody else had a need for this antique.

At the first crossroads she reaches, she hails a cab. "From jail to jail huh?" the cabby comments, sliding open the foggy window that separates them. Immediately, almost by instinct, Ela jerks her fingers awkwardly, as she has seen interpreters for the deaf do in readings and lectures—lowering two fingers, raising three, circling one, penetrating another, pointing here and there, bending and overturning them, as if the fingers have caught on fire or are feeling numb—and performs exaggerated mute lip movements. "Mute too, huh?" the flat-faced cabby asks nodding understandingly in a general commentary about life's trials to which no one is immune, as most cabbies know. He looks quite disappointed. He wears a brown oily large suit and a black tie around his open soiled collar with a knot so tight and old that it is no bigger than a pea by now. He has a fat nose like the prow of a ship, lidless eyes, loosely hanging cheeks, hairy ears, a blacksmith's shoulders, and strange apelike arms and legs.

Ela thinks: If I nod, he'll see I can at least hear him and then talk his head off to his heart's content even if I don't, and I will be unable to protest or rest. I must avoid all communication. I better act deaf as well. She looks out in the characteristic composed-and-absent way of the deaf. The cabby understands and mutters to himself angrily: "Deaf-mute! Now that's a catch!" The cabby smells like a primitive male rather than any kind of city man. His nails are beaten to the roots.

But suddenly new thoughts cross her mind: Who is this man? Will it occur to him that I am at his mercy? If I don't give him his chance to tell me about himself, he may resent me. We are in a wildness as far as I am concerned, and have far to go. If I can't entertain him with my listening or my speaking, what is left for him when boredom overtakes him after some miles? He can rape me, throw me out, take me to another state, lock me in the trunk. How can I control his thoughts in this silence? So she must hit him where it kills: love for a defenseless brave woman in need. At the mention of love people transform, Ela reminds herself. If she makes him feel like a hero, then she can be safe.

She finds a notepad in her big funny-face bag and scribbles on her knees: I'M CATHOLIC. I'VE MADE A VOW NOT TO SPEAK TO ANY MAN NOR HEAR A MAN'S VOICE FOR A YEAR. A VOW TO ST. MARK. VENICE, ITALY. PLEASE HELP ME KEEP IT. IT IS TO SAVE MY DEVOUT BROTHER, WHO IS ON THE VERGE OF DYING FROM SOME UNKNOWN DISEASE, OR I THINK CASTRA-TION. I MUST NOT BE TEMPTED. MAY THE GRACE OF ST. MARK BE WITH YOU. GOD BLESS.

The note instantly performs the miracle. The cabby beams. He turns and looks at her every few minutes and always breaks into a radiant smile from hairy ear to hairy ear like a proud mildly comprehending father. He is delighted. He continues to smile at her throughout the trip, blinking his eyes sweetly in the mirror. How unusual to find someone who still believes these days! This semi-naked girl, he tells himself with admiration, is the first saint I meet in person; I mustn't speak or I would embarrass myself; God knows what dumb blasphemies might come out of me. This is a chance to get along with God. What strength of character! What self-sacrifice! If she is willing to give up so much, to live without human contact, I'll do my small part. She will go far this little funny-looking pretty punk-saint, I can see that! Maybe she will be Mother Theresa one day! That glowing face of hers is a sure sign. And that poor castrated brother, how lucky to be loved like this! He has a lot to think about now until they reach the women's prison. He even wonders what he might ask of her when she is a saint, how he could learn her name. He imagines every detail she would otherwise have to invent herself. He is busy, removed from temptation or suspicion. Now she can take a nap on the back seat.

Two months earlier:

Still no cunt. I have covered museums, talk-show audiences, department stores, Broadway shows, fancy discos, and ferry boats, calculating that the cunt must take the route of any person alone for the first time in the city, not in order to orient or acclimate itself but to find and seduce the naive clean victims that it has a fondness for. I was certain I would meet it on Staten Island one day, which seemed to be the ideal hunting ground. I made the trip on the ferry every day surrounded by sleepy commuters and wide-eyed tourists shouting and shooting all at once. Click! Click! Those sounds took me back to that hard September day that ended so disastrously, but I hoped those very sounds would attract and excite it. The happy tourists didn't suspect there probably was a wild cunt running loose in their midst. Meanwhile I continued to suffer the proximity of picture-crazy lenses and flashes directed thoughtlessly at any which direction, and eventually came to see a smirking cunt in every lens that snapped around me. I reminded myself I was pursuing the Box of Pandora and had to stay firm and relentless until I stepped foot on mound number f/32 and planted my flag into it.

On my thirtieth visit to the mammoth ungraceful metal statue, I finally saw it! What a surprise it afforded me! It was posing between Liberty's colossal legs, holding on to the bronze dress right at the spot where the footlong iron vagina of the Lady would have been inserted if she had been naked or if her sculptor had chosen to add one outside. There it flickered proudly, reflecting the light, shining like a mirror, like a movie star. It must have taken a long time for it to crawl out to that precarious area and I was upset I hadn't seen it sooner. It was practically impossible for me to climb so far out there. The brilliant cunt seemed delighted to be photographed and pointed to by the awed tourists. Beaming out like a lighthouse, Liberty's lively cunt looked over New York like a conqueror! The sea wind blew through it giving it an orgasm. It flapped like the American flag and seemed to have grown out of the bronze folds like a ripe magic mushroom.

I climbed the endless stairs without stopping to catch my breath as if running for my life. In a way I was. I was so mesmerized that my eyes were still flooded by its light and I could only see blackness inside. At the appropriate floor I looked through a smutty window and was frightfully disappointed: nothing there. This hide-and-seek in which the wily deceitful cunt had all the odds in its favor and was physically built to win had begun to exhaust me!

Since then I have often considered: Are my eyes my only

weapon—starting to deceive me? Is it possible that it will continue to go by unseen by everyone else? That no one will recognize it? If the world saw it for what it is, it could be caught at once; if every hand it hid under and every knee or nipple it hung from wasn't blinded by habit and decorum, then it would have been trapped easily by the strong legs or underarms or elbows it attaches itself onto and even attacks. Unfortunately people are blind to the unfamiliar and to the unattached. What can a single disassembled misplaced sluggish and flat observer like me achieve? I trudge, stump, lumber, and slug after it diligently, but I am not built to be active. Oh, if only people understood that this is not a metaphor!

Ela opens her eyes to a grim reality: her cunt is an angel. A silver halo hovers over its lips and it wears thin white wings. It sits alone in the middle of a huge gold-studded throne, a long solid gold couch that could come from the Topkapi palace. There are bellydancers with slanted eyes dressed in silver and gold transparent garments that flow as their bodies undulate, and tall eunuchs with tiaras, heavily embroidered vests, thick lips, and fat colorful birds, probably parrots, perched on their shoulders who crisscross the room bearing trays laden with nargilehs, masks, eyepatches, diaphragms, cameras, and red leather whips. It rains gold dust that whirls in the silently blowing wind.

Her cunt is laughing with evident abandon, opening its lips wide, looking up, vibrating as if to an unmelodious pop tune screamed by hollow-cheeked elongated drugged boys in shredded polka-dot pants and '60s wigs. Luckily there is no sound. The cherubic cunt jumps up and down on its throne, squirms and does somersaults. The halo stays intact. A white bird, perhaps a stray pigeon from the park or the Holy Spirit, flies straight to the edge of the throne, perches there and chirps inaudibly but with fervor, then slides the tip of its pink beak into the cunt's lips, which snap shut at once. The bird flaps its wings a few times in excited or desperate hurry, but remains perched with its neck bending into the cunt's mouth and its beak trapped. When it finally withdraws, in a slow jerk, something dark and squirming is held dangling from its beak. A worm? A bug? A sperm? An eye? There is a close-up: it's a purple, almost black, tongue.

Ela sees with horror that her cunt has lost its tiny tongue. It can no longer speak for itself. Perhaps Ela was its tongue, she hastily interprets. Or perhaps it has lost its clitoris in a gruesome accident. Perhaps it gave sex up for Heaven. Perhaps it can no longer come. She fears this vision implies that her cunt is in trouble. Her cunt will die! Alone! But that would be the worst possible turn of events, it must not die separated, without Ela around it! They may be separated for eternity!

They have arrived. There is no TV in the cab. It was all a dream. As Ela wakes up she remembers that she hates cabs because they make her feel old. The servile driver opens her door, bowing and glowing. His primeval smell pervades her. The smile is now permanent on his face as if glued on. Predictably, he says: "Please, I want no money for the ride, I'm moved by your story, I want to be a part of it." Then he realizes with embarrassment that he is not supposed to speak at all, according to her vow, and for a second covers his mouth with his wrinkled callused hand and shakes his finger as in "bad, bad!" then shakes his head right and left, then opens his arms up from the elbows and shakes them left to right like a Japanese theater actor, and his entire body motions one non-stop "no" while his head points toward the meter. She nods and smiles humbly. She thinks: I'll keep the same note to give to the cabby who drives me back. The man is waving at her outside the gate now, clasping his hands together upward, in a handshake with himself, perhaps to wish her luck, like a coach outside the ring. She has taken off her jacket and vest during the ride, so now she holds them on her birdlike arm feeling flustered from her nap and as she crosses the arid courtyard toward the imposing building she looks like a shining knight in armor. The few people there have an impulse to cross themselves.

This prison seems to Ela more austere, cold, dangerous. She thinks: In another situation I could use my cunt to get what I need. The possibility of it is not much to offer now. I must depend on words. What torture! Here the guards are overweight, fearful, tight-tongued, disciplined. They hear her request sternly and lead her at once to the supervising jailer, also the prison director, an anorexic platinum blonde in tight uniform who moans: "You're a striking woman. Do you need my advice?" They sit down and discuss love and life. They agree in general.

The anorexic jailer: "Aren't we what life is willing to put effort into?" Ela: "I am so cheap." The anorexic jailer: "Food makes me feel unwanted and guilty like a base criminal." Ela: "Have you been to San Blas? When women get their first period they paint their faces black. The dye stays on for a year. I find that provocative and sexy. Perhaps I will do it tonight, cover my face with ashes. I'll hold a candle under the mirror." The anorexic jailer: "I met a Mexican gal here who had known Castañeda, and she explained to me why food is poisonous. Can you fall in love?" Ela: "I was in the sauna in Santa Barbara when a thin Mexican laborer peeked in and immediately sank his probably infected teeth into my cunt on impulse. It was a nice surprise." The anorexic jailer: "I cannot even begin to picture what happens to food inside us. Were you naked?" Ela: "Obviously. He must have come to clean the pool." The anorexic jailer: "When we love we have a habit of saying: 'Give me from your mouth to eat.' Love can kill me. Could you have loved him.?" Ela: "I will tell you a secret:

1. The more you want, the less you must show it.
2. The greater the desire, the stronger the hate.
3. You don't meet the wanted enemy without your mockery.

"I make a better strategist than Mao." The anorexic jailer: "It seems that you believe in reincarnation! Me too. My favorite character is the Hunger Artist. I was happier then, proud, in that cage." Ela: "No one has ever hurt me. It works."

They are standing across from each other, like tough-talking lovers in a *film noir* exchanging words that are bullets from their hearts, over a long shiny desk with a metal paperknife, an ink pen, a Perrier bottle, a box of toothpicks, and some syringes on it. The anorexic jailer often pats down with bony yellowed fingers her smooth perfectly combed hair that reminds Ela of the Caribbean sand and looks as if it were painted on her skull.

The anorexic jailer: "If I were writing about you, I would say: something in her denies participation." Ela: "I do enjoy undressing in front of old paralytic men in wheelchairs and lying naked at their feet to sunbathe. The impossible turns me on." The anorexic jailer: "I would be happy if it was impossible for me to go to the bathroom and evacuate; that function disturbs me profoundly. During work I often fall on the ground screaming, frothing from the orifices. I don't know what comes over me." Ela: "I've come to ask you for an orifice. A prisoner of yours." The anorexic jailer: "Did you say for Orpheus? I believe that was a brand name in antiquity. I am not a great consumer. I stick my thumb into each hole to stop the flow, but this liquid is every-where: behind the bars, inside my bedroom, on the sheets, corroding everything. I dream of plugging up all the holes. I spit. I vomit. I feel it flow out of my pores in my sleep." Ela: "Mirrors have this effect. I often watch my mirror sail on: it flows all day carrying on its surface a white corpse. I must find her before it's too late. I was told she came here because she bit some cock off." The anorexic jailer: "But that's common practice. Splendid. I will ask the girls to check in the files. What name does she go by?" Ela: "I am not sure by now. She's generally called a cunt." The anorexic jailer: "That's an insult I believe. Doesn't she have a Christian name?" Ela: "She was brought here after she murdered or kidnapped a series of cocks. Does that ring a bell?" The anorexic jailer: "I hear many bells. Do you believe the world is liquid? And how long has she been here?" Ela: "Oh, well, she's wet, petite, tense, sometimes pink sometimes silver, very quiet, but she likes lots of action." The anorexic jailer: "Is she the one who just went on hunger strike? That's excellent. Easy to find. Let me ask around. Wait in my office. You can smoke. Please don't eat anything."

Ela thinks: This director must also suffer from a rebellious cunt. In the jailer's plush yellow velvet armchair Ela dreams her cunt is an orator, a scholar. It stands on a podium, with an apple stuck between its open stretched red lips, like a pink roasted pig on a platter. In fact there is only an apple held by what looks like the rubberband of a slingshot. There is a blackboard behind it where the stuffed cunt scribbles with a white stick: WHAT MAKES APPLES AND WOMEN AN IRRESISTIBLE MATCH?

Two thousand years later: From the dining room chandelier of her ancestral home hangs Ela's old lover—K? obviously an Aryan, naked—upside down from his feet which are wide apart and held with ropes from the crystal. He has a gigantic erection and it is funny seen in reverse. His hands point frantically to it or else to his tied feet as if begging her to free him. He screams incessantly: "Ela please!" These are the only two words of any language that he knows. She rests her elbow on her waist, pinches and twists her lips with her fingernails and mutters: "Don't expect me to be so spontaneous. I must first see what I reveal by such a gesture, what symbols are lurking here, what is your hidden metaphor, what I take from this, etc." She asks him to shut up so she can think. A workman—the gardener, part Dutch, part Latino—suddenly sticks his head curiously through the verandah door eager to help. Ela walks toward the wailing hanging lover, stands before him and opens her arms wide hoping to hide him from the other man; "We have to weigh this option carefully first," she confides to the diminutive gardener.

Then Ela walks down the long messy corridors of a preppy '50s hospital, next to a tall woman speaking in Italian and the two of them, dressed in skimpy bright sexy bikinis and barefoot, peek into each sick man's room and crack jokes. She laughs heartily and squeezes the woman's cheek. They notice another of her lovers through an open bathroom door, strapped naked with a white cord inside a toilet, that appears to overflow around him. His mouth is taped shut, but his sweating goggled eyes gesture that he begs her to help him, he is terrified and desperate. The gay Sicilian proposes that they shoot him; they have no camera. So Ela suggests: "Let's swim first." In the pool another of her lovers is making a big show of himself, fluttering, raising his handcuffed arms and drowning in noisy splashes and gasps. And it goes on. Her lovers come up everywhere, bound and gagged. Are they making fun of her childhood fantasies to save people?

The anorexic jailer wakes her up with the following story: there was a vaginal parasite who looked like a cunt brought in two days ago by some whores. The police weren't involved; the inspector had no idea who she was, had no FBI file on her, no social security number, they couldn't even handcuff her properly. There were no murder charges against her, but whores who are trustworthy and regulars here brought her in a sealed shoebox, she was that small, and said she should be kept off the streets because she was emasculating all the customers and they were losing trade. It turned out she attacked the pimps first and got them out of action. She couldn't be caught and she couldn't be shot with a gun as she was an open hole, nor hacked up because she moved constantly and never slept. Maybe a bomb would destroy her, but bomb-builders traveled in different circles from street women. The pimps were scared shitless of her. She was even worse than that alien in *Liquid Sky*.

She was trapped into the Macy's shoebox by a pretty virgin kid who had just that day come out on the street from Milwaukee and she felt something suck on her pussy, she thought she had got a bad infection already, but it didn't smell fishy, it smelled like old orchids and oxidized apples. She put a mirror in front of it and saw a different layer of labia shining over her own, so she pulled it away even though it hurt a lot, for the other cunt wouldn't let go willingly, the kid was bleeding, it hurt as though it was glued on her and she had to tear it off, but those pink farm girls are tough, so she even had the presence of mind to put it in her new spike-heel shoebox and tape it shut, and she took it to the older women who immediately brought it here, not knowing where else it would be safely removed from their world. So we know the monster drops its guard and likes to sit on young women's genitals for some reason; perhaps to recharge itself like a dead battery. But as soon as a man tries to penetrate it, it strikes fatally. It is hard to believe those old wives' tales. The inspector went to check if crack could cause massive trips like that, and if in fact any pimps had been castrated. Both answers were positive. The anorexic jailer limply lifts her deep-set, colorless eyes and opens her skinny arms in a gesture of weakness and disapproval. When she lowers them, always in slow motion, she smiles bitterly and continues with the story.

In that shoebox the new criminal lay swathed in a long strip of red fur. Her identity, if one could call it that, or her predicament, was revealed when she was stripped to be deloused. There was nothing there. Seriously. She didn't have anything, she was just a big hole, just as the women said, and so she was released at once. The whores begged the jailer to keep it here, promised to do plenty of sleuthing, even to pay for its keep, anything. Ela: "Big? How big? What do you mean by 'big'?" Not big enough to trip over and fall into, that much was certain, the jailer assures her, not like an open well, for instance. Ela: "Why did you let her go?" One had to put away something, the jailer explains, in order to keep society calm, so it is useless to imprison nothing. That goes against logic and rules. Ela: "Where did she go?" The anorexic jailer: "That is not a jailer's business. You must contact the police. I can send you to the inspector in charge of the investigation. Why are you so interested in Ms. Cunt?" Ela: "I think she is mine."

The anorexic jailer: "Ontologically speaking, there is no such thing as 'mine.' The liquid around us is a disease. In this liquid all floats loose, nothing belongs to us, not even our bodies and senses. But to drain this liquid is to kill us all." Ela: "But now I live without her." The anorexic jailer: "We each feed off death to stay alive until all death has been consumed and life and death become interchangeable. That is why I loathe food. Do you shoot up?" Ela thinks: How long can our separation last? When will my cunt learn its lesson, get some experience and come back? Is this a time of growth for my cunt? All this is making Ela terribly hungry. She leaves the jail and looks for a sushi restaurant nearby.

I had to predict the cunt's next escapade and be there waiting for it with my net spread open, so to speak. I needed to sit down and pore over all the information I had gathered to discern a pattern in it that would enable me to plan correctly, so I walked into Ray's World Famous Pizza and ordered a slice of eggplant and pineapple. As I waited at the steel counter for the flustered Lolita in a funny red cap to sense me, my glance took in a short energetic Romanian cook singing off-key in his native language and making a show for the pedestrians of throwing the round dough up in the air and catching it into more flour while rolling it to make the crust. It shimmered in the light intriguingly but since he obviously hadn't noticed anything unusual I looked away and kept my suspicions at bay.

I paid, sat on a narrow stiff tall stool, put the paper plate that sank under the steaming slices onto the gray linoleum and tried to concentrate. But the silver light coming from the cook's hands was too piercing by then and too familiar. Could it be what I thought? Could it have grown to such proportions? For the dough twirling around in the air in front of the open window was clearly much wider than the cunt Ela and I had known. Yet that beckoning light could never be mistaken. And here I had sat down preparing to calm myself and develop a plan. That bright cunt was again making fun of me, upsetting my life, stirring me up inside! I couldn't sit back and not try to grab it!

I coolly walked up to the small eager cook and began a conversation on the nature of his job, how long he had done it, where had he learned, did he like it, it looked so difficult and yet such fun to throw the light dough up in the air and catch it, like a game, a Frisbee, like juggling, I would like to try it, would it be okay if I gave that thing a spin? He was flattered and unsuspicious. He nodded and looked around to see if more customers admired his talent now that interest was peaking. My hands were shaking. I knew I had to hold on to it no matter how slippery it would be and how smooth I was, and run away at once.

But a new shock awaited me. "This one," he said, "is ready; they need to make more pizza, so we start a fresh one. Then you can play." I complained: I wanted to do what he just did, not be handed a raw lump of water and flour. "This one has had hard work; you'll ruin it," he argued and without further ado passed it on to a helper who lay it on a black thin rusty-looking tray and smothered it with grated mozzarella. I shouted: "No!!" I sounded as though I was being gutted; for so I felt. The pedestrians stopped at the roar of my voice and some ran in. Everyone got up from their seats to watch and help me in my time of trouble. "Don't do it!" I repeated in the same shrill voice, unable to imagine how the cunt would keep itself from getting roasted and consumed for $2.99 a slice, but equally unable to explain to those mechanically performing their boring menial jobs that they were threatening to ruin the most valuable cunt in the world.

If I dashed to save it, I would be easily outnumbered and stopped, and possibly arrested and locked up. If I tried to buy it now, they would insist on selling it to me cooked. I would have to buy that cunt cooked, and, in the meantime, hope for the best: that the cunt wouldn't fall into lethargy in the extreme heat and be baked like a cannibal's delicacy, but it would look for and possibly find an opening, a slit or corrosion in the old sooty hellish ovens and come out through that escape fumigated but intact. So I held myself in check and watched them complete their funereal ritual, cover it with wreaths of onions and garlands of shredded peppers and submerge it in rich thick tomato sauce and then bury it with a long shovel deep into the ominous cavernous Erebus of their ovens. I broke into silent tears.

Later, they produced a nice-smelling hot pizza which I bought, although I had no way of knowing if it was the correct one and how many had been cooking in those ovens at the same time. There was nothing in the least unusual about its appearance, it certainly did not look like flesh, but I forced myself to eat the whole thing. I spent the day feeling sick.

At this point Ela has reached a dead end: she hates cops. She avoids cops the way others avoid syphilis or food. She sees cops as the brutal blind instruments of conquerors, dictators, and masses. She would never go to cops to ask for a—her—cunt. She hears the script of their reactions in advance: "So it's missing, we'll find it for you all right. How big was it? What shape and color? Did you two have an argument? What were you wearing when you lost it? Did you look weird? Did you have underwear on? What color? Pantyhose? Sheer? A short skirt? Uh-uh! Were your legs open? Were you lying down? On what? Can you show us how? Were you awake? Were you drunk? Were you alone? Did you see it leave? Did you call a doctor? Where is his report? Have you looked through your underwear drawer? Were you looking for trouble? Did you have a pet name for it? Was it tight? How tight? Does it have any other physical characteristics? Scars? A mole? A white beard or a dark mustache? What color is your pubic hair?" They might even ask her to reenact the crime. Ela and cops are two antithetical species. She cannot talk to them for more than one minute. She has run into a deadlock.

About a month ago:

The cunt is now on the talk shows! What degradation! So it was not eliminated in the oven fires of Ray's Pizza! I was shocked to see it! I watched it flirt with Carson and spread its lips open in front of the camera as if they were legs. I first saw it quite accidentally one night when Ela left the TV on mute, for it is her habit to use it as a lighting effect; she likes the blue flickering light coming out of the closet when she fucks or sleeps, for it gives her the impression that another terrifying battle takes place in the next room. That night, while she fucked a lonely Buddhist monk from Tibet who spoke no English, I found out that her cunt had become the new queen of the "in"! That figured! It was a keeper of the secrets of the "in." I was both glad and disappointed that Ela was spared the spectacle.

I turned on the volume. The image of Ela's cunt filled the monitor! Johnny held it on his desk with some discomfort, as he does with all the monkeys and obnoxious pets that visit his show. Why was she making a fool of herself? Even a severed cunt can have dignity! Johnny was asking her who she really is. She leaned back away from him, smiling flattered and mysteriously, tipped her cavity open, and shook with her mute laugh. She was not camera shy. He informed his audience, in way of introducing her, that she was the latest craze on the East Coast, something like the Cabbage-Patch dolls (an insult that went by her unnoticed, for she had been called "doll" in the past and it always brought good fun with it); no one knows what she or it is, he said, where she lives, where she has come from; we only know that she can come, he winked and the audience clapped on cue; we don't know who owns her, who manages her, or how she made her way to the top, but here she is! V! Viva V! Johnny said her name had been inspired by her winning streak, her power and her suggestive shape. So the cunt had now acquired its own name! She was a bona fide individual!

She comes in and out of the spotlight unpredictably, Johnny told us after the commercial break; she comes and she goes. The audience clapped again, because the applause signs lit up. She refuses to be examined by scientists and zoologists whose interest has been aroused by this unrecognizable creature; there are speculations on the existence on earth of a new, more developed species, Johnny explained. "If you have any information on this bombshell, V, call the toll-free number flashing on your screens now," a commentator's voice announced.

Meanwhile the cunt started to smoke, blowing perfect rings of smoke up into the air through her hole. She was quite famous for those rings, it seemed, and she enjoyed smoking immensely. At first I assumed they were the fumes she habitually produced, but the cameras soon zoomed in to the phallic object trapped in her lips. She looked sensual, serene, and almost civilized. She sucked on to a big cigar with all her abysmal might, and then let out the most exquisite fragile huge circles that went up one after the other in parallel layers forming an inverse pagoda of steam that floated in the air a few minutes before it puffed off and vanished. Was that her homage to the creators of toro? During the show she did not appear interested in much more that her fat brown cigars.

That week Ela's cunt was also on David Letterman, literally. At first they had a cigar-smoke-blowing contest which of course she won. He simply exhaled haphazardly making nothing recognizable with his smoke. She blew out smoke-men and women and babies, with a big ring to designate the body, a small for the head, and oblong connected rings for their arms and legs, with little loose hair on the heads and smiling mouths and dots for eyes and shoes and umbrellas and with blown-up genitals, and they hovered in the air for—David timed it—five minutes. She was an expert already. She now had a craft! A performing gimmick!

Then she leapt onto his head and sprawled on it like a pink glowing toupee. Everyone cheered her gall approvingly. So she dangled and swung like Tarzan from his nose. She slipped onto his lips, prevented him from speaking, then onto his crotch.

She became very excited during this show. David explained that the condition for her coming on was that no one would touch her of their own will. So when she refused to leave the set, there was nothing to do but let her spend the hour all over David who, like a good sport, revealed a boy's discomfort to get laughs, frolicked with it, made funny wrinkled faces, and mispronounced his words and took part in the merrymaking allowing her to steal the show from his other guests, for the audience did not listen to their stories and their jokes, busy watching the little down annoy and arouse the host. She did not come on to anyone else. Who knows what happened after the lights went off and the cameras stopped rolling. Perhaps he had a taste of its foremost talent first hand. Knowing Ela's cunt, I was sure it got what it wanted.

Ela sits in a workday outfit of a simple long straight sequined black dress of the '30s and skims the week's events in a stuffy *New Yorker*, the appropriate magazine to read in the Public Library, using it as one uses a toothpick, while she is taking a break at the end of another arduous fruitless investigation through human knowledge in search of her cunt, when she sees the announcement that gives her new hope: Tania Maria is playing at the Village Gate tonight, two hours after Jessye Norman performs at the New York Philharmonic. Ela despises the Gate almost as much as the Philharmonic, but, of all people in the world, those two divine female baits send her lawless cunt into the most exquisite ecstasies. If they sing, she knows it will be there. So Ela is going cunt-fishing again; the day is not over yet.

In the early evening of this day of systematic search, after her visits to the zoo and the prisons, Ela arrived at this public mausoleum of surplus information and money to research the history of other cases of violently emancipated cunts. The impersonal open space conjured up images of a desolate empty hangar and of her own cold spacious and deserted inner cavity, which depressed her. With uncharacteristic tenacity, she stayed to conduct her search. Besieged by the usual gazes, glimpses, glares, leers, and inspections, she summoned a chubby homey balding Semitic albino gay librarian with close-clinging thighs who sat at the desk to assist her; a polite melodious single-breath voice broke out of her and reverberated through the marble hall, thawed the frigid air, disoriented the attentive regulars and inquired: "My dissertation examines the behavior of women without genitalia, the lives of women who lost their labia somehow, and of the labia themselves. I need information on what happens to them and to their genitals. I must focus on the fate of the dismembered genitals. Can you help me?"

The small chlorine-blue red-rimmed well-read eyes lit up, the librarian pursed his thin lips and pledged himself to the cause. He silently led her, like a hospitable mole, through complex corridors to the contents of bulky medical encyclopedias, immense dictionaries of excisions, abscissions, and recisions, special publications about unexplained genital defects, annuals of anatomy, medieval records on women-monsters, dusty studies in teratology, diaries from macabre operations on live peasant women in the Renaissance, treatises on female castration from the Enlightenment, reviews of the tortures performed on hundreds of female servants' genitals by nobles with knives, scissors, and iron rods, firsthand accounts of South American sexual tortures on female political activists, sexual witchcraft practices, memoirs of libertarians and prostitutes, pillagers' excesses during well-known and unknown carnages, anthropological diatribes on scarification, purification and fertility rites of various tribes, reports on mishandled abortions or clitoral castration, archaeological evidence tracing women's initiation tests from lost civilizations, religious and philosophical theories on the contaminated female genitalia, post-Freudian interpretations of dreamed vaginal stabbings as activated penis-envy, until her head throbbed painfully and her white-haired quietly enthusiastic gay helper, his thighs touching even more often than three hours earlier, looking like an ant that has been dragging behind it the carcass of a locust for a few days toward the nearest anthill, wobbled unflinching into the Sci-Fi section, but Ela said: "No more."

Thus Ela perused hundreds of annotated bibliographies, indexes and tables of contents, only to find that there are no more than five documented instances of the practice she came to call 'decuntation'—she coined the term exasperated by the lack of any concise scientific vocabulary for these cases in the history of the world. The letdown: not one humble word on the fate of me excised genitals; not even whether they were fucked, burned, buried, baked, thrown to the dogs, given to the children, made into slingshots, mummified, preserved in salt, used as parchment, sent home as spoils. The common thread: after the amputations they were publicly displayed as depraved signs of victory. She wondered if her own decuntation was to be her claim to fame, her reputed fifteen minutes in front of the lens.

So she receded into an armchair in Periodicals to rest and think of a new strategy for the rest of the day. Her eye fell on the

New Yorker. She picked it up to empty her mind, and the rest is yet to come.

After the *Letterman* show, which became a classic, the latest craze and sport in the hip-yup circles is smoke-ring blowing. People practice for hours, scratch and burn their throats and lungs trying to create the simplest designs, like a smokefish or a smokebaby, but most are still making small balloons. By now V is on television blowing smokevalleys with smoketrees and smokesunsets and smoke-picket-fence-houses. Contests are held on every campus and nightclub, but no one so far can break her record. She is the champion, the idol, the star.

Her fans are organizing clubs and collecting everything that comes out with her image on it. The V-fans get together on the weekends to blow smoke and exchange memorabilia and information and addresses of people who have seen her in person. They vote her honorary president and invite her to fly to remote areas of the country to give a live demonstration of her talents. She goes, smokes for them, laughs, but lets no one touch her. Dark rumors of sexual perversions suddenly rampant in town break out when she leaves.

All over America, old retired couples in thick glasses and sneakers, in trailer parks all over the country, black adolescent mothers with headphones on their ears all day, rapping and shouting to many chubby babies, ex-marines and ex-athletes traveling by train or bus across the country back and forth, upper-middle-class businessmen playing putt putt golf on the weekends in the suburbs, nurses, neo-nazis, nerds, neurologists, nereids, the needy, all wear atrocious T-shirts with her pink horny wet likeness exposed on their chests proudly. They do not see what it is. They don't revel in the nastiness, they see it like a trendy new "Wheel of Fortune." I wonder: Would they like their own genitals advertised on every paper, on sale in every supermarket, stuck into the mouth of every toddler as a teething aid or as a sucking rubber toy, worn by every Joe on the street, massively reproduced, sold below cost in big close-outs where the crowds run to buy three for one? Poor Ela! Poor cunt!

V is the hottest new commodity. In the Village Ela is relatively protected by the V-avalanche, since she shops at thrift stores or mini-boutiques, eats in Japanese restaurants, and hates window-shopping. But she has a few fashion weaknesses and one of them will certainly lead her to her cunt's exploitation. For V has become one of the biggest trends ever: the entire Western world is bombarded by V posters, V notepads and pens, V hats, V ties, V sheets and towels, V perfume, V lollipops, V candy, V gum, V chips, V lunchboxes, V make-up, V cameras, V blenders, V grinders, V choppers, V juicers, V kites, V furniture, V cartoons, V storybooks with titles like "V takes the Kremlin," and of course loads of V underwear and erotic paraphernalia. Even Thomas Pynchon's book, although unrelated, tops the bestseller lists. In the dunes, the heart of the land, hers is the most familiar image since Jackie O became a widow. A huge rollercoaster is being built in Disneyworld in her famous shape of "curvaceous triangle," painted pink and named V. A new skyscraper is being erected in Paris, designed by a famous Japanese architect who was inspired by V; it will be named "V la France." As there are no royalties to be paid to anyone, any small-time local merchant and any hard-thinking tycoon can safely invest in V and use it to sell. Everyone industrious is capitalizing on this happy-go-lucky cunt, rolling in big dough.

Ela walks home from the library to avoid being stormed by subway passengers and cabdrivers. It is late rush hour. Ela changes outfits in a toilet and traverses the crowds on Madison. She likes to feel the bodies around her. She goes through the most frequented places. Trump Tower. Gold waterfalls. Pretty pampered women pour out onto the pavements from the stores. Ela stands out in black flurry Victorian bloomers, bandplayer's hat, sixteenth-century gold court shoes with big bows, white embroidered transparent chiffon blouse, and a long saber hanging sideways from her copper Spanish Navy belt that links in front with a chain. The crowd bestows its usual passionate attention on her and she exposes herself glibly to its appreciation. The humid dusk seems buried in car exhaust.

To her discomfort, Ela runs into a lover—K.? the Russian masterpiece she had some years ago, whom she vaguely remembers that she had promised to marry but left town nauseated two hours before the ceremony, as is her habit with planned weddings. It always shocks her to recognize a face that is not her own. K.: "How are you?" He looks down at her with his shy slothful eyes and she assumes he speaks to her cunt. His pale skin is soft like rose petals; she would like to embroider it with silk thread. He has the most beautiful lush white hair she has ever seen. His gaze is frighteningly deep, like a well in which she throws a stone, waits to hear it hit the bottom and, when she gives up laughing, hours later, she hears a distant faint sound of stone touching stone; it is the gaze of a sleepwalker. Otherwise, his eyes are soulless and drowsy, eyes that can calmly watch a lion tear a child to pieces or a man screaming with a stake in his gut under the hot desert sun. He wears a white Comme Des Garcons shirt, a black stretch miniskirt, long thick black tights and shoes, and an exquisite black vest that had to be designed by an artist.

Ela rubs her belly absentmindedly and asks: "Why is 'fuck you' an insult?" The thirty-three Indian bangles on her thin wrist jangle nervously. K.: "Now I only fuck short foreign women who look like folksy rough-cloth purses and I listen to a Bulgarian women's chorus during sex." K. inquires about the men she fucks these days and reminisces about a "butterfly" remote-control clitoral stimulator Ela used to wear which he loved to operate by sitting on the other side of a classroom or office or family dinner table, and pushing the round red button, and watching her jolt, writhe, moan, sigh, scream, laugh for minutes on end, and come in front of the perplexed spectators. Ela waves good-bye. But K., like all men, is feeling descriptive: "I miss your cunt; your crunchy buttery junky cunt. I'll wait for it as long as it takes. I've found out how much it's worth." Ela feels she is an impostor. She does not tell K. that it is gone, *kaput*, too late, that she misses it too, that if he ever sees it, would he kindly tell it so. She says: "I think every cunt is low in calories."

As K. looks at Ela, he remembers how transparent she always looked, his agony that she would turn into smoke and disappear and elude him, his fear that she would crack like glass, as they were walking hand in hand, and how he kept wondering how such a creature could exist and how the world had suddenly become so beautiful, how Ela's laugh could light up the universe; but he had always pretended that she was as real as he felt he was.

Ela: "Solitude is sentimental: it prolongs the handshakes, it loves nostalgia, it imagines that the awe of being next to another being is universally felt." K.: "But women handle depth better." Ela: "Not hunger." K.: "I will always be in you." He used to shout that when he came, it was his battle cry.

Ela liked his long shiny ringlets that were dyed a different color every week, his lace tights worn under torn jeans, his very long-muscled limbs, his shapely hard naive buttocks, his sculpted stony chest, his oversensitive timid skin, his soapy scent, his physical modesty, his movie cameras always nestled cold and yet inquisitive on his slumped shoulder like watchful birds far more perceptive than K. himself, like ever-present eyes or witnesses, and finally his manly hoarse thundering Herculean voice that made no sense coming out of his elegant Nordic face and shocked her every-time. She liked his slow uninteresting speech that made impatient anyone who was not absorbed by the divine looks of the speaker. She liked his vague gaze reminiscent of the blank maddening Oklahoma plains he had come from and the icy lakes his race had once populated. He was adopted by rich parents, and Ela often thought that K. was as Oliver Twist should be: a boy taken in by the nobles because of his elegant wrists, his politely intimidating height, his frail ankles. He was a huge man, with a huge clean cock, silent and selfish. She starts to leave again.

"I have spent the last three years getting ready to be able to sleep with you, correctly I mean, and I feel I can do it now," K. discharges. K. smiles like an indolent Narcissus and his delicate long priestly fingers make indecent designs on his dusty lenses as if he stands waiting for the adults to finish talking.

K.: "Every night I see a fast-moving mad-angled close-up of your body undressing, piece-by-piece." He looks foolish, artless, unscrupulous, irresponsible, unequipped for anything but to be enjoyed by those smarter than himself, for no thought can ever be possibly formed by the white rose of his brain. They are the characteristics Ela enjoys in a man. K.: "I am hearing E. speak, oh my God, I can't believe it, I stand here listening to E. again! If I don't watch myself, I'll do something silly."

Most of all, Ela had enjoyed the ignorance visibly throbbing in him. K.: "How much do you weigh? I shall have to lift you." Ela thinks: What will I do? He is so dumb, so innocent, so out of it, so tempting. K.: "You do have eyes. I presume they see. They look unreal." Ela: "I need to go to the bathroom." K.: "I can never see the pulse in your neck. Mine is hurting." Ela leaves. K.: "I have seen your legs. I have seen your breasts. Enough. I will go mad."

One month ago:

Three-D Arts hologram watches, earrings, or pendants with glowing eyes, mouths, mummies, scarabs, or spiders on them skillfully laid in leather or snakelike silver coils constitute one of Ela's concessions to generic taste; she likes to wear them, compete with them. This is how she first sees her cunt's image on a U.S.-made product. She recognizes it at once in Manic Panic, it is her own cunt smirking on a watch, she buys it and goes mad: Where is her cunt after all? What has it done to itself? Who has this much access to it? This is a deeper wound.

She still doesn't even remotely realize the dimensions of this international consumption. She thinks her cunt has been used, or abused, by artists and passed on to queer manufacturers. She is cut off from America. Her mirror stays quiet.

As soon as she leaves K., Ela stops in a sports bar and goes to the ladies' room to look in the mirror. She supposes: What if it has grown back in and I haven't noticed? She wants to make sure. She takes off one leg of her bloomers, lifts up her leg on to the shiny yellow sink, leans back so she can see, takes a deep breath, sees nothing new there, and loses a tear to anguish. A tipsy brunette in white comes in. She smells like bitter almonds and has a well-rested pretty face; not the sort of beauty that can only be faced with a weapon in hand. Ela points into the mouth of her open thighs and explains: "I thought I'd check that nothing was wrong down there." The brunette asks: "You need help?" Ela considers it for a while. She would like to follow her earlier lesbian act with an altogether different prospect. She can't imagine how a woman like this would fuck and that intrigues her. But she has only a few hours before the end of the auspicious day she set off for the recovery of her lost cunt. She can always get back to Daisy. She notes down the brunette's number, thanks her, pulls up her bloomers, and walks out.

Ela has acquired the good habit of firming her asshole as she walks, pulling it together to check if she still feels her labia meet. It is at least toning her ass muscles. Her labia used to function as her jaws. She has also started to place her middle and ring fingers joined together on her pubic mound in a quick habitual gesture resembling one that people including her dad—make by placing those fingers on the middle of their foreheads or their temples, in order to concentrate: a slight push. Suddenly she feels as if she is driving faster and faster into a dead end.

She passes a small gray Russian Orthodox church and realizes: I need a priest! A priest will make me feel whole again. Only a priest can make me feel like a woman now. She goes in, but the priest is out. She makes an appointment to confess. The old deacon says: "I am not a deacon, I am a sacristan. How urgent is it?" Ela: "I am unable to commit suicide." The deacon: "No! You're young. Stay and talk to me. Why die? I'm Albert. It is best if you leave God out of matters of life and death. The Almighty can be quite indelicate; when it comes to the nuances. Nice to meet you." Ela: "Because you-know-what happens to be God-knows-where." The deacon: "You're who? I advise you to select a patron saint instead. I would be happy to suggest some for you. Won't you ruminate with me?" Ela: "Russians are my favorite lovers; they are an untapped resource. I visit Moscow often and take them by the dozen. Is the father Russian?" "He is Lithuanian," the deacon disappoints her. He wears what looks like a sexy Roman toga. It reminds her of the producers' party for which there was an invitation in her mailbox this morning. It will be packed, since everyone living wants to be in a film, and she may gather information about V. She tells the deacon in parting: "In the olden days one could walk on the sea, I hear. The ocean was flat like the Scriptures. I wonder what made it so wet."

Five months earlier:

Sitting on the wooden floor of her loft sipping Napoleon, Ela had an idea: if someone did steal it but grew tired of its demands, or found it but didn't know where to return it, she should make herself discreetly available to them. Otherwise she risked losing it out of sheer cowardice. She decided on the simplest bluntest course: reach them through the personals. If they found something that looked valuable, they would check to see if it was advertised missing. Since it couldn't have gone off far, she only had to place an ad in the *Village Voice* personals. Everyone read them. She could even post them up. She sipped and composed:

(1) A WOMAN WHO MISSES HER CUNT (no, change that) A WOMAN WHO NEEDS A CUNT (sounds like lesbian whine) A WOMAN WHOSE CUNT WAS LOST (was lost one day?) A WOMAN WHO FEELS HER CUNT WAS LOST (right on the emotion) A WOMAN WHO FEELS HER CUNT WAS LOST FOREVER (vague and clear, keep it) IS SEARCHING FOR IT (awkward) IS LOOKING FOR THE RIGHT PERSON (be more direct); LOOKING FOR THE ONE WHO'S GOT IT. FINDER WON'T REGRET. ANY REWARD NEGOTIABLE.

She dreaded the letters of response. She had to locate an agency that would read them for a fee. Ela hates receiving mail; it reminds her of how alone she really is not. She thought: Isn't a cunt out of context useless, and vice-versa: a woman out of cunt? We can do nothing much apart: I am bound to find it.

(2) VERY PARTICULAR (nicely bossy and tough) SENSITIVE (no, only men say that) AC/DC (for safety) ATTRACTIVE (necessary) DISCREET (is that negative?) FRIENDLY (reassuring for novices) SEXY (weak) FILTHY (tasteless metaphor) HORNY (more metaphor) YOUNG FEMALE INVITES (old worldish) SEEKS PERSONABLE (flatter the beast) UNATTACHED WHITE SUPER-TIGHT CUNT FOR SEXY FUN (and deaths) AND LONGER TERM RELATIONSHIP. MY PAD. I'll go to the end of the world, but what's the use of advertising?) FEES ACCEPTABLE.

Ela goes home to change for the night. She looks around at the smooth slick shiny sparse loft with the steaming mirror in the middle and feels like an empress; slowly, unknowingly, month after month Ela has been crossing the mirror's borders. She fears that she now belongs to another world. She doesn't know where. She can't touch herself any more. She can't feel being touched. She can't remember coming. She feels she is a secret. She is lighter. She doesn't need the mirror. She feels beyond.

She changes into a Mae-West-as-Delilah gown: gold, tight, majestic, endless, a beam of light. She writes a postcard to her parents: "It's not easy to picture black when you wear it. Maybe I've been sitting on the wrong grave. All day I form my first and only word: 'Come' in my mouth, so when the moment comes, I can too. I never ate so sweet a word. Love me." It has a picture of Gala nude swimming into an empty frame holding on to a mirror. This has calmed her.

She drops it off in a mailbox and hails a cab. The stuttering driver is a Nepalese wife importer who runs his marriage service on the side; by the time he gives her a brochure and enumerates his socially important possessions from the Park Avenue penthouse down to his Panasonic radar-detector and "Frère-Jacques" jingle-car-alarm in order to seduce her, they have arrived at the Philharmonic; he doesn't accept money, she gets out with a sigh. She moves like a statue of gold. The blue sky stirs gently and lovingly toward her. She throws back her head and laughs. Even in that vulnerable angle she looks beautiful.

At the entrance a snobbish herd is milling around, looking each other up and down like adversaries, flaunting clothes, bodies, escorts, pretenses, terrors, smiles, accents. The wind lifts Ela's dress making it easy to walk up the steps. The well-coiffed heads turn up: is it an ascension? Is she going up to heaven or coming down from it? They want her to love them. They want to be on her side. They want to succumb and rest inside her. Seeing them, Ela wonders: Isn't it comical that I should wear a dress, jewelry, that I should comb my hair and take food and need a cunt? Do I have no choice but to attract people? Should I point a gun at them? Will it make a difference? I am a trick performed for company. She gets seated. Wrapped in yards of crisp red satin, the dark diva comes.

On the first note, Ela floats into a heaven of contentment, of grateful inebriety. Her eyes close, her ears open to the marvel, her body is drenched by the ineffable. She gasps for air. She swims in a fluid net of light that pours in and out of her. She forgets about her cunt. She comes.

Jessye Norman looks directly at Ela's eyes; she waits for them to open and pierce her like the archangel's sword and burn a charred hole through her; she wonders if the girl shimmers from pleasure or divinity. Ela feels J.N.'s eyes leave indelible prints on her lids as if the archetypal woman were extinguishing her cigarettes on them, but doesn't flinch from the agony. Ela wonders: Does she know what unbearable maddening pleasure she gives? Does she understand I am consumed by her? Is she aware of her tremendous power to heal, to exorcise, to arouse?

Ela mutely calls: Engulf me, scorch me, singe me, smolder me, swallow me, engulf me in your dark ardent female mass, unroll for me the fuming passion of your vastness, the enormity of your flesh, I lie at the bottom of that torrid gushing throat, don't stop!

It is her scintillating cunt that comes to her. The joyous cunt thinks the magical voice comes from inside it. Ela doesn't notice the culprit jolting about in her resplendent lap, and the audience can't distinguish her brilliant cunt any more than they can see the shape of one crystal in the heavy chandelier of the ceiling. The hedonistic cunt instinctively seeks Ela at the time of its heightened pleasure and enters wave upon wave of orgasm, quakes, convulses, wriggles, and expands, jolted about as if hit by electric current.

At the end both women drip with sweat and pant. For an instant that won't end Ela opens her glinting eyes and they pour themselves into one another, lost in the perfect hyperbole that is the other. The overheated cunt lies unconscious on Ela's golden lap like a tumbler who has performed his fatal cartwheel. The wanted cunt, disappearing behind its own vapors, knocked out, is within arm's reach but Ela doesn't grab it. If Ela lowered her cleansed eyes now, if she were not suspended absolutely still and gasping, her thighs would feel it and with one simple swift move, she could repossess it. Wasn't that her purpose? Instead, they lie together like kittens basking in the sun. Ela offers the world her best smile. All three for a moment are in love.

When she comes to, the black Siren is bowing. Ela jumps and turns away to leave. Love exists only for fleeting seconds, Ela knows. She must not look with her everyday eyes at the Mistress, speak to her, scrutinize her, touch her skin, her wrinkles, her exhaustion. She cannot love J.N. if she doesn't sing. As she makes her way out in the midst of the applause, Ela notices her own slippery marvel slung from her belt and swinging to-and-fro like Me-Jane in the jungle. So why am I possessive of this cunt? she asks; I wasn't possessive of it when I had it. Let it live free. The gay cunt tickles her as it comes down, like a child on a slide. When Ela reaches the curb, tight and ablaze, she has second thoughts, but the cunt has disappeared.

I watched an expert on the news discuss the V-personality. He perceived that V could easily stand for Vanity; V has a flair for publicity and big audiences. It arouses her to be seen. Unfortunately that is also her greatest self-protection: when aroused, she secretes some kind of silver unidentified liquid that wraps her like a cocoon and makes her extremely slippery to touch, impossible to grasp, and difficult to see. She also emits a temporary fog at random occasions that so far don't seem to follow a pattern. She exhibits some sort of memory and critical faculty, for she carefully avoids those who have tried to imprison her or seem eager to and does not even go near anything like a machine or any other scientific instrument, which could scan her, with the exception of cameras. She is too intelligent to be a form of proto-life, and she must belong to a more evolved type of meta-life. No other creatures from her planet have yet appeared, with concrete proof, on our world. This makes her hard to study for we don't see her interact with her own kind. So far her only instincts are for exposure, performance, and freedom. She never sleeps, rests, or hibernates. We don't know yet what she subsists on.

I learned nothing new about the cunt, but admired how far human imagination could reach. A confirmation that, even under such dire circumstances, deeply enchanted me. Those inventions of the mind were the only benign effects of the V-epidemic.

Meanwhile, no one thought to connect the latest series of sexual attacks and grisly murders to the famous V. No one but I ever traced those hundreds of heinous crimes to her.

Ela feels gloomy and confused in the cab. She thinks: The street-light and the buildings are beating against one another, as I remember the bare feet of monks beat, when they crowded frantically by the parlor window at dawn to watch the bare-chested sailor boys, looking like tiny violins exploding in the air, like thin trees whitewashed up to the waist and from the waist up like bronze sardines galloping inside a fishermen's net, disembark with a comical smell of premature lemons; at that instant it was obvious to everyone there that a lot had ended and so the photographers and the murderers gathered their liquids and their tools and left.

There is another passenger, a shy hollow shaky Filipino boy feigning an Ivy League accent: "I asked the driver to stop. I am grateful for the chance to look at you up close. What are you made of?" Ela: "Dreams. Light is a spasm." The skinny cabdriver comes from Jordan, studies computers at Queens College, has a girlfriend from Java who cooks good Chinese food and decides that Ela is a movie star. He wants to kiss her. He asks for her autograph. He stops his cab at every traffic light, unrolls his window and calls out to the other drivers: "I've got a movie star in the car! Follow me down to see her come out. She is unreal, man! I am in seventh heaven! I have a dream!"

The Filipino: "One last question: Is there life out of the rainbow?" Ela: "In spring, I like the orgiastic creatures that elude and recede before me. In winter, I like the taste of beautiful boys for breakfast, the sweet sausages of their tongues, the berry-flavored jam of their lips, the hot pancakes of their hearts, and creamy milk from their cocks."

The Filipino gets off with her on Bleecker, pleads to escort her, pays her ticket, buys her cognac, finds a front table, sucks on his cigarettes like a boy, and explains proudly that he works on Madison, is on a diet, has just lost forty-five pounds, feels connected to her, and has never before been drawn to a woman or man. His dream is to act. His nightmare is having to face the Sphinx. She feigns the attitude of someone present. But, true to his promise, he asks no more questions. She thinks: A nightmare is nothing exotic. Relations with others are collisions of nightmares.

A sleek sleazy mafia-handsome wrinkle-free Jewish Moroccan film producer in an Armani suit, geometric haircut, and fat rings on his fingers, introduces himself smiling his white teeth, gives Ela his business card, a typed list of his investors, his current shooting dates and locations in New York City which include the New School and Unique, squints at Ela as if he is looking straight into the sun and says: "I want to fuck every woman alive!" Ela: "Start with my grandmother who at ninety-six is low on offers, for after the first few thousand women there won't be much of you left or she may die, so here is her number." Her breathless voice spreads out like molasses.

Ashamed of his bad pick-up, the Moroccan looks to the men on the other tables: "Feminist! I watched her eyes open like flying saucers when I said that line." In fact Ela's blinding eyes roam the basement like searchlights: is the cunt here yet?

The place buzzes with small, youthful, fashionable Orientals. Ela wonders if her cunt will stay, knowing it has no predilection for them. But the heat of the music will claim it. The Filipino or the Moroccan or someone else talks about himself and his sentences become a monotonous hum in the background, a private elegy with no hope for answer that reminds Ela of men speaking to her as she falls into post cum stupor. This time, she warns herself, I have to shut off the angel's mouth and hold on to my cunt, if it comes. In the dark her eyes look like holograms.

She thinks: Too many vanquished cocks have been rinsed away from between my legs like ripe rats that scurry through the city sewers, squealing that when they enter me, gleaming feathers float on the mirror; in the meantime, the ice inside me expands.

Tania Maria comes onstage in a long loose housewife blouse that covers her abundant thighs, short black stretch pants, and high stiletto heels, and stands by the piano. Her eyes resemble torches. T.M.'s tropical reckless beguiling voice vibrates through Ela from toes to hair, gives her gooseflesh, tears, spasms, orgasms, blackouts.

She gasps, moans, swings her ass on the chair, immersed in the voice, her body talks, her silver head falls back, she shakes her hips on each unpredictable beat. She feels a full oblivion as if she occupied a gap, a non-space. The oriental crowds sit still, expressionless and drunk. They watch the yowling scatting Brazilian maenad as if she were a TV screen. From time to time they ogle Ela. She stares into T.M.'s dark, cruel, volcanic, monkey-like, greedy, gypsy's face, her powerful protruding teeth, her bony legs going up and down like a locust's, her hourglass body that Ela would give anything to see naked now, and to dive into, while T.M. woos, coos, and calls in new vowels and her own rushing spontaneous meaningless words.

Ela thinks: With what ardor she sees me, how long her breaths are, bound under water she could still sing to change the minds of the gods, how her eye relishes me, she will devour me, in a single preverbal gulp, this is true language, I feel it in my groin, I want that uncontrollable voracious voice inside me mingling with my tears and digestive fluids and cum.

Her cunt comes on the round tin table, vaulting, hankering, yearning, pining, twisting, overwhelmed, thrown in exalted rapture. It froths and oozes like a disturbed earthworm and gooey circles of saliva-like liquid stain the table. No one notices; it twirls around the cognac glasses and over the mouths of the beer bottles.

The two women hunger for each other. Ela looks at T.M.'s teeth, and asks: Take me, take me, take me. She sees an immense inflated breast, a single backside cheek of sea in front of her eyes tickling and lulling her, prodding her on.

When everything is over, her cunt lies sprawled out on the sand-covered dance floor behind her, clear in the fake moonlight, gaping upturned and phosphorescent. Ela looks away to avoid the suddenly aged T.M.'s glare, and she sees it. But again she has forgotten why she is persecuting it, what she could ever want from this poor exhausted epicure. As from one old Quixote to another, she winks at it.

Outside, the world is full of extras. The overzealous Moroccan offers to drive her home. Ela is still in a daze. He leads her to a tall sexy swanky Silver Cloud Rolls, immaculately clean and glowing. She slides in: it's the perfect fit. He offers her champagne from the bar. She prefers to fill the car with champagne and bathe in it and drive through town submerged. He shuts the door quietly as if he fears waking someone up. She is radiant gold serenely displayed within a sturdy metal work of art. He wants to be seen at this moment by everyone he has ever known. She doesn't look human. He has fanatical almond-shaped eyes, suddenly pink shapely lips, a thin nose, a trim body, big but elegant hands and he is not stingy with his smile. She rests back feeling loved and protected by this machine. He runs his dark hand through his glossy-back-combed-hair every few seconds and steals febrile glances at her making sure she is still there. She caresses the sublime leather textures of that metal swan. He shows her the jar of Grey Poupon he keeps inside the spotless oak cabinet. She wants to live in this strong smooth curvaceous dome from now on as in an invisible moving cocoon or heat-and cold-resistant silver foil. His dark skin shines like expensive polished leather. She wants to take it in her bed, her bathtub, her mirror, to carry it comfortably and weightlessly coiled around her body at all times like a snail's shell. He fidgets a lot. She wants to masturbate. He wants to have her at any price. She wants to make it come. He snorts some coke. At her doorstep, he holds the door open, rigid like a uniformed chauffeur in his long open coat. She glances back into the mouth of that cave, hears the call of its wild roaring body and thinks: Does this prove I myself am an object? He asks to come up. She tells him: "Some people like to have sex while looking in front of the mirror. I find that to be excessive. I think one mirror is enough."

From the upstairs window, the car looks insignificant. She is more happily hungry and hungrily happy than she has been in months. She doesn't recognize the effulgent wet marble eyes that meet hers in the mirror. She conserves her heightened senses for one purpose: to understand. She pulls together her resources, holds her temples, shuts her eyes and begins to think:

Once, a lone blind snail slowly crawled out of V onscreen, I believe at a game show. It turned its nervous antennae this way and that, carrying its heavy spherical home on its back, and looked intent on going God knew where, but far and fast; It was completely unaware that it had just crossed the circle of the most wanted cunt, it had efficiently and moistly penetrated the world's tightest and first emancipated cunt; it felt no pleasure. I realized then, to my mirth, that the record was broken, that her power was waning, that this was the first living being to go into Ela's cunt and come out unharmed and unaffected. And in the solitude of the closet I cheered the little champion.

How badly does Ela want her cunt back? Why is she unable to want anything enough to go out and get it, as the locals say? Why did she not take it by force when she had the chance? Is this quest a matter of blind pride or is it a joke?

Ela feels that without a cunt she will close off and retreat into the dreams that take place in her head and that she will be happy. And why not? Does she hear a calling? No. Does she owe it to the world to be part of it? No. It turns out that her cunt was her main link, her bond, to the world outside her, her cunt was her opening into the world.

Now she is finally free as she always dreamed to be, free as a child. Why search for it then? She no longer needs people! Now, immediately, she can go to the empty family house on the deserted beach and live alone off the land, among the flowers, the cacti, the fruit trees; she can swim, fish, and sit alone for ever after thinking up stories to please herself.

She shivers and thinks: I can't look anymore. I will go off by the sea and live on fish until I die. Without a cunt. So what. There are people who are born that way. I used it a lot for a while, had the experience. Do I go to a doctor and let him cut off bits of my thighs or ass to put together an ugly wrinkled funny-colored new cunt? If someone could tell me what to do!

She decides to call overseas. Ela: "Hi, I feel I am not a woman." Mommie, an ethereal serene sculpture of white marble on the receiver, with the softest sweetest voice, replies: "Baby...why?" Mommie lingers on each syllable as if she has to think to remember the next sound in every word. Ela: "Mmm, something is missing." Mommie: "Of course, honey, there is always something missing, that's how things are: parts of them are missing!" Ela: "It's not that; it is like I am missing." Mommie: "Don't do a thing! Don't think! Rest, relax, take a bath, get a facial, go on a cruise, get a massage, wax yourself, and don't have sex!" Ela: "I have done all that." Mommie: "Sex is exhausting, darling, it's a lot of hard work, you not only take, you give! Why take? Or give? Take a nap in front of the mirror." Ela: "I feel like I don't have a womb." Mommie: "That's not bad. Go and get X-rays! Lay your breasts on the metal." Ela: "But it's true!" Mommie: "Darling, truth is a lower-class notion." Ela: "If you were here, you'd see for yourself." Mommie: "I'll take a little trip, and come, we can go shop for silk." Ela: "No. I like missing you."

Ela thinks: This panic keeps me young. She feels nausea again. She runs to the bathroom. She is sick of being sick. She thinks: I will wear a sign: PROUD TO BE ILL.

I think: We die for words over and over, why not die for a cunt?

Ela in a silver concoction of space-age punk boots, a taffeta dress in the shape of a spiral orchid, tight long gloves and hat in the form of a cobra, worn in memory of her departed cunt, decides to go to the party in Soho. She can't be alone with her decisions. Despite the rustling of her clothes, she runs the ten blocks there in order to kill her energy and fear.

An immense black doorman lets her in with an obedient canine smile, without asking for her invitation and ID. Ela feels taken for granted: Is seeing believing? She looks up with reproach. The beast thinks she is making eyes at him. His manicured nails, faultless skin, soft voice, and dreamy expression surprise her and remind her of the other oversized monsters she met today. He looks down for a moment at his new livery, as if trying to choose between that and the pursuit of Ela. He is bald. He has the neck of a bull and the eyes of a werewolf. She slides inside.

The suite is thronged with people dressed in black and silver. Ela looks around: only one small vision in pink—pink leather skirt, pink leather jacket and beret, pink fishnet shirt and stockings, pink suede pumps, pink messy hair—stands out in the back among fans. She thinks: Crowds used to be so enjoyable; I miss the crowds that used to gather on the docks: what foreign mouths were those, what blinding reflections off the army coat buttons; children chased peacocks, tin wastebaskets rolled, drums called, splendidly detached lithe dumb green wombs were on sale, limping lepers begged "please deprive me of my wounds," cries of fucking cats, as if hundreds of babies were butchered or raped, merged with the racing sirens that couldn't catch up with all the fires, until the first sunlight stabbed the tourists in the eyes.

A man in thick-rimmed glasses and a silver tie who looks like Allen Ginsberg spits in Ela's mouth: "Cut that sexy stuff out! If you keep it up, I'll have to go out and solicit." Simultaneously, a ghostly white-wigged inarticulate male in a Freddy Kruger outfit who could be Andy Warhol's double or specter exhales in a gossipy voice: "What do you think of the men? I need an honest informed opinion." Within the minute a third thin ugly bespectacled young man, dressed in a paper silver suit stuffed at the crotch with noisy newspaper dramatically bulging, who must be Keith Haring's ghost addresses her: "We aren't well because we don't fuck." Ela: "Mommie warned me to eat men like fish. Until you develop the immunity of the locals, she said, you can get hepatitis from seafood."

A short myopic editor with black curly hair, thick lips, and sneaky eyes pushes his round face into hers and ascertains: "The new fashion is to be asexual. Lots of beautiful, horny, asexual people. Convents are multiplying like rabbits. The word in the street is: 'Be priests!'" Warhol's spook continuously whispers in her ear: "Mmm, I. Who do you recommend here? Whom would you try?" She points absentmindedly at the first waiter who passes by holding a silver tray. "Surreal," Ginsberg gasps in response, "so you too are eyeing the grocery boys! Of course!"

Why did I come? Ela asks herself. Going to parties is a form of suicide. A fat-bellied balding Arab whom she identifies as Adnan Khashoggi on parole, with childish eyes and undefinable consonants, slurps a double martini, fingers a long cross-eyed Czechoslovakian model and tells Ela confidentially "American anti-intellectualism is a CIA plot. The CIA invented AIDS, the floods in Bangladesh, the market crash, and modeling." Andy's phantom rasps in her ear: "Huh, look. How many men here have you tried personally?" Ginsberg announces: "It's my time to strip, jump into the vodka punch, and howl. Are you coming?" Ela: "I see neon, art deco, a balcony like Babylon's gardens, a pool, torches. Miami. I am in a travelogue!"

A chorus of partyers chimes: "Everyone we know has AIDS. It's 'in'!" The leader of the chorus: "Who doesn't have AIDS in this room? Raise your hand!" Ela: "I must make a confession. My cunt is a razor. When I masturbate, you understand, it's messy."

A six feet green-haired woman in chartreuse jersey slacks inter-rupts: "Do you think the world should be inhabited?" Ela: "By no more than, say, two or three of us." Chorus: "An orgy!"

Ela thinks: I came to lose myself. A recently disinherited British count heroin addict with day-glo skin, Savile Row suit and a black umbrella: "The roar of the water outside is deafening. We'll have to run into the sea to find refuge. The tropics will make it. The North won't survive. The intellectuals will die; only fishermen and villagers will swim on." Warhol still bothers her ear: "Well, I. No quickie for me." Ela: "A necrophiliac had a thing for me and I went for it, he killed me to have sex with me, I came the instant I died which might have been too soon because immediately this necrophiliac committed suicide and masturbated to the end of time." The day-glo count: "If our bodies cannot adapt to the sea, grow fins, scales, and so on, there will be no humans left."

Private security men and bodybuilders stand outside the bath-room and allow one person in at a time. Various brawls and stripteases start. Waiters in drag are flying onto the carpet, asses up. Ela's eyes search the crowd for someone not reduced to chaos by the mere effort of living.

She is again intrigued by the fanciful pink girl smothered under a heap of flushed men on the couch. She thinks: I see in her eyes the gleam of a knife. She cuts decisively through the packed rooms, approaches her, sees the girl's smile and stops dead. Then, with the instinct of a hound, she pulls out her party invitation and studies the silver smile printed under the announcement. Yes, it is the same one. That is where she saw it before. It is a familiar smirk. When Ela had seen the notice: OUR MARCH 21ST COMING OUT PARTY: COME FIND OUT WHOSE, she thought the silver logo was Jimmy Dean's mischievous grin. But now that the same smile appears in front of her, in a shroud of steam, she recognizes it with terror. Is it possible? Andy's phantom: "Look, I don't know… But wow!"

It is the typical grimace of her cunt, which she had seen often in the mirror, then later on the pavement and through the jar. If nothing else, she still knows her cunt when she sees it. No? Could it be a coincidence? A close resemblance? The oversized asymmetrical labia are there, in the smile, they are not mouth-lips, the tiny hard clitoris hiding much lower than normal is in the place of the tip of a tongue. Are there many more cunts like hers wandering and smiling around free? But does this mean she can no longer even recognize it when she meets it? Ela decides to embarrass herself if she must.

Ela bends in front of the pink creature until her silver face nearly touches its lips, her silver ass high up in the air, her silver brows perspiring, and whispers: "Excuse me." Her voice is an intimate breathless tickle that gets under the skin and permeates the blood. Inquisitive hands land on her ass. She calls: "Come." This, she thinks, it will recognize. Andy: "How unglamorous though."

The pink cunt puckers its lips until they wrinkle. Ela: "I don't know how to put it, but, you must surely agree, we know each other from far back. How do you get along without me? For my part, I've tried abstinence, but the thought of it, knowing that I can't fuck, eats at me. If abstinence was a choice that you hadn't forced me into, it might be different." Ela takes off one glove to touch her cunt. The cunt retracts like a snail's horns. It shrinks. Now Ela is certain: the intoxicating scent—which was Ela's—of hot wet sugar with lemon and old orchids rises under her nose. Andy persists: "How interesting. Yes, really." The day-glo count has also steered through the crowd to find her and suggest: "I propose that we march together into the nearest mass of water."

Ela: "What better position could you have asked for, you had your independence, I never believed you escaped of your own volition. Is it possible that you wanted more attention." She wonders: Why doesn't it run away? Is it willing to come back?

The cunt keeps its lips pursed and still. White steam evaporates from its pores, enveloping it and Ela's face in a romantic silver Felliniesque cloud. The day-glo count: "I do not ask for much. I would like to help Charon push the boat, then sit back on the bank smoking, watching each boat disappear on the black waters of Lethe." Ela: "Did someone kidnap you or not? You look pale. Is anyone taking care of you?" The cunt looks down like a child being reprimanded. The day-glo count: "No one, you are right. I've waited for someone to say this all my life. Let us go to death in the sea. Do you know boats of madmen were sent off into the ocean with provisions to stay away from shore and die at sea? It was a sane practice for centuries." Ela: "What have they done to you? I see traces of abuse." Andy's buzz tortures her like a mosquito: "Mmm, OK. Fab. Whom can you try next?" The day-glo count: "What about myself?"

Ela reaches out her hand, but her cunt slides down into its clothes; Ela's hand follows it through the fishnet shirt, down the leather skirt, and into the stockings. Somewhere there she loses it. She rips the tiny translucent threads in the gap of the garments, which held it up, and comes out the bottom empty-handed. She searches on the floor under the couch. There is a crowd of moving feet on the rug. She wants to shout: "Open up, my cunt just escaped again!" "Sorry, I lost my cunt!" "Move out of the way, a cunt is running off!" "Someone catch my cunt!" She can't. High heels step on her hand.

Throughout all this, men are kissing Ela's nape, rubbing her thighs, licking her ears, sucking her neck, biting her hair, twisting her nipple, pinching her ass, each concentrating on one area as if they are following an earlier plan. For an instant she remembers being swarmed in the Bahamas by short brown natives who rode astride long wooden poles, yelled: "Come, Missie, Missie!" and hung from every inch of her flesh. A few men still caress the now emptier than before pile of pink holes and leather. She sweats. She can't stand back up under the pressure of the crowd. Andy asks: "Is she your special friend?"

Now Ela is being raided by comments falling on her from every direction around the coffee table: "Are you a princess?"

"Oil money?" "Finally someone who knows her!" "How is it to work for sheiks?" "A ravishing shot!" "You must speak about V!" "Do you need an agent?" "Are you a Soviet double agent?" "Are you V's ex-lover?" "Is V your relative?" "Silver reminds me of the war, the shiny bombers on V-day." "I envy your silver complexion." "Collagen shots?" "V didn't even blow a ring!" "Have you drunk cat's blood?" More people are coming, shouting joyfully. The party is a success. A man in sweats forces a home movie camera through and shoots Ela, shouting into a padded suspended microphone a title: "Dykes." In the throes of this terrible confusion, Ela whispers to the world one concise last command: "Shut up!" She sways, feels the weight of a senile deformed olive tree crash on her, and faints, sucked into its cellulosic bark. The familiar post-faint commotion follows, high-pitched, shrill, sounding like a commune of crickets. Ela's legs are raised at once up in the air, and expensive perfume immediately pervades the room and drenches her.

When Ela comes to, she is being hoisted up and carried off by the black bulky doorman in his gold-braid blue uniform to the cheers of all, as in a remake of *King Kong*. Ela kicks her arms and legs and squirms like a glow-worm for effect. The procession moves on to the street. Shouldn't she find out in time if this gorilla has working eyesight? Does he plan to throw her into the oncoming traffic? He carries Ela like a feather, apparently disappointed that she is not heavy enough to force his muscles to bulge out and his anger to rise. She meets his hard lethargic eyes. This time I will speak, she thinks, I've little curiosity left for these games. I already know, for instance, that he will climb onto some marble arch or monument next. Too predictable.

"I have no glands," Ela bellows at the crowd, "no guts, no follicles, no cum. The moisture on my flesh is dew. I am a planet in orbit, I perform my rounds unconsciously." The doorman stands heroically on top of the expressionistic statue on 59th at the Central Park entrance as if he is perched on the belfry of Notre Dame. The cluster portrays three scantily clad muscular youths contorted in terrible pleasure or pain, dying of sex or murder; they are the symbols of Eternity, Nationalism, Capitalism, or three similar ideals.

The crowd expands; tipsy suited businessmen, colorful joggers, streetsweepers, late-working secretaries, callgirls and gigolos, rich old maids, gay playboys, horsecarriage drivers and cops join the partyers. I hate Victor Hugo, Ela thinks and calls to her audience: "Close your eyes." The limpidity and luster of her voice has a bracing effect like sparkling oils that purify the blood. Her eyes look as if a spatter of sun and sea came between her eyelids. The crowd, now with closed eyes, hears her whisper: "Yeah! Let go. I love the way your body moves." They realize she is a guru, a priestess, who can relax and advise them into perfect meditation until they wake up as new people. She probably travels around the world with her black guard and assistant performing cleansing spiritual rituals for free. The devotees now move rhythmically in trance, like people at a reggae concert. "Up and down. That's the way. Open. Breathless. Great." The believers hear her breathe near them, in them, as if through individual earphones. They visualize sea waves and sighing mermaids. "I touch you. Here. Feel me. Relinquish. Easy. Give it to me. Lie down."

The crowded auditors are now on their backs on the pavement at the entrance of the park, their eyes always closed, their lips parted, their limbs loose, their hearts at ease. They abandon themselves to a better being. I will never understand this, this power of language, Ela thinks. They lie stretched out in front of her and below her, moving slowly, erotically, up and down on their buttocks. They glow. She remembers standing on the school verandah watching her classmates stretch and exercise on the hot schoolyard at dead noon, as she hovers in midair watching this massive democratic midnight masturbation in her honor.

Once it was my dream, she thinks, to die coming on the busiest widest avenue stormed by people of all ages and creeds touching me wildly, irreverently; I would be immense; that touch would awaken them, jolt them into a revolution; as I would come, the dream goes, the people would rebel, change the world. My deadly orgasm would end all fear, faith, sacrifice. But nothing heroic for me today, I will pass. My attachment to some silly cunt disgusts me.

For the benefit of that noble savage who holds her in one palm like a dead bird and absentmindedly rubs his rigid erection with the other, his livery torn, his eyes lurking, his strength shaking her, Ela shrieks her muezzin orgasm call. This shatters all resistance. The crowd sees the face of the god. The doorman comes into his own hand, then falls back relaxed as a puppet so that his loose form hangs from the statues by sleeves, knees, and elbows, and now joins the erotic complex as an integral part. Ela slides out of the iron arms of the monster and decides to give the New York

City Transit System one more try. She runs swiftly into the open stinking mouth of the subway.

Two months earlier:

I had not had a lead for days although I was committed to the pursuit of Ela's cunt. As I was waiting for the train on my way back from the pier one day, I glanced down in front of me and saw the cunt right next to my feet on the old yellow line. It was flapping about on the dirty subway floor, neglected, dusty, unnoticed, playing with the remnants of a Butterfinger candybar, screwing itself around it and jumping about like a kitten, stained with black subway coal and melted chocolate. My heart broke at the sight. In my excitement, I took a step toward it, shouting: "Now let me help you!" I plunged toward it certain that this time it could not escape. The poor devil was trapped between my advancing feet, positioned so they could raid it from every side, and the edge of the platform.

In that instant, slowly as if sorrowfully, the cunt rolled off the platform. I moved forward, eager to grasp it, but staggered. The headstrong cunt was hanging precariously from the parapet, planning to fall onto the tracks. I hollered: "No!" It was clearly threatening to jump in front of the Eighth Avenue Express and be brutally cut up by the New York City Transit! Would it survive such an onslaught? I stopped dead. I had plenty of indication that it was unaware of its own worth. It might easily kill itself in self-defense on my account. That I could never bear. I was afraid if I took the next step, it would let go of its hold and throw itself onto the tracks to be squashed into Jell-O by the coming train whose lights I saw in the mouth of the tunnel. I could not cause its destruction. I retreated without taking my eyes from it, hoping it would climb into the subway car, where I could then catch it. But when the train stopped and its doors opened, the wanton cunt disappeared under the avalanche of feet rushing in and out of the doors.

I had lost sight of it again! I needed a quick decision. I judged it to be unable, because of its size and strength, to hop over the gap into the car. I gambled on its exhaustion, which I assumed led it to contemplate its self-extinction, and I lost. When the doors shut, the recalcitrant cunt was nowhere in sight. There was no deformed silver mass lying anywhere among the tracks, no wet silver trail on the grime. Did someone kick it accidentally into the car? Did it jump into the train on its own strength? Did it climb onto the shoe or into the pocket of a passenger who struck its fancy? Now that I had the time to think more carefully all these other possibilities occurred to me.

I began to question my luck.

In an empty rattling subway car Ela thinks: Did my cunt throw the party? Was my cunt the guest of honor? Did she "come out"? It explains its picture printed on the invitations. Is it friends with that crowd? Who took the photo? Can the cunt see now? Where does it live? How does it survive? Who would believe this? Should I believe it?

So other people get close to her and take portraits of her, but I am kept at a distance. I, who carried her for twenty-two years and kept her happy no matter what the cost and how much it disgusted me later, because I felt I had to feed her; like keeping a pet boa, having to throw live mice into its mouth every week, hearing their desperate squeals and her grunts of bliss as she swallowed them whole and spat out seconds later leftovers and bones and sat back quiet and full for some hours digesting them, their juices still dripping out of her; I, who adjusted to her savagery, as I wouldn't do for anyone else, but I felt I was part of her, I couldn't very well get rid of her where she nestled. If I knew then that I had a choice, I could refuse, but after I gave up my preferences and impulses for hers, after I spent my youth tending to her, cooking special meals for my needy beast that refused to grow up, after I grew used to her, and in some ways even identified myself with her, how am I expected to feel now that she denies me? We were after all united in flesh, not in metaphor, and I became who I am because of my union with her, we were one; I didn't abandon her in a gutter, she had no reason to leave, all I wanted was to have a better look at her. So how can I not feel betrayed and deserted now? It enrages me to see that little porcupine take off to conquer the world leaving me, the one on top, the one in charge, leaving me gaping. I am unable to comprehend it, I am not trained to take that in, accept it and live with it.

Ela is suddenly surrounded by a group of hard-muscled under-sexed Cuban youths in leather jackets who ululate at each other in monosyllables. They look her up and down, lost as she is in her silver shell, and want to break through to her: "We can't decide if you're more pretty or rich. We've got one stop to rape or rob you. But you must pay attention. When we brandish a weapon, show your fear. Do you want us to cut you, huh? Would you like your face slashed to look like a scaffold?" Ela looks at them without seeing them, but reflecting their street-bred shiny valor. Her breathless voice echoes through their bodies striking them as the most sincere sound they have heard, an inner voice of knowledge: "I am always exposed before an anonymous Other. There are two kinds of people: those who watch and those who feel they are being watched, whose mouths look careful even in rest, whose hands stay always pleasantly placed, who exude peace and walk as if they parade in a beauty pageant. I must carry myself as a huge aesthetic burden of unfathomable implications, auras, readings, and I can never see others out of unadulterated curiosity, or gain profits from those who see me. I do not take. I cannot."

The Cubans sense that they must study this speech and use it in their work, that it will lead them to success and wisdom. They now speak in Spanish, kiss her hand in turns, and leave the car walking backwards. Latinos know a fairy when they see one.

The week before:

One morning, while Ela listened to the Requiem in her black silk robe, it crossed her mind to teach her cunt and this dopey country a lesson. She could call the sucker publicly by its name and publish the old photos that show it as a white severed fly sensuously sprawled out on unsuspecting persons. They are the proof that Ela knew it long before it became famous.

As its owner, Ela would receive a chunky percentage of the profits from all the V-offshoot products; she would strike it filthy rich; not that she has any use for money, but she feels robbed of her cunt although now it seems as if it left of its own accord. If she has to live staring into it everywhere around her, the least it must do for the years that she nourished and protected it is to acknowledge its past connection with her.

Ela would be an instant celebrity. She would outshine her cunt easily. Her cunt's power and talent is in fucking; and unless it can exploit that in public, and with the public, it will be a passing curiosity. Ela, meanwhile, would go on the talk shows to tell her story; the tabloids would make her a favorite front-page topic. She could become V's unauthorized translator and biographer, called in to explain its behavior. She would be mentioned in the *Guinness Book of Records*. She would speak at length about the pain of women who lose their cunts. Oprah would break into tears and remember a time in her childhood when she herself, albeit for a short fortnight, had been abandoned by her malicious vagina. Housewives would call up on live shows to confess the loss of their vaginas. For the first time, thousands of women would come out with the shocking truth. Countless cuntless women would be pouring out their hearts! People would realize that their genitals are by this point in history quite separate from them and science should make them optional, portable, transferable, disposable, so that they could wear them just for sex like lacy lingerie or edible gel.

Ela would be admired for her honesty. She would socialize with the Hollywood brats, date Lowe or Beatty, talk to B. Walters for an hour about her insecurities, pose in *Playboy* semi-nude, publish her dreams and diaries, visit the White House and third-world countries, marry a few times, attend charity galas and buy houses on both coasts. She would be a pillar of the world. She would never make up with her treacherous cunt. How horrific!

DEADLY CUNT DOWN

Daily reports of more wild-running cunts coming into New York and the suburbs are alarming city officials. Experts claim that the cunts ran off on their own, when they were not properly fed, or they had been repressed, and initially gathered around the Catskills area. There they began to hunt in packs and multiplied to dangerous numbers. After spreading terror upstate, becoming bolder and hungrier, they are now sweeping down into the city.

It is impossible to calculate how much havoc they have already caused, for many of the assaults go unreported, but the situation can only become worse. The killer cunts hide during the day and attack men by moonlight in remote suburbs and seedy areas of the city. They "rage and rave and rant and raise the devil" residents report.

No killer cunts have been apprehended as yet. Police hounds, specially trained squads, guerrilla forces, and the National Guard have pooled their resources and are hunting for them around the dock, but so far the police's only success has been to save the lives of three partly devoured and abandoned victims, after being called by neighbors who heard the cries.

The police are distributing artist's renditions of the "beasts" based on the survivors' descriptions. They are the only pictures of them available, but the cunts certainly do not look half as menacing as they are alleged to be.

City residents have been requested to report any signs of public fornication or of a sexual attack, but New Yorkers have a reputation for ignoring criminal acts in which others are the victims. All city ambulance services are on twenty-four-hour stand by.

There is no precedent for such unbridled sexual violence. City officials have decided to declare a state of emergency in New York City If the city closes down, including such nerve centers as Wall Street, the country and the rest of the world will feel the blow. Suggestions of moving business and U.N. headquarters to Boston or Washington have been made, but the manpower required and the costs involved for such an undertaking render it impractical.

Psychiatrists and sex specialists have eagerly offered their services to help understand the "killer's motive" and interpret the killer cunts' instincts. No pattern of the killers' preferences or movements has emerged however, other than gender. They attack anywhere, any male. Killer cunts are definitely mankind's new and possibly greatest scourge.

Lunch hour protest marches are being held every day in New York and candlelight vigils take place every night. Gun sales are skyrocketing. Churches and cemeteries are overcrowded, and priests work overtime to meet demands. Group memorial services are now available. The victim toll has reached the one hundred mark.

Men fear to travel alone at night and go out only in groups, accompanied by police escorts and bodyguards. These precautions, however, have not reduced the number of men found dead in ditches and sideroads every morning. Experts fear that, in a population as large and diversified as New York's, the cunt crisis may prove impossible to contain for some time.

In her dark loft, in the light of a match as she lights a cigarette, Ela sees her face in the mirror and it is new: it is suddenly light, devoid of greed. Her lips that used to crave cum look harmless as a fresh open strawberry, no longer pale, but bright red. The sweet putrid smell of sex and love that always rose out of her cunt and her loft has been replaced by cool clear air. Her ears, usually so tense and sensitive to sounds, look relaxed, like seashells. Her body that had become a coffin for spent men feels young and new again.

"And I wonder, why, why, why, she ran away, and I wonder, if she would stay, my little runaway, my run, run, run, run, runaway…"

OUT OF CUNTROL

In the past week the killer cunts have begun to come into crowded city areas. They allegedly tear into the flesh of the unsuspecting, they toss themselves at helpless men. They give no warning: no yelps, groans, or grunts are heard, and the sound of flesh being sucked and ripped is the first sign the pedestrians have that they are being attacked. The pain comes next.

Cuntsucking marks have been identified on the corpses of three thousand four hundred victims so far. We quote the testimony of a rare survivor: "They rammed me against the trees in the [Central] Park, I just gasped, but I kicked and flung [the cunts] off my genitals, I knew that if I went down I faced a prolonged tormenting ending, I yelled my lungs off, as I felt my life being taken from me drop by drop, chunk by chunk, trapped in the mouth of a crazed life beyond all appeal or humanity. It was worse than dying of rape."

These events have caused worldwide shock. Sympathetic heads of state have expressed their deep concern to the mayor of New York. International men's groups are dispatching squads of men to replenish the declining male population of the city. But even such volunteers are decreasing as the deadly sexual assaults receive more international coverage.

The new plague has replaced AIDS as the major public concern, since cunt assault is today the number one killer of men in New York. AIDS seems harmless in comparison and has already faded from public memory; for, as some diehard gay-rights activists have pointed out, "cunts are much more democratic in their distribution of death."

Does she miss me? Ela wonders lying awake in her round bed. I made her life easier, I made it simple for her to get whom and what she craved. I had the language! I kept up the appearances, played by known rules and secured her prey.

Isn't she having trouble, with her overt ways, finding mates and taking what she wants out of them? Does she like to do everything for herself? Does she like to be misinterpreted, given the wrong thing, taken for the wrong thing?

As things turned out it would be easier for me if I had given it a name. I could call now to it silently with longing, without feeling ridiculous. How can I express it: "Cunt, cunt!" "My cunt!" "My cunt, my cunt, why did you forsake me?"

Many men whom Ela knows had names for their cocks; they would say: "Romeo is up on the balcony," "Ronnie wants to make a statement," "Tiger is roaring out there," "Marco Polo is on a new expedition," "Let the Pope give you blessing." Ela did not think they were funny. She saw them as unnecessary metaphors and looked down on these attempts to humanize or exorcise instincts. Now she sees that it can be useful and comforting on occasion.

Ela's Mommie's vagina is Penelope. Ela grew up hearing Mommie complain: "Penelope is infected," or "He goes straight for Penelope, you know the type," or "In this bikini half of Penelope is showing," and she referred to Dad's cock as Ulysses. She did have a quiet, unobtrusive, faithful Penelope between her thighs, content, chubby, a nice fluff.

But Ela's cunt was too nervous, stubborn, and argumentative to grow fat like a eunuch. She knew early on that there could be no name for it, no "nice, civilized way of referring to it," as Mommie advised her to do. It was a nameless primitive elemental urge more attractive and destructive than any mythical females. So Ela thought when she was in its grip, at its beck and call. Now it seems cute, and sexy in a harmless "Hustler" way, on the face of Ela's new 3-D day-glo watch.

"The soldier came knocking upon the queen's door, said I am not fighting for you anymore I've watched your palace up here on the hill and I

wondered who's the woman for whom I kill, how hungry are you, how weak you must feel as you live here alone and you are never revealed, I see you now and you are so very young but I've seen more battles lost than I have battles won and I've got this intuition that it's all for your fun, now will you tell me why? She said I've swallowed a secret burning thread, it cuts me inside and often I've bled and she shut herself up like a fan..."

Ela is torn between two forces of equal opposite gravity, so she can only stay still. She can give in neither to her desire to live in total isolation, nor to the urge to jump into the thick o f things and seduce the world. She used to give in to her cunt instead, which at least followed one single-minded direction and kept her busy, so she did not have to choose either extreme. That is why now she can neither abandon her footloose cunt to its fate and live happily alone, nor come out into the glare of the world to demand what is hers.

NO DISCUNTENTED WOMEN

Who are the women whose cunts are wreaking havoc? This is the question everyone has been asking of late. Why haven't they come out in public? Where are the bodies that initially hosted all the dissatisfied cunts? If the reasons for the killer cunts' appearance were established, many believe that their lust could be controlled. Yet, despite the authorities' guarantees of full anonymity and of all the psychiatric help that might be required, women have been indifferent to pleas for their cooperation.

Right before dawn, the phone rings in the closet: one of Ela's anonymous commonplace lovers whines into her machine: "I have what you want!" She grasps the receiver eagerly and holds her stomach in her other hand carefully, like a sharp blade. Ela: "Where?" Commonplace lover: "Are you sick?" Ela: "Are you well?" Commonplace lover: "Why are you cold? You sound stuffed up." Ela: "Is she there with you?" Commonplace lover: "For me there can be no other 'she.'" Ela: "What do you want for her? To hand her over to me? Name your price." Commonplace lover: "You've always been dad's little girl and mommie's little girl. It's time to change." Ela: "Are these your demands?"

Commonplace lover: "Don't you want to be self-sufficient one day?" Ela: "You know what I want." Commonplace lover: "Do you want to be my little girl?" Ela: "Are you blackmailing me?" Commonplace lover: "You said I was no use because I didn't grab my cock and fuck some strange woman for you, you said people seduce people to tell them what to do, so I should seduce her so you could rent her place upstate; you said you needed a cock for yourself, to convenience-fuck; I told you I wasn't a cock; you said if you had a cock you'd like to fuck men's asses. That was the last time we made love." Ela: "Are you reading her a poem? Is this a bedtime story? Is she all right?" Commonplace lover: "When I couldn't have you, my cock drove me nuts. It hurt like hell." Ela: "When did all that happen? To whom? What is the point? Who are you? Is she gagged? Is she hurt?" Commonplace lover: "I thought everything out. You can have it, without the rest of me! Get your wish, Ela!" Ela: "Where is it? How did you recognize it? Is it in one piece?" Commonplace lover: "Well, now I've got it for you. I have it wrapped in a dinner napkin right here in my lap! But it's bleeding badly. I cut it off with my Swiss Army knife." Ela: "You cut it! Is it wounded? Again?" Commonplace lover: "Didn't feel a thing. It's my homage to you." Ela: "Stay where you are. Don't move, don't call anyone, don't touch any knives. I'll be there in three minutes. What's the address?" Commonplace lover: "When you come, you'll have a real living cock to take home with you!" At that, Ela hangs up.

She thinks: men are sick. All they do is tell me stories from the past. So much beating around the bush. Why do men have to run to show me every time they get violent? I need a bath.

A CUNTAMINATED CUNTRY

A man in Long Island allegedly saw his male-dominated household raided by the killer cunts and two of his sons were murdered.

The entire nation is alarmed, since up to now the killer cunts have refrained from attacking groups. That had afforded men a certain degree of security. Suddenly they feel endangered in their homes and in the company of other men. This has caused panic among workers in such male-dominated industries as auto plants and the docks. Many of them have failed to report to work this week. Men refuse to go anywhere unaccompanied by women, as women have been respected and unharmed by the "beasts" up to date. Dozens of lonely men, mostly bachelors, have committed suicide in fear of a more horrendous end awaiting them in the killer cunts' labia.

According to what the Long Island victim, fifty-two, a divorcé, told the reporters from his hospital bed, he was having breakfast on Monday, 9 A.M., "when out of nowhere an army of little pink creatures broke in through the doors and windows! They swooped down at my crotch, but despite the pain I was so angry I managed to grab one my hanging onto my flesh. I am an NRA member after all! I shot at them, but they are impossible to aim at because they are very small and always moving. In fact, one of the bullets landed in my thigh, but I didn't know it until much later. The pull at my genitals was so much more intense. I was saved by my sons who had just then walked into the kitchen. The killer cunts all dispersed to attack the boys and I fled. I have six boys, two of them are now dead and the other four lie in this hospital in critical condition."

When the troops finally arrived, the killer cunts probably decided that they would be outnumbered and took off. But the soldiers felt defeated. "I can't imagine what we'll do when they start hitting schools or monasteries!" one sergeant told the reporters. "If they develop a taste for orgies, men are doomed!" he predicted. "I'll never forget the physical humiliation as long as I live! No man is safe on this earth any more!" the tragic father added before he was taken away for plastic surgery.

At dawn, Ela notices: The daylight tries to break the windows. Every day the light tries to break the mirror.

It is early morning now. There are mechanical noises, excited birds, loud wide-eyed crowds, and bright windows. Ela closes the shutters and takes a bath. In three hours it will be a day since she woke up yesterday with the knowledge that she would have her cunt back. She should have asked the mirror before trusting that intuition, but it seemed empty this morning and she was in an excited hurry. It hasn't been present lately.

In the bathtub she thinks: Without sex, I am becoming soft. My brain feels overworked, my lips stiff. I should be reciting Eurydice's last lines: "and all terror defied, no past is mine, no future: look at me!"

Ela covers herself from hair to ankles with a transparent black-diamanté gauze punctured with tiny silver moons; her pores give out an unreal light. She wears red Russian boots and feels like a sturdy peasant. She takes big steps and chooses: I won't look for my cunt ever again. All ambition is vulgar. It is so embarrassing to want something. I have made my decision. This afternoon I will move to another town. Maybe Rio.

She decides to go back to that church and tell the priest the truth: since she has no cunt, it's not a sin to fuck her; a priest between her legs would be soothing. She decides to do her laundry first. An easy cleansing act. It is too early in the day to deal with a priest. She walks, coughing, dragging an immense pink laundry bag behind her to the laundromat. On the way she passes outside the Mary Boone Gallery. The trendy art inside is so flashy, boisterous and funny that Ela always strolls through the gallery on her way to the wash. Mostly out of habit, she glimpses through the glass window hoping for an eyeful of kitsch. Then she freezes.

The two adversaries exchange blank, fierce glares. She runs in a blind fit of rage. It waits for her on a gleaming oval shield. They are looking each other in the blind eye, eternally pitted against one another. The tension cuts ice.

She turns and enters the gallery. She can no longer think coherently about this affair. She shouts: "Are you following me? I find you everywhere. Leave me fucking alone!" A pert early riser from New Jersey looking like vanilla-flavored yogurt, interferes: "Excuse me Miss, would you mind? I have mission to photograph this piece! I'm due next door a minute ago." Ela: "Be a star. Show off. Get in the magazines. Go on Broadway. Act the sap. But leave me out of it, I want no part of it. I won't blow your cover. But don't try to get me to believe this identity crisis." The still-photographer now looking strawberry-flavored: "The curator is out, I have a job to do, and how am I expected to deal with all the freaks who walk in here." Ela: "I thought you were the most imaginative free babe in the world. I was just a foil!" The still-photographer, bending under the weight of straps, tripods, cameras, film, and shooting schedules: "Are you the model? I used to be a model myself. I may be a simple social climber, but I only fall for European women." Ela: "Ungrateful cunt!" The cunt is spinning. The early riser turns *chocolat* and stammers: "Miss, you turn up in every picture! Try to stand more to the left while giving your speech. Bend your head backwards and shake that silver fountain of hair."

The opponents take in the might and madness of the other, quickly glance behind them, inhale, hold their breath, unleash their love, and charge through the thin glass.

The rebel cunt is the centerpiece of the new op-art exhibit, which is built on a performance piece, judging from the muscular mulatto who hangs from the wall in an X, naked, his cock painted silver to match the cunt. He seems nailed on the wall from his hands and feet. He reminds Ela of a famous Da Vinci drawing. His eyes, apparently popped out, bleed. He is alive and probably the artist himself. His dry mouth hangs open and an obese black cockroach sits on his dark purple tongue. His tongue looks badly bitten and cracked. This crucified man is asleep. He may be one of the gurus who sleep on nails or torture wheels in front of an audience. All around him stand tall metal sculptures and a drippainted jungle of masks, teeth, newspapers, condoms, nuclear waste, broken TVs, stereos, cameras, and pink confetti. In the center of the room, on top of a tall crystal stand, alone on an oval mirror lies the frivolous cunt, pretending to be an object. Ela's first question is: "What's all this frippery?"

Now it stands up on the mirror and apparently in direct reaction to what Ela says at that instant—jolts, twists around in circles, lies on its back, pants, or pouts. It walks back and forth on its invisible feet, absorbed in thoughts. This is the first time that it seems to pay attention to any words addressed to it. It looks sincere. It changes colors from silver to deep scarlet red. It bends down and looks (?) at its own reflection. It does flips in the air. It leaps straight up and down, higher and higher. What is it trying to communicate?

Ela: "It seems we would know it if we belonged somewhere, for instance you between my legs, not out in the open. But we don't." She speaks as if she is singing a lullaby. Ela: "Do you deny that you are after all a cunt and an important part of me?" The cunt makes no sign of denial. Ela: "We're misfits." The cunt nods.

I am once again the felicitous observer of an unprecedented, gratifying, perfectly executed spectacle. In all my years—has it been only years?—as their loyal voyeur, I have never seen either one of them so animated. Never before has either one confronted a person, or a person's part, with such conviction.

The cunt pops off the mirror leaving behind a wet sparkling circle of steam, and throws itself with a high backflip at Ela's moving lips. For a split second she is so stunned she almost swallows it. The syllables stop midway in her throat crammed together in a jam. She is choking.

Ela asks her cunt: "Am I experiencing the paralogism of love? Is this a claptrap? Is it joy that overflows from me like an ocean?" Her cunt is crying. It drips. Ela confesses to her cunt: "I have been learning to approach something outside myself and incorporate it. Or is it the reverse? I am learning to stand back from something inside myself and examine it. I am becoming see-through. Does it show?"

I see that I have been deceived. This is a simple moral fable. I mistook it for something else entirely, a *roman policier* or a comedy of manners perhaps. I expected to cut into Gordian knots, to fulfill age-old prophecies and prayers. I expected more suffering. I am bursting with unanswered questions: Will the cunt stay permanently with Ela, will it be detachable? Will it grow roots and silver webs and hang from her womb like a tiny spaceship? Will it turn into a lens at will?

Whose will? How will they compromise? Will its irresistible appetites and stubborn fits and legendary abilities persist?

In that heartwarming moment Ela takes out her tongue and wipes her lips and pulls the little burning cunt into the warm enclave of her mouth; not as a bullfrog catches its prey, but as if she simply licks the corner of her lips. She realizes that she can swallow it now in no time, and end her conflict. The cunt would go back inside her where it belongs. She would let her body conduct the trial and distribute its own justice, either by digesting and then excreting the guilty cunt or by reinstating it to its old prestigious position. She closes her soft wet lips. This gives it a taste of its own poison: an awareness of what it is, of how it feels to those inside it, of what it does to others. The cunt has its first real look in a mirror. It does not fight in her mouth for its life. It likes being there.

Suddenly someone or something—Ela does not turn to look—crashes through the glass windows and falls with a roar. Glass shatters everywhere into numerous pointed sharp shards, staging a breathtaking show of light, a towering exhibition of force and despotism, a gorgeous explosion of frail rainbows. The doors, the windows, the frames, the display stands and the walls made of mirror or glass crumble like a crystal toy palace. Shards of every shape and size from the hardly visible grains that nestle deep into the skin to the monstrous guillotines that fall from the mirrored ceiling, pour *en masse* on Ela and her unprotected cunt. Something is gone amuck, Ela thinks.

In Ela's mouth her cunt bends from side to side shyly like a child who knows that it deserves a spanking but that it will be forgiven because it is doted on. It taps on her tongue to test its consistency, it skates, slides, and falls on it to check the texture of its surface, it wraps around to feel its muscle, embraces it with pressure to judge its strength, whirls on every millimeter of it to see how agile it is, surprises it with sudden jolts to test its endurance, and, as slowly as a snail, proceeds further into the crimson recesses of her mouth that is waiting holding its breath.

Ela does the same thing: she tests her cunt's power, resilience, flexibility, at the same time and in the same way that her cunt becomes familiar with her. Both feel pleased.

It does not please me that the cunt has returned of its own free will. I cannot accept that. I feel used. I should have led Ela to her cunt. What else was my purpose here? Am I the failed intimacy? Blind and invisible?

My eyes have nothing more to show. So I poke them out. For, as it was once for Oedipus, there is nothing left for me to see. I possess no memory of my own and no self to be remembered. I am shattered. I am discarded like a cracked and cloudy mirror.

It is a frenzied discharge, a lovesick paroxysm. Ela feels it personally directed at her. It is nothing as simple as an earthquake. She is surrounded by fury and shock. Something is in hysterics, she repeats to herself. What?

I think for a while there I was myself. Suddenly the two of them became one: Ela and her cunt, Ela and her reflection, Ela and I, I am not sure. I did not suspect this conspiracy. How cruel of her to leave me in the dark, hanging about like a clueless blind phantom. Did I not unfailingly take her side? Was I not always present, always clear, always selfless? Why was I destined for betrayal? Why was I the object?

Ela bravely confronts this assault. She stands under the heavy rain of glass and sucks on her little cunt whose display has broken and fallen into a sad heap of shards on the floor. Ela feels her cunt leap in her mouth like a heart, excited both by their proximity and by the unmitigated spasm that takes place outside. She bleeds where she is cut by the falling shards. She laughs, caught in the beauty of the blast. She looks into a frothing mouth of glass and loves it and laughs louder.

Its taste reminds Ela of a semi-liquid fruit that she has eaten in India called *targola:* a semi-transparent, imperfectly round, very smooth, shiny, fragile fruit with juice in the middle which is fragrant and mildly sweet like fresh coconut water and spurts out suddenly when one bites into the soft white flesh, leaving a milky, thick, and oily aftertaste. She has to summon all her self-control to stop her teeth from giving into their instincts and biting through the core of her cunt.

All around her hundreds of sparks and specks dance in the crisp air. As she stands in the heart of that spewing volcano, that uncontrollable consuming blow-up, that jagged Armageddon, she senses the cutthroat orgasm. Then the great white-hot breath quells. Dead? Asleep? Fulfilled? Happy? Ela wonders.

She looks around. The artist lies murdered under broken mirrors. The photographer has turned into a pillar of salt, like Lot's wife. His camera stops clicking. Too bad. The curator is still coming. He will never understand.

At the end of that majestic show, Ela cannot help herself: she gives its maker a standing ovation.

The world watches silent. It stands still, even devout. People all around America hear Ela whisper into the microphone: "I love you." They don't know she is speaking to her cunt.

From the ruins of glass rises a dense cold fog. Ela leans on this thick swollen wave of misery with admiration, without fear, and considers it a biblical episode where all life unites into one solid shattered mass, as at the end of a long journey. Only, here, the world that Ela knows has just broken itself.

The creatures that come by night to steal the blood of the living, the undead who lurk ready to change shape in the dark, have won. I did not expect it differently. They are creatures of their imagination. I fought against hope. As do the brave.

Distracted from its regular daily chores, America stares dumfounded into an immense superimposed screen of silver steam that hovers in front of the buildings, the sky, the fields, the objects of the world. Ela's mirroring face that stares into them from so near and looms before them so large, transfixes the American people. They see Ela and hold their breaths; they see her cunt, and their hearts stop. Sucked into the suspense, the terror and the magnitude of the moment on screen, victims of their own eyes like those privileged to see Medusa, these vacuous lonely childish people are blessed and doomed, from now on, to do nothing but absorb the action on the big atmospheric screen in bliss.

Ela does not feel the eyes of the world turned on her. It does not occur to her to look around for her audience.

She is licking her cunt, both as a cat bathes a blind newborn and like a fiery lover. She smells it, she tickles it, she wants to kill a prized lamb, for her cunt was lost to her and now has come back. The rest of her body does not sag with jealousy; it joins the celebration as every nerve feels the purifying pleasure that the cunt causes in her mouth. Her scalp tingles, her fingertips caress the air like tentacles, her limbs bubble, her spine shivers. The words that had been locked in her throat blow out in a slow endless exhale, almost a wind, which lasts for so long that when it stops she cannot remember how to breathe; it empties her insides until she is an airless cavern.

The mirror looked in the mirror and desired a fusion. It gazed into itself and saw a blank gap. It gazed into the Other and shattered.

Her cunt cuddles in her mouth. They both feel loved.

Later, the cunt withdraws and, with one of its backflips attaches itself like a slug on Ela's pubic mound over the gauze that covers her loosely. It hangs preposterously. She touches it lovingly, as she might lightly feel a lover's hand while they walk side by side in the street. She smiles in a new unfamiliar way: a mute joy, too big for her lips, pushes from behind her huge blinding eyes, almost causing them to burst.

So Ela walks out of the gallery waving her hips in her characteristic sensuous manner, taking quick small ginger steps, and goes back to her loft with her sparkling pink cunt hanging on to her black-diamanté gauze, from the exact spot where it once hid under her clothes and inside her skin. Ela does not think.

A giant Ela floats lost in herself on the celestial screen. America tries to touch Ela as she hovers complacently in the sky.

Ela lies facing her cunt. She looks at it and laughs. She masturbates for days. Her cunt greedily explores every part of her body. The sensation is beyond dreaming.

She sees the sea rise into a single wave like a solid breast. A salty breeze blows through her labia. The breast hits against her face. She is washed in mists. Completely still, feeling the cool breeze come through her like through tree leaves, Ela has a silent orgasm.

Her cunt is a small round silver boat. Miniature brilliant webs grow from its shiny skin like the silver strings hanging on a Christmas tree, and like mirror chips. Zoom in: From the webs hang tiny cunts whose labia open and close continuously like the mouths of tropical fish breathing in an aquarium. The new cunts are so small and so tight that they are certainly not usable.

Why She Found It

In the beginning of all there was the mirror, on every side, wide open. The mirror created everything. I first opened my eyes (or was it its eyes?) while going through the mirror; or coming through the mirror: from my safe mirror view, this and the other side were identical. The mirror taught me how to talk, walk, defecate. I dressed up for it, smiled into it, wore the "fuck me" look on my face to please it. I discovered myself in the mirror: something outside of me was myself. I was always in the picture, and everyone else was blurred. I existed by excluding myself. My otherness was clear. I could see behind my back. No one would dare come.

Since then, I sleep with the mirror and wake up to it. I go into it at impossible times or come out of it at impossible places. Living through the mirror is not a sequence, an addition, a story. I say mirror words. My breasts have a mirror smell. My words mirror my mouth. My smell mirrors my breasts. I have mirror feelings. Great fatal crippling passions become impossible in the mirror. The glass breaks from too much love or hate or anger. So I cannot be held. I am exempt from volume. In the mirror, *la dolce vita* lasts for ever.

Though I look as if I don't care about anything, I hold on to my hiding place: the mirror. The mirror is not a closed erect system. It is a river. When I look into it for over a second, I no longer recognize myself. I never focus: the mirror overwhelms me, so I live in continuous orgasm. The mirror invents foreplay and afterplay. It prolongs sex. The mirror is the source of all suspense. It cannot obey. It is inconsistent. It is a revenge. A zero. Like looking into the firing squad, or into the lens.

My reflection looks at me, not at herself. The image of me doesn't see what I see. It sees what I cannot see. Both my presence and my absence are announced. Each side wants to taste the heart (the death) of the other. If I move too close, it (or I) will float away (or drown). The mirror, like a camera, freezes my eyes. Its (or my) impersonal stare beckons to be identified: ice. Men become attracted to the look that tells them: "Don't come."

My eyes are self-contained: I (or you) see my (or your) reflection in them: they are convex mirrors. Men desire me (or my reflection) to acknowledge (devastate) them. Men see the mirror as real. So they live out of place. Then the mirror looks like a window. Men have to be heard. So they narrate. I am the object. Imperative by my nature. I say: "I ask you to obey." Men desire the evil eye: the gap between my flesh and my eyes. Men say: "I want to know what you are thinking." Living in the mirror is a continuous rehearsal. I have no loss. What I see is compelling enough to make me leave (or come) at once.

When I come, I slip in between the two of them; between you

and me, or you and yourself, or you and him or her or her image. It is not an assertion or an insertion. Unlike a man saying: "I'm coming in now" or "Tell me when to come" or "Am I in yet?" or "How does it feel?" or "See what a Jewish cock can do?" I am open to all comers. My coming does not end the suspense. I come for the fun of the curve. Men ask "Did sex come before everything?" or "Whom do you think of during sex?" or "Why don't you see from my perspective?" or "Do you realize there are two sides to a couple?"

Whispering in confidential tones, I foresee the following in response: "I come in front of you as if nothing has ever happened. Do you invent everything? That you see? That I am? My body is only the pretext. A few say love is impossible; or love makes everything else impossible; or love is fine only once. Others say that love is war or love is not war or love is a strategy with expediencies, retreats, artifices, crisis techniques, all based on the exception rather than the rule; or love is what keeps us from degenerating into norms. I say love is the search for the mirror. We can't know if love bridges us or if the proximity separates us. We can never satisfy our love, our deep desire to be transparent, even when we are transparent; for love secretes a dark thick fog independently from the lovers. Love likes only roads that have never been traveled. Lovers pose only problems that cannot be solved. So when choosing a new mirror, remember that the mirror will outlast your presence. A mirror cannot see you."

I, for one (or two), never know where I am. I live in water and glass. I cannot be distinguished from the screen. I am not transfixed. I hover beyond. I am always seen. But because I have always been secretive, and because no one has ever discovered me, I think it suffices to cross into the rippling glass and pretend to disappear.

About the Author

Eurydice was born on Lesbos and brought up in Alexandria and Athens. She has published two books of poetry, one in Greek, and has written two novellas—*scree* and *Amfi-trite*. She holds a B.A. in Creative Writing and Fine Arts from Bard College, a Greek University degree in Minoan Archeology, an M.A. in Creative Writing frm the University of Colorado at Boulder, and is a Ph.D student in comparative literature at Brown University.